"Real people with real flaws and palpable emotions [illegible] ay at your heartstrings in this u[illegible]'s greatest Jewish heroine. Jill [illegible] yle makes Esther's story relatab[illegible] dable, and its details fascinating. A must-read for every [illegible] ction fan."

Mesu Andrews, Christy Award–winning author of *Isaiah's Daughter*

"In *Star of Persia*, Jill Eileen Smith breathes new life into the tale of Queen Esther, and those whose lives entwined with hers, by weaving together richly crafted descriptions, well-researched historical detail, and her usual flair for retelling biblical stories with a fresh perspective."

Connilyn Cossette, ECPA bestselling author of the Out from Egypt and Cities of Refuge series

Praise for Jill Eileen Smith

"Readers will appreciate that Smith infuses this well-known story with emotional depth and a modern sensibility not typically seen in historical novels."

Publishers Weekly on *A Passionate Hope*

"Smith's fresh retelling of the story of Ruth and Naomi portrays these strong biblical women in a thoughtful and reflective manner. Her impeccable research and richly detailed setting give readers a strong sense of life in ancient Israel."

Library Journal on *Redeeming Grace*

"Readers who enjoy historical biblical fiction will find this book, as well as the other titles in Smith's Daughters of the Promised Land series, fascinating."

Booklist on *Redeeming Grace*

STAR OF PERSIA

Books by Jill Eileen Smith

The Wives of King David

Michal

Abigail

Bathsheba

Wives of the Patriarchs

Sarai

Rebekah

Rachel

Daughters of the Promised Land

The Crimson Cord

The Prophetess

Redeeming Grace

A Passionate Hope

The Heart of a King

When Life Doesn't Match Your Dreams

Star of Persia

STAR OF PERSIA

ESTHER'S STORY

JILL EILEEN SMITH

Revell
a division of Baker Publishing Group
Grand Rapids, Michigan

Published by Revell
a division of Baker Publishing Group
Grand Rapids, Michigan
www.revellbooks.com

Printed in the United States of America

Library of Congress Cataloging-in-Publication Data
Names: Smith, Jill Eileen, 1958- author.
Title: Star of Persia : Esther's story / Jill Eileen Smith.
Other titles: Esther's story
Description: Grand Rapids, MI : Revell, a division of Baker Publishing Group, 2019. | Bibliography: p. [275]-278.
Identifiers: LCCN 2019017717 | ISBN 9780800734718 (pbk.)
Subjects: LCSH: Esther, Queen of Persia—Fiction. | Bible. Esther—History of Biblical events—Fiction. | Xerxes I, King of Persia, 519 B.C.-465 B.C. or 464 B.C.—Fiction. | Women in the Bible—Fiction. | GSAFD: Bible fiction. | Historical fiction.
Classification: LCC PS3619.M58838 S73 2018 | DDC 813/.6—dc23
LC record available at https://lccn.loc.gov/2019017717

ISBN 978-0-8007-3778-8 (casebound)

Published in association with Books & Such Literary Management, 52 Mission Circle, Suite 122, PMB 170, Santa Rosa, CA 95409-5370, www.booksandsuch.com.

Baker Publishing Group publications use paper produced from sustainable forestry practices and post-consumer waste whenever possible.

To every man and woman
who is willing to take the risk of trusting God
in the middle of a crisis and do the hard things.
To those who will step up when faced
with your own "such a time as this."
This book is for you.

Prologue

489 BC

Vashti moved through the palace gardens, cradling her bulging middle After three years of marriage to Xerxes and two pregnancies lost, she had feared she would never bear a child. Even now she feared. What if the child was stillborn? What if she died in childbirth?

She moved through a walkway of flowering almond trees, her maids following closely behind. What she wouldn't give to talk to another woman, but she cared nothing for Xerxes' concubines.

She crossed her arms. Surely the child would be a boy. Xerxes' heir. Perhaps that would keep her husband from wandering to the beds of other women, though she knew him too well to think him capable of being faithful to her alone.

Still, her child would be his first. Even when he married Amestris, a spoiled child of royal blood promised to Xerxes once he took his father's throne, no one would be able to take her child's place as firstborn of the king. Vashti felt her jaw tighten with every thought of Amestris and the insistence of Xerxes' mother, Atossa, that this was best for all. After all, she'd reminded Vashti often enough, "You are not fully Persian, my dear." Never mind that she was the granddaughter of Babylonian kings.

She shook her head. Thinking of Amestris did nothing but cause her worry, and she needed peace and rest lest she disturb the babe. Still she paced, restless. She walked toward the gate that separated the palace grounds from the residents of Susa. As she looked out at the city, she spotted a young girl skipping beside her mother, her thick, dark curls bouncing beneath a neatly tied beige linen headscarf. The girl turned her head and looked toward the imposing palace. Vashti drew in a breath. Such large, inquisitive eyes! The child was already beautiful and not yet grown. Vashti smiled. How many suitors this child's father would have to fend off! At least her father would have choices. Something Vashti's father never did.

The sting of loss over what she had never known faded as she placed a protective hand on her swelling belly, and reminded herself that Xerxes was at least an attentive lover when he was in need of her. That he favored her was satisfaction in itself, though she often wondered what life would have been like if she had been born in Babylon, the city of her ancestors, instead of in the conquering land of Persia.

You should be grateful that one day you will be queen. You have privileges others do not.

She knew that. Didn't she remind herself often enough?

She looked again toward the gate and saw that the child stood near, peering at her through the slats.

"Hadassah, come!" the girl's mother called.

A sudden urge overcame Vashti, and she moved closer to the gate. She spoke to one of her maids. "Call the woman and the child to me."

The maid complied, and a moment later, the woman and her daughter were ushered into the gardens. The woman bowed low, but the child simply stared at her with those large, dark eyes.

"I hope I did not startle you," Vashti said, motioning for the woman to rise. "Your daughter. She is beautiful."

The woman nodded. "Thank you, Your Majesty." Clearly the woman recognized her, though Vashti was not dressed in her royal finery as the crown prince's wife.

Vashti met the woman's gaze. "You called her Hadassah. You are of Jewish blood."

"Yes, Your Majesty." The woman glanced about her as though the meeting made her uncomfortable.

"Do not fear. I hold nothing against your people. I simply wanted to see the child." And to speak to someone about birth and raising a child, though others would do the job for her. "Was it difficult to birth her?" Vashti asked, despite her better sense to keep her thoughts to herself rather than make them subject to public gossip.

The woman looked at her feet, then lifted her head and offered Vashti a slight smile. "I can tell you what it was like to birth my sons, but I did not birth Hadassah. She is my husband's cousin. She is orphaned, so we adopted her."

Vashti released a breath. She could trust a woman who would reveal such knowledge. "How did she become orphaned?" Vashti longed to kneel to the child's height, but in her condition she could only look down at the girl. She moved to a bench and sat, inviting the two to join her.

"Her father died of a fever before her birth, and her mother died shortly after childbirth. Hadassah has been with us these past six years."

"And may I ask your name?" Vashti looked at the woman, then coaxed the child to sit beside her. Hadassah glanced at the woman for permission, then climbed onto the stone seat.

"Levia. My husband is Mordecai. He works as a scribe at the king's gate."

Vashti touched the child's curls, suddenly hoping her child would be a girl despite the need to bear a son. "Then he is a good man," she said without looking up. "It is unfortunate the child has lost so much."

Hadassah looked into Vashti's eyes and searched her face as though she was seeing beyond her ability to comprehend. She reached a small hand to touch Vashti's face, then placed a hand on Vashti's protruding middle. "You will have a baby soon," Hadassah said. "You are pretty and have kind eyes."

Vashti sat straighter. She took the child's hand. "And you are young to say such things."

"She has always been a bright child," Levia said.

Vashti nodded. She had no reason to detain the woman or the child, yet a part of her longed to do just that. At last common sense won out, and she cupped Hadassah's face and slowly rose. She looked at Levia. "Take good care of her. She is one who could come to great favor or great harm for her beauty."

"Thank you, Majesty. I will be extra watchful for your warning."

Vashti dismissed them, wondering what had caused her to say such a thing, yet feeling some strange sense that she had done well. She watched Levia, with Hadassah in hand, walk toward the gate, where Hadassah looked back at her and smiled. Warmth like the break of dawn after the darkness washed over Vashti, and she wondered if she had touched the face of an angel.

PART ONE

This is what happened during the time of Xerxes, the Xerxes who ruled over 127 provinces stretching from India to Cush: At that time King Xerxes reigned from his royal throne in the citadel of Susa, and in the third year of his reign he gave a banquet for all his nobles and officials. The military leaders of Persia and Media, the princes, and the nobles of the provinces were present.

For a full 180 days he displayed the vast wealth of his kingdom and the splendor and glory of his majesty. When these days were over, the king gave a banquet, lasting seven days, in the enclosed garden of the king's palace, for all the people from the least to the greatest who were in the citadel of Susa. . . .

Queen Vashti also gave a banquet for the women in the royal palace of King Xerxes.

On the seventh day, when King Xerxes was in high spirits from wine, he commanded the seven eunuchs who served him—Mehuman, Biztha, Harbona, Bigtha, Abagtha, Zethar and Karkas—to bring before him Queen Vashti, wearing her royal crown, in order to display her beauty to the people and nobles, for she was lovely to look at. But when the attendants delivered the king's command, Queen Vashti refused to come. Then the king became furious and burned with anger.

Esther 1:1–5, 9–12 NIV

CHAPTER One

Six Years Later

Hadassah moved through the market, basket on her head, Levia one step ahead of her. "Hurry along, child," Levia scolded. "The crowds are growing too great."

The market had been quiet when they'd arrived after their visit to the well and preparing the morning meal. But now, servants of visiting nobles and governors from the king's 127 provinces descended upon the shops. Hadassah could feel Levia's tension and protectiveness.

"I'm coming," Hadassah assured her as she picked up her pace and came alongside her cousin's wife, the only woman she had known as mother. She glanced behind her and noticed the servants streaming from the palace halls. The palace stood in all its grandeur like a towering sentinel in the center of the city.

Her heart skipped a beat as she and Levia nearly ran

through the cobbled streets, and she breathed a sigh of relief as they finally entered their neighborhood. The clay brick home looked like every other in their small community, all clumped together with little space between them, owned by those subject to King Xerxes. While the Jews tended to settle together, Levia's husband, Mordecai, had kept them slightly apart—a few blocks away from other Hebrew people.

Most of the Jews had returned to Jerusalem several years before, but Mordecai had followed his father in service to the king and felt compelled to stay. Sometimes Hadassah wondered if they would have been better off to go with their people, to be free of the wild debauchery of Susa. But when the king moved to Persepolis for the winter, Susa was quiet. Peaceful even. After a cleansing rain, Hadassah could stroll with her older cousins to the hills outside the city. Life felt safer during those times.

They reached the house and hurried inside. Levia shut the door and leaned against it. "How long is this revelry to go on?" She wiped her brow and moved into the cooking area. "A person should not have to feel like a thief stealing spices from the market."

"But we aren't thieves, Ima." The endearment had come early in her life. "We purchase what we need."

"I know that, sweet girl." Levia touched Hadassah's cheek. "I just hate to be so rushed, as though I'm sneaking away before I'm caught."

Hadassah smiled. Levia was always dramatic in her telling of tales, while Hadassah cared more for Mordecai's matter-of-fact, often earnest way of sharing the day's news.

"How long does Abba say the governors will be here?" Hadassah took the basket from her head and unloaded its contents—muskmelon, carrots, eggplant, pistachios, garlic, and a sack of beans. She looked forward to tasting all of it with the evening's meal.

"Mordecai knows nothing." Levia waved her hands as if batting at flies. "What good does it do to work at the king's gate and know nothing of what goes on in the king's house?" She pulled out the jar of flour ground earlier that morning and set about to knead bread for the evening. Levia began early in order to use the community oven first. Perhaps one day Mordecai would be able to build a grand oven for them in their own courtyard, but he'd been too busy to work on anything since the king had called together the leaders of the provinces to Susa. If their old oven had not crumbled to where they could no longer use it, Levia would not always be in such a hurry.

"Perhaps Abba will learn something new today," Hadassah said. She realized that Levia would hurry no matter what the circumstances because she was simply anxious, and to expect her to be anything than what she was would do no good. None of it mattered regardless. Hadassah loved Levia just as she was. "They've already been here five months," she added, setting the vegetables on a board to begin chopping them.

"How long can men sit around and just eat and drink?" Levia clucked her tongue. "Such a waste of time."

Hadassah nodded. She had never seen drunken men, but Mordecai had often told tales. It was said that the king drank far too much for his own good and couldn't make decisions when he was in such a state. Yet Mordecai had also told them that the purpose for this grand celebration was to gather the leaders from every province where Xerxes ruled in order to plan a great war. The war his father, Darius, had planned to wage before his sudden death. In the uproar of Xerxes' coronation and marriage to the Persian princess Amestris, then the birth of their two sons, there had been little time to leave Persia. Apparently now, Xerxes was ready.

"Hopefully, it will all be over soon." Hadassah took some of the flour and kneaded a batch to be made into a sweet pistachio treat, while Levia prepared two round loaves of bread.

"Yes. Hopefully."

Silence fell between them, a pleasant camaraderie Hadassah enjoyed, though sometimes she wondered what life would have been like had her own mother lived.

"Do you remember the time we stopped at the palace gardens and Princess Vashti talked with us?" Levia's comment brought the memory to mind.

"I was just a child, but I remember she was kind."

"She was carrying Xerxes' heir and gave birth a few months later. I wonder if her son will have any standing at all in the kingdom, with Amestris bearing two sons in two short years of marriage."

"Vashti is the first wife. Her son should rule after his father." Hadassah recalled how bold she had been to even touch the future queen's face.

"Yes, but Amestris is the wife of royalty. She wed Xerxes after he was crowned king. My guess is that her sons will rise above Vashti's boy." Levia glanced at Hadassah. "It's a shame, really. Vashti is truly a queen. Amestris, from what the gossips say, is a cruel person."

Hadassah shivered. "I am glad to have nothing to do with any of that. I want to marry a Hebrew man and move to Jerusalem."

Levia scowled ever so slightly. "You are too young to marry, my child. As for Jerusalem, the walls are not yet built. It is not safe."

"Perhaps by the time I am ready to marry they will be built and we will all move there together." She smiled, hoping to diffuse any doubt in Levia's mind.

But Levia shook her head. "Walls take years to build, child. As for all of us moving together—Mordecai would never do so. He could have gone before our sons were born and chose not to. Personally, I am glad of it. The rumors coming from Jerusalem say that rebuilding the temple was no easy task." She bit her lip. "No. It is safer to stay here, despite our drunken king." She lowered her voice and met Hadassah's wide eyes. "But you must not worry, dear girl. Mordecai will always keep you safe."

Hadassah merely nodded. There was no sense in disagreeing with Levia when she began worrying about Hadassah's safety. It was something she could do nothing about. She wanted peace, but she enjoyed adventure too. Sometimes she wondered if she would ever know her own mind or what she wanted in life.

Not that it mattered. Girls didn't get to choose their futures. Mordecai would pick a husband for her one day, and she would belong to him. Others would always make choices for her—at least the ones that mattered.

Hadassah sighed. She would think about her future later. For now, she simply wanted peace and time with her cousins and her friends. To be a girl, and not have to worry about the things that troubled Levia. She sensed that day would come soon enough.

CHAPTER Two

Vashti looked up at the sound of the door opening. Little feet pounded the mosaic tiles until her son flopped onto the couch at her side. "Maman, you must come!"

Vashti laughed at the dimpled grin on Gazsi's face. She set her needlework aside and took his young hands in hers. "And what is so important that I must see?"

"Omid showed me a place in the wall where we can look down on the dancing, and they are playing games and singing. Maman, you must see it!" Gazsi's earnest look gave Vashti pause. She glanced toward the door, where the eunuch in charge of his care stood at attention.

"Omid, did you take my son to see the king's celebration?"

Omid stepped closer and bowed low. "He saw only a little, my queen. The noise was so great that I could not keep him from constantly asking to see. It will not happen again, my queen."

"See that it does not." She would have called the celebration by a far worse name, for to her it was simply drunken revelry, but she knew to Xerxes it was much more. Her husband had a great war to plan against Greece, and he had no intention of losing. Thousands of men, some known as the Immortals, would march out within the year to subdue the Greeks in order to fulfill the promise Xerxes had made to his father, Darius, before his death.

A sigh escaped. If only her husband didn't think six months of jovial merrymaking need be part of war planning. He was showing off the grandeur of Susa and the riches he possessed. And his power. His wealth most definitely showed that he also wielded great power. His father and ancestors had already conquered so many nations. Only Greece stuck out like a stubborn child who would not submit to Persia's rule. Xerxes intended to make sure they were put in their place.

But that did not mean her six-year-old son needed to be party to or witness to his father's actions or plans.

Vashti stood, still holding her son's hand, and walked to the window of her suite of rooms. She pushed the curtain aside and pointed to the beautiful flowering gardens below and the hills beyond the rooftops. "This is a much better sight to gaze upon, my son." She bent to look into his eyes.

His dark brow furrowed as though he did not believe her. "But there are no games or dancers. It's just an old garden, Maman." Gazsi pulled his hand from hers and crossed his arms over his small chest. "I want games."

"Then we will have Omid find some appropriate games for a young boy to play. And perhaps it is time your tutors teach you all of the things that hide beneath the garden's beauty. There is more there than your eye can see." Vashti patted his head, then gave orders to her servant to call the boy's tutor and gather some young boys to engage him in games.

The servant left, and Vashti settled on the couch again while Gazsi pulled out carved images and set them up in battle array as though he were the one planning the war with Greece. She looked on with a hint of dismay. No other children had been born to her these past six years. She could not bear to have this one grow up and leave here to go to battle with his father. But if he took the throne one day, war was inevitable.

Unless Amestris's son Darius was declared king over her son. The thought troubled her. Amestris troubled her. She had always known things would change when Xerxes took the throne and married the woman his mother had intended for him. But she hadn't expected her mother-in-law to turn so strongly against her.

"She is Persian, my son," Atossa had said to Xerxes on a visit to his chambers, knowing full well that Vashti was nearby. "You know you cannot have that half-Persian woman's child wearing the crown after you. You must marry a woman of royalty—of full Persian blood—once you wear the crown. Her rights will surpass this foreigner's, and you will never need fear that woman's son usurping the throne of your rightful heir."

Atossa's words still stung, though three years had passed since the coronation and Xerxes' marriage to Amestris. It hadn't helped that Amestris had already borne her husband two sons while Vashti could claim only one. *Am I so unworthy in his eyes?*

But she knew that was not the truth. Xerxes had been devoted to her for sixteen years before his coronation, and even with the addition of Amestris and many concubines,

Vashti remained his favorite. To Atossa's dismay, Vashti bore the title of queen above Amestris, something that brought a smile to Vashti's face when she thought on it. Still, she did her best to think on other things.

The noise of the men's revelry drifted to her from the king's rooms and audience chamber. His private court was located at the opposite end of the palace from her privileged, secluded rooms. He had promised never to put her in a harem, and thus far had kept his word. How long she would retain the title of queen, however, was a question that often surfaced. Amestris clearly had set her sights on wearing the crown and sitting at Xerxes' side. Vashti determined she would not let that happen. Not as long as she had her son to protect.

She glanced at him sitting on the rug, making war noises and loud battle cries. She must do more to make sure he was taught all he needed to take his father's place and not allow *her* sons to wedge their way between Gazsi and Xerxes. A boy needed his father. Especially the firstborn. And she would do all in her power to protect his place as the rightful heir.

"Please make them stop!" Amestris walked from the nursery, where her two young sons wailed in protest that she refused to hold them. She'd held them long enough and needed time away from them. Ungrateful children.

She pushed past her maids, who hurried to coddle the boys, and headed to the door that led to her small private court. It was not nearly large enough in comparison to what Vashti had at her disposal. The woman had no business being queen. Atossa had assured Amestris that marrying her son would give her the status of rightful queen and Vashti would take second place once Xerxes was crowned king. But none of those promises had come to pass. Apparently Atossa did not know her son as well as she thought she did. Xerxes, despite the fact that Amestris had given him two whiny children, did nothing to place her above Vashti. Vashti, the favored one. Vashti, his first love.

She felt sick at the very thought. She paced the court, cursing its size, determined to insist that Xerxes give her bigger rooms at the first opportunity. But he was so wrapped up with the governors and rulers of the provinces that he hadn't been to see her in months.

He'd probably been to see *her*, though. Amestris felt her hands clench of their own volition. How she hated that woman. She really must do something to change her situation. If only there was a way to get rid of Vashti completely. Or at the very least have her demoted from her high place. Give her a taste of the life she should be living.

How to do such a thing, though? She couldn't just go to Xerxes and ask him. He was in love with the woman, foolish as that was. No, she needed to think. To plan. But the more she thought on it, the more hopeless any sort of change seemed. She moved back to her rooms. At least her children were quiet now. She rubbed her neck, cursing the headache that had assaulted her in the courtyard.

This was not the life she had intended. She was a princess. Royalty. She deserved to rule, and one way or another she would change her circumstances. No matter what she had to do to achieve her wishes.

CHAPTER Three

Hadassah bent over the plants in the garden, picking weeds from between rows of cucumber, leek, radish, and melon. The plot of ground was small compared to those in the yards of the homes she had seen on walks to the marketplace. But Mordecai seemed to prefer the small, obscure house to one that might afford them more space and allow them to hire a few servants. Of course, she did not know whether Mordecai could pay for anything better, and Hadassah did not mind the close quarters, except for those times when her neighbors fought or babies cried in the night.

She rubbed the dirt from her hands and leaned back on her heels. The sun beat down on her covered head and a bead of sweat trickled down her back. Levia would have called her inside to rest at this time of day, but she had gone several blocks away to help her son's wife with one of the children.

Hadassah enjoyed the time to herself, though she took care to stay near the house as Mordecai had asked.

The revelry of the past months had risen to such great noise that Hadassah was glad for the instruction to stay as far from the palace as possible. Nearly six months had passed, and Mordecai had assured her that the governors and satraps would soon go home, if palace informants were correct. "But," he told her, "it is said that the king plans another feast immediately following this one."

"What?" Levia was spinning wool but allowed the spindle to come to a stop as Mordecai explained.

"Apparently the king wants all of Susa to celebrate with him. His plans for war against Greece have gone very well, and all of the people in the citadel are invited to celebrate." He paused. Rubbed a hand over his beard. "I am expected to attend as well."

Levia looked at him while Hadassah continued to wind dyed wool into a ball. "For how long?" Levia asked.

"They say it will last a week. The invitation was to all the people, but they meant the men. You and Hadassah must stay far from the palace, even if I do not come home for a week." Mordecai seemed troubled, but he said no more even when Levia pressed him with questions.

No doubt Mordecai had remained silent for her sake. Levia would talk privately to him when they were behind the curtain of their chamber. Hadassah often heard muffled conversations, though she rarely understood the words. They were protecting her. Always protecting her.

She straightened, then stood and moved into the cooler house. Water filled a skin they had drawn from the well that morning, and she took a long drink. A knock on the door startled her. Who would come visiting in the middle of the day? Had something happened to Levia or Mordecai or one of their grandchildren?

She crept to the door and peered through the window beside it. Jola! She hurried to let her friend inside.

"What are you doing here?" Hadassah motioned Jola to sit and offered her a drink from the skin she had just used.

"Is that any way to greet your best friend? I came to see you, of course." Jola plopped down on one of the cushions in the house's main room. "Ima was resting, so I snuck out." She grinned.

Hadassah smiled. Jola's mother would not be upset with her once she knew where her daughter had gone. But Jola would cause her no small amount of worry in the meantime. "You will be confined to your house for days."

Jola chuckled. "It is worth it to get away for a few minutes. Aren't you weary of everyone hovering? And all because the king decided to have a six-month-long party. Why should we be worried about being seen? They all act like someone is going to snatch us up and take us away."

Hadassah sat beside her friend and wiped her brow. "Abba seems to have good reason for concern. The city has been overrun with hundreds of extra men. I don't think he trusts any of them."

"I suppose they will stop worrying once we marry." Jola's face took on a dreamy expression. "Do you ever wonder who they will pick for you? I've had my eye on some of the boys who come to the meetings. I think it will be fun to help Ima choose."

Hadassah laughed as her friend dramatically fluttered a hand over her heart. "We are too young to wed yet," she said, wondering who fascinated Jola so much. Mordecai stayed away from the meetings most of the time. Though he did his best to follow the laws of the Hebrew God, he avoided mingling often with their people. "I wonder if they are afraid." The words were out before she realized she had spoken.

"Of course they are afraid. They want to keep us pure until the marriage bed. In this pagan land, we are in more danger than we would be if we had gone back to Israel with the exiles." Jola looked thoughtful. "Do you ever wish we'd gone back?"

"I meant I wonder if they are afraid of being together as Jews. Why does my abba keep us from most of the meetings yet observe the Jewish law at home? Are Jews truly in danger here? If we were, surely our families would have gone back with the other exiles." Hadassah picked up a piece of straw that had come loose from a basket and chewed on the end.

Jola gave her a strange look, then shrugged. "I don't know. Ima thinks so, but we've lived here for more than seventy years and the Persians have never treated any people in a treacherous way. They don't even make us give up our God for theirs. I don't know what your abba fears, unless he knows something we don't. Then again, maybe he doesn't like the rabbi."

Hadassah laughed, but inside she knew it was more than that. She could feel something beyond their simple conclusions, but she had no idea why she sensed Mordecai had reasons for secrecy toward his fellow Jews that he would not tell his family.

"So answer my question now." Jola stood to explore the cooking room for dates or nuts, something she loved.

Hadassah followed her. "Which one? Do I wonder who

they will pick for me to marry, or do I wish we had returned to Jerusalem?"

"Both." Jola laughed. "I'll tell you if you'll tell me."

Hadassah gave her friend a sociable scowl. "I'm curious about Jerusalem. I wonder if my parents would have gone back if they'd lived. And I'd like to see the city. But Ima tells me the walls are not done. I don't think she likes it when I talk about wanting to go back."

"She loves you. She fears losing you even in marriage, if my guess is right." Jola bit off the end of a fresh date. "Now answer the other question."

Hadassah leaned against a wooden table where they chopped food. "I will have to accept whoever Abba picks for me. Perhaps Ima will let me help pick the man. When I'm old enough. And twelve isn't old enough yet."

"Thirteen is." Her friend gave her a smirk. Jola was a year her senior and had just turned thirteen.

"Fifteen is better. Ima insists that is the earliest she will consider someone for me."

Jola finished the date and gave a dramatic sigh. "I will have baskets of dates at my wedding, and my beloved and I will feast on them throughout the night."

"I see I have lost you to your dream world again. I suppose you will marry a prince as well?" Hadassah gently pushed Jola back toward the sitting room. "Though now it is your turn to answer your questions."

"A prince? Nay. A king!" Jola laughed and Hadassah joined her. Of course, neither of them would wed a prince or a king, for there was no king left in Israel. "There are a few young men who come to the meetings. I haven't decided which one I like best yet." Jola crossed her arms. "And I would only return to Jerusalem if I could go with the man I pick. If Ima gives me to someone awful, I am not leaving Susa!" She waved her hand in a flourish. "I will be forever exiled in this pagan city."

Hadassah pondered Jola's words, knowing that most of what she said she did not mean. Both of them would marry men from among their people and do as they were told, even if that meant leaving Susa. Women did not go against the customs of their men, and men did not go against the customs of the Jews, whether Mordecai wanted to mingle with their people or not.

CHAPTER *Four*

Vashti entered the king's opulent rooms, which were decorated much like other parts of his palace—with blue and white linen curtains fastened to silver rods that hung from marble pillars. Xerxes' couches were crafted of gold and silver and cushioned with lamb's wool. The floor sparkled of alabaster done in a colorful mosaic pavement of turquoise and black-and-white marble.

Since his coronation, Xerxes had spared no expense in redecorating the palace to his liking, and each time Vashti entered his apartments, he seemed to have added some new vase or tapestry or vessel of gold to adorn the walls and shelves and tables of gold and silver. When the sun shone through the tall windows, the effect nearly blinded her.

She moved into the large sitting room, where Xerxes sat lazily on one of the couches. She bowed low and kissed his signet ring. He took her hand and pulled her onto his lap. His breath touched her ear.

"How I have missed you, my love." He traced a line along her jaw. "How beautiful you are."

"And how handsome you are, my king." She submitted to his lingering caress. He had a way of wooing her that still caused her heart to beat faster despite their years of marriage. "I have missed you as well."

"Six months with little time for anyone but the military men is more than enough time away from my favorite wife." He cupped her chin and deepened his kiss.

"Did you accomplish what you wished?" she asked once he took a breath. She leaned away from him to better see his face.

He nodded. "The men are ready. We will leave for war within the month. The Greeks won't see us coming. At last we will subdue them and rule those rebellious Spartans and Athenians with the iron resolve they deserve."

Vashti tilted her head. "Surely you will treat them as you do the other nations you have subdued."

The lines along his brow furrowed, so much like her son's did when he pouted. "Once they are subdued, we will see. It depends on how much trouble they cause me." He laughed. "But I did not call you here, my love, to discuss what I've spent six months planning with the governors and satraps. Come, let us eat something and talk of other things."

He led her to a table filled with rich food, and she sat after he did, allowing servants to fill her plate as they did the king's.

"I have something to tell you," he said after eating a mouthful of fish. "I'm going to give another feast for seven more days."

At her look of concern, he held up a hand. "Do not worry, this one is for the people of Susa, who have put up with the additional people in the citadel and city for so long." He paused. "I want you to give a feast for the royal women at the same time."

She nodded. Of course she would do his bidding. "It will be an honor, my lord, to serve you." The royal women would include his wives and concubines and the noblemen's wives. And his mother. But it was Amestris whom she wished she could keep from attending.

"Good." He took a bite of bread and washed it down with wine in his favorite golden goblet decorated with the sun, moon, and stars. He leaned back to look at her, a smile curving his lips. "I will hold my celebration in the courtyard, while you can invite the women into one of the banquet halls. I'm sure your attendants can help you bring it together by tomorrow."

Tomorrow? Her mind whirled with so much to do. But she only nodded.

"You might ask my mother to help," Xerxes said, interrupting her thoughts. "Or Amestris. I'm sure both women would enjoy something to do."

Vashti's jaw clenched, though she bid her expression to remain neutral. "Yes, my lord. I will see what can be done, though I'm certain my servants can handle the details." She would stay up all night if need be, making sure things were done her way.

But as he led her to his decorated bed, where they had often shared their love, she knew she would have little time to plan a feast while he slept beside her.

Vashti slipped from the king's chambers before dawn and hurried to her rooms. "Omid!" She called the eunuch's name before her feet had fully crossed the threshold. "Gather my servants—every last one of them. I need a banquet put together today and invitations sent to every woman in the king's household and all of the wives of the nobles." She whirled about, spotting Gazsi rubbing sleep from his eyes as he moved from his chamber to her sitting room. She paused. His nurse would need to remain with him, as would the servants who watched the other children of Xerxes. She looked at Omid. "Only the caretakers of the children are excused from helping. This must be as lavish a feast as the king is giving." Xerxes would expect it of her. Of course he would.

But if she didn't ask for his mother's help, she would probably hear of it from him in a week when the feasting ended. Coming war or not, it would do no good to distress Atossa. Or Atossa's favored Amestris.

A sigh escaped, and she cinched the neck of her robe tighter. She needed to bathe and change into fresh royal robes before she called for her mother-in-law or Xerxes' second wife.

"Omid."

"Yes, my queen." The servant bowed low. "What else may I do to help you?"

She looked into the kind face of the eunuch. "Once I am ready—give me until the sun rises halfway to the middle of the sky—send for Atossa . . . and Amestris. The king would like them to be included in the planning. But I want to get started before they come."

"Understood, my queen." Omid smiled.

Could she trust him? Surely she could trust him with a simple statement if she could entrust her son's care to him. Even if the man did show Gazsi things he was too young to see in the king's court.

"I will need you to handle the servants. Have Jahan take the children." She turned then, signaling his dismissal. Her maids descended on her in a flurry, and suddenly it seemed as though the entire court of women had come alive with activity.

Vashti worried her lip before she caught herself. She lifted her head and drew in a breath. She could do this. She could even handle two women who were her constant nemeses. She would prove to her husband that she was still his best choice for queen.

"A banquet with only one day to plan?" Amestris plucked a grape from a silver tray in Vashti's meeting chamber and glanced at Atossa. "Not even a full day. Am I to understand this is the king's doing?"

Vashti nodded, and Amestris couldn't help the kick of jealousy in her heart. *She* should have been the one to plan such a feast. She tapped one foot, wishing not for the first time that she had some way to rid the kingdom of this woman. This half Persian. But she smiled and held her tongue.

"I've had the invitations sent, and the food is being prepared as we speak. The hall will be ready for the evening meal. I wondered if either of you had suggestions on how we should seat the guests?" Vashti clasped her hands in her lap, her look serene. How smug she must be beneath that smiling demeanor.

They quickly worked out the seating arrangements, and Amestris excused herself before Atossa left. She had no desire to be alone with Vashti. The woman would work to make her son king simply because he was Xerxes' firstborn. Amestris would have none of it. Her Darius would be his father's successor, whatever it took.

She straightened, lifted her chin, and made her way through the women's quarters to the courtyard and gardens that separated the king's area and the rest of the household. The place where Persian nobles often gathered. It was a risk to meet one of the king's advisors, family or not, but Amestris needed Uncle Memucan's advice. A walk among the gardens with the man and her eunuch as guard should not garner suspicion. At least that is what she told herself over and over again since she had requested they meet.

She glanced behind her at her servant Shahin, then looked ahead toward a secluded area of the garden and saw Memucan waiting for her. She drew closer. He bowed slightly at her approach.

"My queen," he said, offering her a slight bow.

"Would that were true," she said, her jaw rigid. "But we both know that it is not."

"And something that you cannot change, for the king delights in Vashti." Memucan turned and Amestris fell into step with him, her guard two steps behind. "But I am sure you have thought of ways to discredit her. Have any of them worked?"

He seemed amused with his question, raising Amestris's ire. "I've done nothing of the kind. You know Xerxes would not take kindly to me speaking against her. What do you think I'm supposed to do?"

She was frowning and she knew it. She forced her lips into a grim line. Be cool and calm, like Vashti managed to be. Why was it so hard to copy the woman's ways? It could not be so hard to act a part one didn't feel. Hadn't she done so all of her life? But she had not come upon a foe as difficult as the woman her husband loved.

"Do not think me callous, my queen." Memucan's handsome face held a furrowed brow. "You know I have always favored you among the king's women." He briefly touched her shoulder. "Even if the king married one of my daughters, I would still consider you their queen. Unfortunately, Darius the First gave Vashti to Xerxes long before he wore the crown, and he has remained besotted with her."

"She is too beautiful." Saying the words pained her. "Xerxes is drawn by physical beauty, and somehow Vashti has remained exactly as she was when he married her. At least that's what Atossa tells me."

"Perhaps her beauty could be used against her." Memucan's words made Amestris stop.

She faced him. "You have a plan?" Her mind whirled with ideas, none of which were of any worth.

"No. Not one that would work the way you hope it will." Memucan stroked his chin. "But do not worry, my queen. Eventually, Vashti will do something that will not please the king, and then we will make the most of the opportunity."

"I cannot think of a single thing she could possibly do that would upset him enough to get rid of her." Amestris did not stop the scowl this time.

"Perhaps we will know it better when the opportunity arises." Memucan touched the small of her back. "Trust me, my dear child. You know you have always been the favored of our family. I will do whatever I can to see that your son Darius and not the son of the usurper follows his father." He met her gaze. "We will find a way."

Amestris gave her uncle a small smile. The truth was that

he would have given one of his many daughters the privilege he offered her, but she was the mother of the heir apparent. He had no choice but to help her if he wanted to further his place in the kingdom.

"Thank you, Uncle. I am counting on you." She turned and walked back to the court of women.

She could count on Memucan. Couldn't she?

CHAPTER Five

Hadassah followed Levia to the home of her oldest son, Taneli. Darkness blanketed the streets, but lamps cast light from the shadows onto the paved stones between Mordecai's home and Taneli's.

"I should have brought more pastries," Levia said, fretting in her usual way. "What if Niria invited more women from among our family? Her mother is near. She would have invited her mother."

"I'm sure we have plenty of food, Ima." Hadassah hefted a basket filled with the delicate pastries, shifting it to her other hand. Levia carried one as well. They had spent the day baking, and Hadassah was anxious to rest with her cousins' wives and enjoy the laughter of family and the antics of the children. Someday Hadassah hoped to have many sons and daughters.

"It is good to come to visit with family again," Hadassah

said as they crossed the threshold to Taneli's home. The warm atmosphere that greeted her put her completely at ease.

"Yes," Levia said. "I will enjoy it more though when Mordecai is home to join us. A few more days. This feast, this keeping ourselves to the shadows or indoors, has worn me out." Levia tsked her tongue as Hadassah put her basket on a low table in the food preparation area. Her cousins' wives busily arranged fruit and nutmeats and cheeses and olives on silver trays and set them on low tables in the sitting room. Children ran in circles, squealing and chasing each other throughout the house. Hadassah ran after two-year-old Isha, chasing the giggling toddler down a hall toward the sleeping room.

"I've caught you!" Hadassah scooped the child into her arms and held her close, rewarded with warm hugs.

"'Dassah! Play with us?" Isha squirmed to be set down, took Hadassah's hand, and tugged her toward a corner where a pile of carved wooden animals sat. Obviously Taneli's work, though some of them had been Hadassah's as a child.

"Of course." Hadassah sat on the floor opposite Isha and joined in as several other children plopped beside her. She told them the story of Noah and the big ship he built and then filled with every kind of animal.

"Even lions?" one of the boys asked. "And camels?"

Hadassah smiled. "Even lions and camels and horses and apes and lizards of every kind and more birds than you can imagine."

The children laughed and turned a small table upside down to make a pretend ship. Hadassah listened to their animal noises and the conversations as they took turns being Noah. At last she stood, brushed off her tunic, and moved back to the sitting area to join the women.

"Taneli claims the king grows drunker by the day," Niria said. "It cannot be good to have the ruler of such a vast kingdom no longer in control of his thinking." She flitted about the room, serving Levia and her sisters-in-law along with several other Hebrew women who had joined them.

"I've heard the same thing," a neighbor said. "Some say he is always this way."

"Mordecai thinks he is worse than he was when the governors and satraps were here a week ago." Levia jumped up to rearrange the tray of sweets.

"I don't suppose he could have remained drunk for six months while planning a war." This from her cousin Sakeri's wife, Keran.

"Unlikely. But it is a concern to have the whole city in such an uproar that an invading force of women could conquer us!" Levia's comment came in hushed tones.

"Only if the women were us," Keran said. "I doubt the guards at the gates are allowed to leave their posts. The king may be merry with wine, but not all of his advisors will be as besotted as he is."

Hadassah listened, her mind whirling. How she loved times with these women, listening to their combined wisdom. She paused a moment and thanked God again for not leaving her an orphan. She had Mordecai and his family, and she couldn't imagine loving anyone more.

But what must her cousins and Mordecai be facing as they ate and drank with the king and the rest of Susa's men? She tried to imagine what the palace looked like on the inside and what Mordecai was forced to deal with each day.

"Nevertheless, Mordecai is still concerned." Levia picked up a spindle, and Hadassah smiled. Her ima could never sit idle.

"Let us talk of more pleasant things," Niria said, offering the tray of sweets to the woman next to her. "The feasting will soon end and we will all forget this week. What could possibly happen during a drunken feast other than foolish men asleep in odd places and women alone waiting for them to come home?" She laughed lightly. "Now tell me, how shall we divide the preparation of food for Passover? Assuming we are going to celebrate it next month?"

The conversation drifted to life's simpler things, and Hadassah half listened to the women and half listened to the children playing in the back room. The women were right, of course. The king often put on lavish feasts. If nothing else, King Xerxes was known for his drunken carousing and his obsession with war and women.

A sudden compassion for the queen filled her. How hard it must be for the woman to have her only rightful position crowded with more wives and plenty of foreign women. Hadassah shuddered at the thought.

She hoped Mordecai would someday give her to Gad in marriage, though even Jola did not know this was her secret longing. He belonged to their tribe of Benjamin. He would grow up to make a good husband. And he was her friend. At least he was during those few times she was allowed to mingle with the boys in their circle. Perhaps one day he would be much more.

Amestris allowed a servant to refill her golden chalice with wine, though she did little more than sip. She glanced about the large banquet hall, listening to the incessant noise of female voices thrumming like high-pitched bees. Annoying beasts, these cloying women. But necessary annoyances nonetheless. None of them came close to what she might call a friend, though Memucan's wife at least attempted to make polite conversation. His second wife, after the death of his first. Amestris had never quite become accustomed to her as either "aunt" or "friend." She was simply a relative—one among many.

She was looking about for a place to set her chalice when a maid took it from her. She stood and moved about the room, searching until her gaze landed on Vashti. The woman sat on a gilded chair, a single circlet of gold about her head. Xerxes would not be pleased to see his queen hosting a feast he had commanded without wearing her proper royal jewels and crown. If Amestris were queen, she would most certainly let every woman in this place know it. Dressing the part would be nonnegotiable.

Vashti was a foreign peasant and had no place in the king's household, let alone the place of his queen.

Never mind that he loves her.

Bah! She almost spoke the word aloud. Xerxes did not know the meaning of love. He favored Vashti's beauty, nothing more. But if the reflecting pools were any indication, Vashti was the most beautiful woman in the harem. Probably in the entire kingdom.

So what are you going to do about it? She hated when her thoughts rambled in her head as though they were a different person. If she had known what to do about Vashti, wouldn't she have done it years ago? Even Memucan could think of no way to use Vashti's beauty against her.

Amestris turned, disgusted with herself. Tomorrow the last day of the feast would commence, and she had yet to figure out a single way to discredit her rival. Vashti did not drink wine and moved about the room with grace, treating every woman in attendance as though she was her favorite friend.

Few women look with such kindness on you.

That did not matter. What mattered was wearing the crown. The true queen's crown. She turned again and stared at the golden circlet. Why did Vashti not wear the heavy headdress filled with jewels so that the women would have no doubt as to her superior status as queen? Why put herself on par with some of the lowest nobles in the room?

A headache began along her temples, and Amestris could no longer bear the mixed scents of perfumes and sweat, which they could not avoid despite the many slaves wielding fans. She nodded to her servants to follow her and headed toward the door. She would sleep, and then she would attempt to think again. Though she doubted either one would do her any good.

Vashti sank onto her couch and pulled Gazsi into her arms. "I've missed you," she whispered into his ear.

He rewarded her with a tight hug and a kiss on her cheek. "Me too, Maman. Will you be away again tomorrow?"

Vashti kissed the top of her son's head and held him at arm's length. "One more day, my son." A sigh escaped. How weary she had grown of the continual conversations that held no significance but to play to the egos of the noblewomen. And the constant need to praise Atossa and even Amestris when she showed her face. Strange that Vashti had seen so little of her these past six days. She had surely been in attendance, but she did not seat herself with the concubines or other wives of Xerxes.

Not that she blamed the woman. Amestris wanted to be singled out as special. To hold first place in Xerxes' life and heart. To take Vashti's place. She'd always known it. The looks from Atossa, the whispered words among the servants, and the scowls from Amestris were reason enough to know Vashti was not their first choice as queen. Only Xerxes thought so. And she trusted that he would not forget their long bond, the one that had carried them through years of childlessness and into the coronation and royal apartments as man and wife.

He wouldn't forget. No matter how drunk he allowed himself to become, he had never done anything to make her fear his wrath. Many others had died under his command, and for this reason men and women all feared coming into his presence without an invitation. His temper could be dreadful. His actions swift.

But he had always treated her with kindness. Gentleness even. Only once had she seen his temper up close, but it was aimed at his mother, not at her. And even then, his mother knew how to cool his ire with a few well-placed words.

"Did I frighten you?" he had said to her once his mother left the room and they were alone in his chambers. "I know I have a quick rage that bursts forth without thought sometimes." He stroked her cheek, then cupped it with his palm. "But never fear, my love. I will never allow myself to grow angry with you. You could never disappoint me."

She nodded and allowed him to kiss her, then applied her womanly charms to appease him and soften his unyielding posture until he was relaxed and at ease with her again. Their love that night had produced Gazsi, and she reminded him often that it was his kindness that had brought about his first son. Surely he would always be kind to her.

She smiled at Gazsi now as he slipped from her hold to play again with his games. If only he had been blessed to have a brother to enjoy these moments with him. Perhaps once this final feast ended, before Xerxes went off to war . . . But she did not ponder long on the thought. She'd had six years to conceive another child and had yet to do so. Amestris had blessed Xerxes with two sons, and he had more by his concubines. When she did spend time alone with him, she felt no quickening in her womb.

She stood and gave instructions for Gazsi to move to his own room and ready himself for bed. She would spend more time with him once the feast had passed. For now, she had one more day to plan—a fact she faced as Omid entered the room. One more day to entertain too many women. Then she would sleep for a week.

CHAPTER Six

Xerxes opened one eye, then quickly shut it, too aware of the blinding light coming through the open windows. When had the dawn snuck up on him? Even his curtained bed did not keep out midday light. He touched his aching head. How long had he slept?

He rose gingerly but still barely made it to the elaborate urn, where he lost the contents of last evening's festivities. He wiped his mouth with a cloth a servant handed him in silence. His servants knew better than to speak to him after a night of revelry. If only the wine obeyed him as well as his servants did. He always managed to pay for his enjoyment for half of the next day or more.

But tonight would be the last night of feasting for some time. He could get through this once his awful headache subsided.

He walked slowly to his gilded chair, where a table sat laden with small squares—a mixture of powdered birds' beaks and myrrh—to help his pounding head. Food would come later, if he could stomach this ancient remedy for his overindulgence. Surely one of his physicians could have come up with something better, but he lifted the gooey mess and popped it into his mouth, barely chewing, then pushed it down with a long draft of water.

Servants stood like statues along the wall, watching him. He ignored them as he fingered another of the disgusting squares and leaned against the chair. What if he just tolerated the drumbeat in his head? He closed his eyes, hating himself in that moment.

He was becoming a glutton and a drunkard. Somewhere in the back of his mind he wondered if his father would approve. He pictured Darius, the great king who had conquered kingdoms like his father before him. If he had not died unexpectedly, he would be the one leading the Persian army to war with Greece. Xerxes would simply accompany him, not be the one in full command.

Why did taking command cause him such hesitance? He could not even seem to make a decision in his own household without the advice of others. Had he ever gone against their advice?

The thoughts caused his head to pound harder. He rubbed his temples, which brought his chief eunuch quickly to his side.

"Majesty, this may help," Harbona said, offering him some white powder and a golden goblet of water.

Xerxes looked at the man. "More birds' beaks?"

Harbona shook his head. "It is from the bark of a tree. It is said to heal." He put the powder in the water, stirred, and sipped from the cup.

Xerxes waited and watched. When the eunuch did not fall over dead, Xerxes drank the rest. One could never be too careful when it came to the king's food and drink. He trusted these eunuchs more than he should. Why had he failed to have the other remedy tested?

He looked out the window over the inner court, where men still slept on benches or were passed out on the grass. He should have them removed until evening, but he had no desire to move, to make any decisions, to sit at court, or to even think. Perhaps he should sleep until evening.

But his body was tired of the bed. He could call for one of his wives . . . Vashti would be comforting. She knew how to help him through these nightmare headaches. Yes, that was what he would do.

"Harbona!" His words were harsh to his own ears. "Send for my queen. I will see Vashti now."

Harbona bowed. "Yes, my lord." He took another eunuch with him and hurried from the king's chambers.

Xerxes leaned back and let his muscles relax. Vashti would help him get through this final day. And she would give him the courage he needed to take on the Greeks. Like it or not, war was coming. He would leave in a few weeks, as even now the army was gathering and heading to Susa, where he would join them. Tonight was his last night to enjoy life as he knew it. Hopefully, he would be returning victorious and could live as he wanted—in peace.

Vashti's servant answered the hard knock on her door. She looked up from helping Gazsi tie the leather straps of his sandals. Though servants usually did such work, she enjoyed doing things mothers did whenever she had the chance. And she had spent too many nights away from her son with this week of feasting. By the time she returned to her rooms each night, Gazsi was fast asleep. So she spent her mornings with him before he headed off with the palace tutors.

"My queen," Omid said, interrupting her thoughts. "Two of the king's eunuchs are here, requesting your presence in the king's chambers."

"Now?" She straightened. What could Xerxes possibly want so early in the day? She had not seen him since this celebration in Susa began. But she accepted her robe and simple crown from her maid and followed Harbona and Karkas toward the king's rooms.

She entered without announcement. Xerxes sat in his chair near the window, elbows on a table, head in his hands.

"Another headache?" she whispered to Harbona.

He nodded.

Vashti removed her robe and stepped closer, kneeling at the king's side. She touched his knee. He looked up and met her gaze. "Another headache?" she said softly.

He grimaced without speaking. She stood behind him and worked her fingers along his temples and neck and the top of his shoulders. Slowly, she felt the sinews in his neck and shoulders soften, his muscles relaxing under her touch.

He leaned his head against her palm. "You always know how to help." He turned slowly and smiled at her. "Whatever would I do without you?"

"Pray we never have to find out," she said, sitting beside him.

He took her hand in his. "I know I drink too much. I allow

myself to be swayed by the men beneath me. I find it too hard to not try to please them."

His admission did not surprise her. Some would have called him weak, but she had known him for so long. He had a deep need to be accepted. Perhaps he was still trying to earn his father's favor—something she was certain he'd never felt during the years Darius lived.

"Your men think very highly of you, my lord. They respect you because you are generous and good, not simply because you are Darius's son. They fear you. You must never fear them." She stroked his cheek with her free hand. "You are the king of Persia. You do not need their approval." She hoped her words convinced him to stop his revelry, his drunkenness, which always caused trouble for him, either personally or in some manner in the kingdom. Never mind the lie that all of his men respected him. She would not speak the truth to him. It would only cause his fragile ego to crack more.

"Perhaps you are right." He squeezed her fingers, then kissed their tips. "You always make me feel better. You make my world right."

"Thank you, my lord." She lowered her head in respect, but he lifted it with a gentle touch.

"Never stop telling me the truth. I depend on you, for there is no one else I trust more." He looked her up and down. "And none of my advisors are nearly as beautiful as you are."

She blushed at his comment, but more at the look he gave her. Compliments from him made her glad of heart, but somehow she did not enjoy dwelling on them lest she conclude he was not sincere. "Is your headache gone then?"

"You have banished it from me completely." He took a piece of flatbread from the table. "And now I am hungry."

"Then you should eat." She took the date spread and slathered it over the bread.

They ate together in silence after he bid her to join him. Sometimes she wished moments like these would never end. But too soon he would move on and prepare for his last night of celebration. As would she.

"I enjoy spending time with you like this," she said as he popped the last piece of bread into his mouth.

He finished with a swallow of goat's milk. "As do I." He stood and offered her his hand. "I will call for you again soon. One more night of feasting in Susa. Then we can live normally again until I head to war."

"Yes. War." She did not hide the sadness that one word evoked.

He took her in his arms. "You will miss me." He kissed her forehead.

"Yes." She searched his gaze. "Please come back safely to me."

"I will. I promise."

He could not promise, of course, but neither one of them was willing to say what they both feared. That he could die in battle. So she smiled and pretended that all was well.

He walked her to the door, and she slipped back into the hall. A few hours of peace until she must don her royal robes and greet the noblewomen one last time. She hurried to her rooms, wanting as much time away from the crowds as she could get.

Hadassah stood in the sitting area, watching while Levia fussed over Mordecai before he headed to work at the palace.

"Must you spend the entire day and night there again?" Levia leaned forward and kissed Mordecai's cheek.

Mordecai gave his wife a fond look, then glanced at Hadassah and smiled. "Take care of her," he said to Hadassah before looking back at his wife. "Levia, you know I cannot disobey the king's edict. He has requested all of the men of Susa to attend his feast. And you know a request does not come with an option to say no. I will go to my work as usual and then join the feasting. Be thankful this is the last day." He kissed her and turned toward the door.

"Be on your guard," Levia warned. "Drunken kings are not safe kings."

Mordecai simply nodded and waved as he stepped into the street. Levia stood a moment watching him, then turned to Hadassah and released a shaky breath. "I fear for him."

"I know you do." Hadassah stepped closer and touched Levia's arm. "You are a good wife to him. But I know Mordecai is cautious. You know he rarely even dresses in the way of the Hebrews to protect us. And he stopped wearing his beard the way the law prescribes in order to work for the king without questions."

"And I fear he will bring down Adonai's wrath on us all by keeping his secrets." Levia moved her arms as if she were swatting a fly, then walked to a low couch, sat, and picked up her spindle. "It is his secrecy I fear as much as I do the king."

"But we live in a foreign land, Ima. Abba would not keep such secrets or break such laws if he did not believe God would understand. Surely we cannot keep every commandment. We cannot sacrifice without a temple. We are barely able to recite the Torah together in this pagan land." Hadassah sat beside Levia and took up a spindle of her own. Once the thread was spun, they could begin the weaving.

"Adonai's name is in Jerusalem with the other exiles. Might we have been safer there?" Levia glanced at the open window. "Though I wonder since the exile whether we are truly safe anywhere."

"Surely God will protect us here, as He has since we came." Hadassah hoped her words were true as she fed the thread through the spindle and pondered Levia's comment. Jerusalem held a fascination for her, and she often wondered if Solomon's palace was anything like King Xerxes' in Susa. Mordecai claimed Xerxes also had a palace in Persepolis, but then it was said that Solomon had built many palaces and fortified towns, his greatest accomplishment being the temple—the very thing the exiles had returned to rebuild.

"Do you not fear, my girl? Have we been in this pagan land so long that you and the people your age see no reason to fear God? Even my Mordecai acts this way. If we truly want our God's blessings, we cannot live in hiding like this." Levia paused to untangle a thread. She seemed more flustered than normal.

A soft sigh lifted Hadassah's chest as she worked with the wool. Levia was clearly distraught. But it was unfair of her to think that no one Hadassah's age, and especially her own husband, did not fear their God.

Hadassah tilted her head to better look into Levia's face. "I fear God, Ima. Every good Hebrew fears Him." Didn't they?

"Not every Hebrew." Levia snapped the thread. "If we had obeyed Him, our ancestors would not have been sent into exile these more than seventy years." She looked into Hadassah's eyes. "I fear Mordecai has become too lax with the

Law. We should be meeting with the others every Sabbath, celebrating every holy day, and doing as our God has taught us to do. How can we go on breaking His laws and not suffer for it?"

Hadassah leaned back and allowed the spindle to stop. These were questions Levia should discuss with her friends. Hadassah was not even old enough to marry, yet Levia often confided in her. She struggled with strong feelings on both sides of the question. Mordecai was her protector, the one who had brought her from her mother's side as she lay dying and took her as his own. She would defend his decisions to do whatever he deemed best to anyone, even his wife.

But Levia had raised her. Taught her every womanly thing she knew. Hadassah understood her frustration when Mordecai seemed to feel the need to please the king even when the king's commands were nonsensical. Sometimes she knew Levia was right, but she did not have the heart to disobey Mordecai or question his words or decisions as Levia did.

"I don't know, Ima." She had already tried to explain her thoughts that surely God would understand. But what if Levia was right? What if Mordecai was wrong to keep such secrets from the Persians? What if hiding their Hebrew identity except from their small family and close-knit clan was an affront to Adonai?

"Well, I do," Levia said, interrupting her thoughts. "And I think we are taking a big risk to hide who we are from our captors. As if they don't already know." She tsked her tongue as if the whole matter were ridiculous. "But Mordecai will not listen. His reasons make no sense, but will he listen to *my* reason? Of course not!" She muttered a few more frustrations as Hadassah picked up the spindle once more.

She let Levia rant while her own mind drifted to other things. Soon Levia would tire of this topic, and once Mordecai was home in the evening, life would go on as usual. Hadassah glanced toward the window, where the last shadows of dawn gave way to the brighter glow of morning. Tomorrow could not come soon enough.

Amestris awoke with a start. The dream had been so real. Surely the gods had visited her in the night with the idea that might give her the very thing she had longed for all these years. A smile threatened, but she squelched it. There was no time to imagine the good when she had no indication that her thoughts were anything more than a foolish dream. She would wait and see.

But first she must get word to her uncle. Memucan would help her. If he was not already too drunk with wine. The fool. All men were fools to become so enamored with Xerxes and continually attempt to please him. Everyone knew he was nothing compared to his father. Could barely judge his people or make a ruling without consulting someone. To ask his advisors was not so bad—most kings did so—but to even take the advice of servants? Xerxes was weak.

The thought spurred her to rise, and she snapped at her maids to hurry with her bath and dress her in her best attire. Then she called for her eunuch to get a message to Memucan to meet her. The man had better show up. Yes, it would be difficult to slip away from the king in the middle of a feast, but if he knew what was good for him, he would make a way. She would give him that subtle warning in her message.

"Is there anything else, my queen?" her maid asked, when

at last she stood dressed in all her finery and royal jewels. Almost as magnificent as on her wedding day. Almost. She would not dare to wear the garments that Xerxes had considered his alone to see, for she had come before him shielded from the eyes of those who would look on. A bride of the king was not to be seen by the common people or even the nobility on her wedding day. Once she belonged to him, she still remained somewhat secluded, kept in the palace, rarely seen in public.

But today would be different. Today that rule must be broken, and the feasting men would look upon the beauty of the king's most favored queen. Xerxes would break all protocol to command such a thing, but if Amestris had her way, he *would* command it. And Vashti would become common in the eyes of every man in Susa and be shown as the peasant she truly was.

Vashti looked out over the gardens from her private rooms and sipped her second cup of reddish-brown tea, trying to relax before she was forced to face Atossa, Amestris, and hundreds of staring women. The call to the king's rooms had been unexpected, but she took courage in his need of her. As long as he needed her, Amestris would be less likely to win him over or usurp her place as queen. And tomorrow she would be free to roam the palace in peace, free of the confines of hostess to the noblewomen.

She drew in a breath and slowly released it, feeling the tension at last ease from her shoulders. In all their years of marriage, Xerxes had never asked her to host so lengthy a feast. A few days, yes. But she had spent many months avoiding the men he had entertained from around the empire, and now to have to be part of his desire for yet more feasting and the resulting drunkenness caused a sliver of fear to creep up her spine. She couldn't tell him, of course, but she hated Xerxes' drinking.

She was much happier to have him thinking clearly, honestly, and soberly than to have him merry. He paid attention to their son, showed her greater kindness, and didn't consume himself with the troubles of his kingdom or other kingdoms he seemed insistent on conquering. Wine changed all of that in him, and she hated it. Her people had fallen to destruction when her father, Belshazzar, and his nobles drank from the golden goblets of the Hebrew god, and she feared one day Xerxes would do something just as foolish and end up judged by some god he had offended.

She set the tea on a side table and took one last look at the gardens. Tonight she would wear her jewels and royal crown. Xerxes would be glad to know she wore the crown, even if she didn't tell him she'd only done so once. She knew he would have wanted her to wear it every night of the feast to show the others the way he favored her. What he didn't know was fine with her. Though she had no doubt his mother or Amestris would report her every move to him.

She must watch Amestris more carefully. Omid would help her do so, as he always did. Perhaps she would send him to check on the woman before the banquet began—see what she did with her time. If he could do so inconspicuously. Yes, that's what she should do. Better to know her rival's actions than to be blindsided by them.

CHAPTER Seven

"What do you expect Amestris to do, my queen? I have had little success in the past in securing information about her. Her servants are loyal. And if I follow her too closely, she will suspect you of spying on her." Omid clasped his hands in front of him. "Though if you ask it of me, I will do my best to be discreet."

"I do not want you to put yourself in danger, Omid. I simply want to make sure Amestris is not somehow speaking with the king when she belongs with the women. I know I sound fearfully ridiculous, but there has been something in her manner these past few days that has concerned me. I would like to relieve my fears." Vashti touched one of her earrings to make certain it was straight, though she knew it was placed perfectly.

"I will see what I can do, Majesty." Omid bowed and left her presence.

She walked to the banquet hall, escorted by her eunuchs

and maids. Undoubtedly Amestris would be there already, waiting, watching. No matter how early Vashti arrived, Amestris always seemed to be one step ahead of her. The realization brought an uneasy feeling to her gut. Why did her rival evoke these fears? But she knew the reason. Amestris's hatred of Vashti could be felt even across the length of a room, no matter how congenial she pretended to be. How glad she would be when this feast ended and she could avoid Amestris at all costs.

Amestris crossed the threshold of the hall of women into the king's private gardens. Memucan met her before she had a chance to fully enter.

"You should not be here. What are you thinking? He is not in good humor or thinking clearly." Memucan frowned and rubbed his clean-shaven chin.

"I need to talk to you, and it cannot wait." Amestris intertwined her arms over her chest and met his fierce gaze. "I've had a dream, and I believe there is a way to coax the king to bring down Vashti."

Memucan glanced behind him, then leaned closer. "Be careful what you say," he hissed. "We cannot know who might be hiding in the foliage or hear of your words in some other way, and then it would be you in trouble. And me for having spoken to you." He stepped back, the scowl growing deeper.

Amestris was not deterred. "All you have to do is convince the king to request Vashti to appear before the men dressed in her royal finery, wearing her royal crown. To show off her beauty to his guests. Trust me, he will *want* to show others what only he is supposed to see. Especially when he is thoroughly drunk."

Memucan stared at her for so long she wondered if he would speak. He rubbed the back of his neck. "You are asking me to suggest that he go against a most deeply held rule of court. No man is to look upon the king's women, not even during the ceremony of marriage. You know this. Do you not recall the heavy veils that hid you from the eyes of all? What makes you think the king would even consider such a thing?"

Good. He was considering her suggestion. She could tell by the fact that he had repeated her request to her. And by the gleam in his eyes. He would like to see Vashti humiliated as much as she would.

"If this was not of the gods, why would I have had such a dream? I have thought for years of a way to expose her for what she is—a Babylonian half princess not fit to rule in any fashion on Persia's throne. And then the thought came in a dream. How can you discount it?" She tapped one finger against her chin and watched him.

His eyes gave away his struggle. "I should not even be talking to you."

She knew then that she had him. "But you are, and you know I am right." She slowly smiled. "Trust me. When it is done and I take Vashti's place, your daughters will rise to places of great prominence. I have greater influence over Xerxes than Vashti ever did." She didn't, but he did not need to know that. Or how inadequate and uncertain she felt.

"I will watch to see if there is a good time. I will not act if there is not." Memucan moved away from her.

"There will be," Amestris assured him. "Trust me."

He turned and left without a word. He might not trust her,

but he would act. When the time was right and her husband was fully drunk, Memucan would plant the idea, and the king would do the rest.

Vashti turned at the sound of footsteps. Omid motioned to her, and she moved gracefully toward him, though her steps threatened to match the sudden pounding of her heart. They met in an alcove to the side of the banquet hall.

Vashti looked before and behind her to be sure they were alone. "What did you learn?" She bent nearer to him and he leaned down, for he towered over her.

"Amestris met with Memucan," Omid said, his lips drawn into a thin scowl. "I did my best to draw close enough to hear their conversation, but I could only piece together parts of it."

"What was your impression?" The meeting could have been about anything, but Vashti doubted it was good.

"I heard your name mentioned. And they spoke of a desire to see you taken down by the king himself. I am sorry that I could not hear more than that. I risked being noticed if I got closer to them." Omid clasped his hands behind his back and straightened. "What would you have me do, my queen? Shall I attend the banquet of the king's men and try to intercept anything Memucan tries to do?"

Vashti smoothed her gown and glanced down the long hall, which led to the outer doors of the room. "No," she said. "I would rather have you here. Watch Amestris and keep me abreast of anything else she does that seems wrong or out of place. She would take my position as queen and favorite of Xerxes in a heartbeat. But the king has never listened to her or to his mother in this regard. And if anyone has influence with him, it is his mother. Memucan will not be able to convince the king of anything he is not willing to do."

Even drunk, Xerxes would not foolishly do something to harm her. He loved her.

She drew in a breath and let it slowly release. "We will continue today as we have all week. If something happens that is out of the normal routine, I will trust you to help me make the right decision."

Omid nodded. "Of course, my queen."

As he stepped back at her dismissal, she wondered again whether there was truly anyone she could trust.

Xerxes entered the court of men amid a lengthy fanfare. Though it was still early in the day, after Vashti left him he'd grown restless. He must finish this week and be done with it. Surely he could stop the desire for fine food and drink, which seemed at times to consume him.

He settled on cushions that overlooked the garden court, where some of the men of Susa had begun to gather. His seven noblemen soon joined him, and servants started filling the golden goblets with rich red wine.

Entertainers and musicians and jugglers filled one corner of the court, and men gathered to watch. Xerxes looked on from above and listened to one of the stories Memucan was telling them.

"My wife tried to talk me out of coming tonight," he said, leaning closer to Xerxes. "She feared I was drinking too much and for some reason seems to think it's a bad thing for a man to enjoy himself." He laughed, and Xerxes joined him. Vashti would never have told him what he did was wrong. She might encourage him to drink less, but she did not have the audacity of Memucan's wife.

"I assume you told her to mind her own business," Shethar said. Everyone knew that Shethar's wife was the quiet, obedient type.

"I did indeed," Memucan said, smiling. "At first I did not receive the response I expected from her. She had the nerve to argue with me."

Xerxes looked at his nobleman's expression to gauge whether the story was true.

"Of course, I could not tolerate such a response." Memucan lifted his chin. "She did not argue long." His eyes narrowed and he sipped from his cup. "I will not allow a woman to rule my own house."

Murmurs of agreement passed among the men, and Xerxes offered a slight nod. A man was to be honored in his own home. Everyone in Persia knew it. Surprising that Memucan's wife was not already more obedient and acquiescing. None of Xerxes' wives would argue with him, especially Vashti. Amestris had tried, but she learned quickly that he did not tolerate such disrespect.

He turned away from his men to watch the jugglers, pondering Memucan's tale. Had the man struck his wife in order to stop the argument? It would not have surprised him, though Xerxes had never found it necessary or desirable to strike a woman. They might deserve death, but those cases were just. Was Memucan just?

He took a long drink, wondering why the tale troubled him at all.

As the midday festivities drew near, Vashti returned to the banquet hall and entered with all of the fanfare of her royal status. Every noblewoman bowed as the flag bearers and trumpeters announced her presence. She took her seat at the center of the room, where a golden throne had been placed for her use. Rarely did she have the chance to sit in a place of such honor, and tonight she would use it to her advantage. The dining and entertainment could go on around her while she watched the women.

She nodded once at Omid, who had suggested the seating arrangement, and settled back, her gaze moving over the room. Amestris sat at the main table with Atossa, a look of satisfaction on her normally pinched face. Vashti looked past her without interest. Let the woman think she had control over the king's advisors. Vashti would not be controlled.

She smiled at the rest of the women and bid them to take their places. Jugglers and dancers took up the center of the room, and servants moved about, serving the women every delicacy of food and drink that Vashti had ordered.

By the time the sun began to set, Vashti had allowed herself to relax. Soon the banquet would end, and she could return to her son and all would be well.

How good it would be to be rid of her continual contact with Amestris. Cunning, controlling, and cruel Amestris. That Xerxes had agreed to wed her had hurt Vashti more deeply than she cared to admit. But it was the price one paid to marry a king. As the daughter of kings, she knew that too well.

Xerxes felt his head spin, and laughter spilled from his mouth at every simple thing said to him. Oh yes, he was quite merry now. But it was the last night he would allow himself to consume so much wine, and tomorrow he could call for Vashti to help if he had another headache.

He laughed at the thought of her rubbing his shoulders, caressing him, and his mind drifted to all he would do with her when they were at last alone again. Such beauty. The woman was flawless.

Memucan was talking again and mentioned that his reason for keeping his wife was her beauty.

Xerxes guffawed at the comment. "No one can top my Vashti's beauty. And she is as obedient as a trained pup."

"Perhaps you would like to prove her obedience to us, my king," Memucan said. "And let us gaze on her beauty to see for ourselves." He smiled, then looked from one man to the next.

Each one of his nobles murmured their agreement.

"Yes."

"What a good idea."

"Send for the queen."

The comments continued until Xerxes wished he had not opened his mouth. But the words were said, and now he had something to prove. These men would not respect him if he did not show them that he spoke the truth.

"All right," he said to an attendant standing near. "Send me the seven eunuchs who serve me." He would dispatch them to fetch Vashti from the women's banquet and show off her beauty to the entire crowd. Never mind that no one but him was supposed to see the queen's beauty, not even her face. He would make it up to Vashti later. She would come for him. She would understand his need.

A commotion at the outer door drew Vashti out of her thoughts and away from the distant buzz of female voices. She searched for Omid, but he no longer stood near. She spotted him near the entrance, where seven men waited.

Vashti squinted, trying to take in the features of the men. Omid spoke with them, his expression troubled. When he stepped back, a knot settled in Vashti's middle. The men were the king's seven eunuchs. She would recognize them anywhere. They were among the very few who served in the presence of the king. She often spoke with them when one or more were sent to fetch her to appear in Xerxes' chambers.

Why were they here now? The banquet had not ended, had it? Was Xerxes back in his rooms, wanting her to join him? So soon after a week of feasting? Curiosity mingled with uncertainty in her heart. She met Omid's gaze as he knelt before her.

"My queen. The king's men have come with a message from the king." Though he kept his voice low, she could hear the strain in his tone.

"Speak," she said, looking briefly at the king's eunuchs.

Omid cleared his throat, and she sensed his discomfort. "The king has commanded Queen Vashti to appear before him wearing her royal crown, in order that he might display her beauty to the peoples and the princes." He had not risen from his kneeling position and spoke without meeting her gaze.

She drew in a sharp breath, which caused her servant to look up. "Now?" What was Xerxes thinking? No one other than the servants and the king was supposed to look upon the beauty of the king's women. Even as queen, she did not sit beside him on his royal throne or stand in public. Not once since she had become queen had he made such a request. Even Amestris and Xerxes' concubines were kept from public view. To ask her to come before his men was to betray a trust. It was degrading and disrespectful of him.

How could he?

She bid Omid to stand before her. He rose slowly. "Is that all they said?" she whispered so only he could hear.

"Yes, my queen."

She studied his square face. "Why would he ask such a thing? It goes against his protocol. He would never do this if he were thinking clearly. Is he drunk with wine?"

Omid shrugged one shoulder. "I do not know, my queen. I suspect so, as that seems to be his custom during such feasts."

Vashti sat in silence, looking over the crowd of women who had grown unnervingly quiet. Each one seemed to focus either on the eunuchs or on her. She searched for Amestris and Atossa but saw only Atossa in her assigned seat. Was Amestris behind this?

Memucan must have planted this idea in the king's head, for surely he would not ask it on his own.

Her ire rose as she looked about the room again. "Where is Amestris?" she asked Omid, keeping her voice low.

He turned slowly, looking left to right. His expression told her what she already knew. "She does not appear to be in the room, my queen."

Vashti fought the temptation to chew her lower lip. Her rival had something to do with this. That's why she'd met with Memucan this morning. Did she truly think Vashti would be so foolish as to humiliate herself in front of all? When Xerxes sobered, he would regret his decision to parade her before them, and it could ruin her relationship with the king for good. He would no longer be able to say that he alone had looked on her beauty, and he might put another in her place.

"Which is exactly what she wanted all along," Vashti said, realizing at Omid's lifted brow that she had spoken aloud.

"Begging your pardon, my queen. I do not understand."

"It is nothing, Omid. But mark my words. Amestris has something to do with this request. She wants to see me humiliated before the king's nobles and the common men. Well, I am not so easily fooled." She swallowed. Met his gaze. "Tell the king's eunuchs that I am not coming. I refuse to break the king's law to embarrass him in such a way."

Omid nodded. "You are sure?" His uncertainty at her answer unnerved her.

"You don't think I should do this?" Whose side was he taking? The old fear that even her closest servant could not be trusted surfaced once more.

"You must do what you think best, my queen. It is hard to say how the king will respond if he has had too much wine to drink." Omid bowed his head. "I will give the eunuchs your response."

He walked back toward the entrance, and she wondered for the briefest moment if she should change her mind and call him back. To disobey Xerxes could cost her. But to obey could cost her more and humiliate them both.

Her refusal was a risk she had to take.

CHAPTER Eight

Amestris pulled Biztha aside as he slipped from the banquet room and headed back to face the king. He was the one eunuch belonging strictly to Xerxes who favored her over Vashti, and by his look, she could not withhold a smile. "She refused then?"

Biztha nodded. "Yes, my queen." He glanced at his fellow eunuchs, who marched ahead of him back to the king's gardens, where the king and his men and the people still celebrated.

"Good," she said. "Come and tell me everything the king decides as soon as you can."

He bowed and she waved him on. He could not show up late behind the others, lest he anger the king.

Vashti would suspect her absence, but soon, if her hopes and dreams were correct, what Vashti thought would no longer matter.

"Where did you go?" Atossa asked, smiling her way.

"I fear I had too much to drink." Let her mother-in-law think she had simply gone to relieve herself. If she had her way, she would be relieved of her nemesis as well. And that could not come soon enough.

Xerxes leaned against his cushioned couch and guzzled the rest of the wine in his cup. A servant quickly refilled it. Xerxes looked at the contents and set the goblet aside. He laughed, giddy with the pleasures surrounding him. Life was good. His men were happy, his own heart light. Soon Vashti would appear before him, and he could show the world that the king of kings was wed to the most beautiful woman in all of Persia. And the entire known world!

He laughed again. He could not help himself, though his advisors looked at him as though he was mad. Let them wonder what made him merry. Surely they suspected how much he appreciated Memucan's suggestion. Hadn't he thought the same thing many times in the past? What silly law had kept him from showing his prize to his men all these years? True, before he had worn the crown, Vashti was not kept as hidden. But memories faded, and to show her now, to show that her beauty had not faded, would fill his men with jealousy.

He chuckled, pleased with himself. How unfortunate that law had been. He had missed out on years of added respect that a beautiful wife afforded him.

Why keep her to himself? She would shine, decked out in her royal apparel and the jeweled crown he'd had made for her when he ascended the throne. It set her apart from all other women, something she most certainly deserved. Ah, Vashti. *How I love you, my queen.*

Had he told her that? Love was not something men thought about in terms of marriage. They wed for status, to carry on their name, to increase wealth. Love was hardly something that entered a man's mind when he took a woman to his bed.

But as he listened to the men's laughter around him, he felt the slightest sobering. If love was real, then Vashti had won his heart. He could not imagine his world without her. Without her tender embrace, her willingness to do whatever he asked of her, and her understanding mind, he would be lost. What man among those here compared to her?

Certainly not in form. The thought caused his heart to beat faster as he considered her beauty once more. After this night, he would call her to his bed and enjoy what his men would only glimpse here. A smile lifted his lips. He reached again for his cup and drank.

The sound of marching feet drew his attention, and he realized that his eunuchs had already returned. He searched among them. Counted seven of them. Where was Vashti?

"My lord." Biztha stepped forward and knelt at his feet. "We took your command to Queen Vashti, and she refused to come and appear before the king and his men."

Xerxes stared at the eunuch for a silent, lengthy breath. The air in the room around him thinned, and he felt as though a spear had pierced him. She had *refused* him?

He drew himself up, anger rising slowly, then increasing in strength with every strangled breath. "What did you say?"

Biztha cowered and moved slightly away from him. "Begging your pardon, my lord. We delivered your message to the queen. She refused to come with us to show her beauty to you and your guests, my lord." The eunuch stilled, his wide gaze displaying his fear.

He should have the eunuchs killed. Every last one of them! "How dare you defy my order! Did I not tell you to bring her with you?" Xerxes' words roared through the court. Silence fell like a pall. "Take them away. All of them!"

Guards appeared and the seven eunuchs marched away, surrounded by the men who would see to their execution. Yet Xerxes' anger did not abate. The eunuchs were weak. They should not have listened to a woman!

He turned to face his seven advisors, each of whom had paled. Good. Let them fear the king's wrath. And let them come up with a good punishment for this "favored" wife. The one he thought he loved.

Love! There was no such thing. If a woman could be so favored as to enjoy his presence and repay him with such disrespect, she did not deserve to have his affection.

Vashti accepted a cup of wine from a servant, her first of the banquet. What could Xerxes possibly be thinking to want her to stand before a whole city of men? In her royal crown? Did he mean *only* her crown? Her face heated at that thought. Surely not. Surely he simply wanted to show her beauty dressed in her royal finery.

Would saying yes have been so bad? Should she even now change her mind and send Omid to catch up to the eunuchs? No. She could not allow herself to be so humiliated, for if Xerxes were drunk, there was no telling what else he might ask of her once she arrived at his feast.

She turned to listen to the conversations nearest her, but her mind whirled with uncertain thoughts. When would this day end? She longed to hold her son and lie beside him to rest, to hear his gentle breathing as he slept. How much longer?

Another commotion at the banquet doors rattled her already fraught nerves. She straightened, lifted her chin, and smoothed her expression. Whatever it was, she would meet it as a queen should.

Hegai, the eunuch in charge of the king's harem, appeared at the door, and Omid met him. They spoke in whispers until at last Hegai came forward with Omid. Both bowed before her.

"What news do you bring?" She met Hegai's gaze. Was that sorrow in his dark eyes?

"The king has sent me with this message." He straightened.

"Where are the eunuchs who came to me earlier?" she asked before he could say more.

"The king has removed them," Hegai said.

Vashti knew better than to ask what he meant by that. Xerxes had a violent temper, and no doubt his messengers had received the punishment for her refusal to obey the king. Sudden sadness filled her that she could be responsible for harm to those men. She looked briefly away, then met Hegai's gaze once more. The message had to be important for the king to send his highest-ranking eunuch.

"Tell me what the king said." She clasped her hands in her lap.

Hegai cleared his throat. "Begging your forgiveness, my queen, but it is my unfortunate task to tell Queen Vashti that because she refused the king's summons, he asked his advisors, 'According to the law, what is to be done to Queen Vashti because she has not performed the command of King Xerxes delivered by the eunuchs?'"

Vashti sensed the heat of Xerxes' anger in Hegai's words. Her stomach dipped in a sense of dread.

"Then Memucan spoke to the king," Hegai continued. "He said, 'Not only against the king has Queen Vashti done wrong, but also against all the officials and all the peoples who are in all the provinces of King Xerxes. For the queen's behavior will be made known to all women, causing them to look at their husbands with contempt, since they will say, "King Xerxes commanded Queen Vashti to be brought before him, and she did not come." This very day the noblewomen of Persia and Media who have heard of the queen's behavior will say the same to all the king's officials, and there will be contempt and wrath in plenty.'"

The knot twisted in Vashti's gut, and she knew without looking that Amestris was smiling at her loss. This was why her rival had met with Memucan before the banquet. Vashti felt light-headed.

Hegai droned on, but Vashti barely heard him for the faint feeling overcoming her. "'If it pleases the king,' Memucan said to the king, 'let a royal order go out from him, and let it be written among the laws of the Persians and the Medes so that it may not be repealed, that Vashti is never again to come before King Xerxes. And let the king give her royal position to another who is better than she. So when the decree made by the king is proclaimed throughout all his kingdom, for it is vast, all women will give honor to their husbands, high and low alike.'"

Dread grew to stunned incomprehension. Never see her husband again? Never enter his presence, listen to his heart, share his love? Was it not just this morning he had called for her and promised his protection? And what of her son? Would he remain while she alone was sent away?

"I'm afraid, my queen, that this means you must come with me. The king's orders are to have you removed from the palace before this night ends," Hegai said, but she heard him as through a long tunnel.

"Omid?" She looked from Hegai to her eunuch, but his face bore no expression. Not even the sorrow and compassion covering Hegai's features. Was he glad of this? Had he sided with Amestris all along?

"I will help you gather what you need, my queen," Omid said. "And I will see about Gazsi."

They both glanced at Hegai. He nodded. "The king said nothing about his son."

Perhaps she would have this one comfort to take him with her. Would the king allow them to live? But he had not ordered her death. Only her loss of position. No doubt Amestris would take her place. She looked at her rival and did not miss the smirk on her round face.

Vashti turned away and slowly stood. She lifted her head and stepped down from the throne, left the banquet hall, and walked toward her apartments.

CHAPTER *Nine*

Hadassah greeted Mordecai, carrying a small oil lamp. "You are home at last." She smiled at him as he closed the door behind him.

He kissed her cheek. "Where is Levia?" He looked about the room, a brow lifting.

"She was here waiting with me, but she grew so weary that she sought her pallet. She asked me to wake her when you arrived." Hadassah searched Mordecai's face. "Should I wake her?"

Mordecai sank onto a low couch and glanced toward the hall, where his wife slept in a small room. "No. Do not wake her. When I join her, if she wakes, I will tell her anything she asks of me." He ran a hand over his face. Somehow he looked older than he had that morning.

Hadassah sat across from him and set the lamp on a low table. "Did something happen?" She had come to read his expressions, and she held a bond with him that he did not share with his sons or even his wife. She was the daughter he'd never had.

He nodded, then leaned forward and placed his head in his hands. Hadassah waited until he lifted his gaze to hers. "The king has done a foolish thing." His words were whispered, barely audible.

"What happened?" she asked again.

Mordecai clasped his hands. "The king and his men drank too much wine tonight. This is not unusual, because the king often drinks much wine. But tonight he broke a tradition of his fathers and ordered Queen Vashti to appear before him in front of all who were there. The tradition of the kings of Persia is that a king's wives or concubines appear only to the king—and, of course, to their servants—but not to the general male populace. Even upon their marriage, they are covered in veils or hidden behind screens, lest a common man gaze on their beauty." Mordecai's chest lifted in a sigh.

Hadassah drew in a startled breath, suddenly fearing for the queen who once was so kind to her. "Did she come?"

Mordecai shook his head. "No. She refused the king's command. And the king banished her from being queen. Queen Vashti was sent from Susa this very night."

Hadassah stared at him. "Where did he send her?"

Mordecai shrugged. "No one knows. She was sent with her son from the kingdom. I daresay she left as quickly as the messengers who carried a decree throughout Persia declaring every man ruler in his own home. As if we needed such a thing." Scorn dripped from Mordecai's lips.

"Is not every man already ruler in his own home?" Hadassah tilted her head, searching his face.

"Exactly. The king asked the queen to break a tradition,

a law even, that would humiliate them both, and she had more sense than he did. If she had obeyed such a foolish command"—he lowered his voice again—"it would have decreased the king's respect in the eyes of all the people. As it is, this decree will likely do the same."

Hadassah sat in silence, processing Mordecai's news. "Who will take her place?" she asked at last.

He made a disgusted sound. "Probably Amestris. No doubt she had something to do with the whole scheme. She is related to Memucan, after all, and Memucan put the idea in the king's head when he was cheerful with too much wine."

Hadassah nodded. "Amestris is not a nice person, is she?" The gossips had little good to say about the king's second wife, mother to his heirs.

"She is not," Mordecai said, standing. "I'm going to bed. You get some sleep."

Hadassah nodded and walked to her room. She lay awake long into the night, wondering how things would change with a new, unkind queen.

Vashti huddled with Gazsi in the curtained litter and jolted every time the men carrying them moved. At last they fell into a steady rhythm, and Gazsi slept in her arms. Sleep would be a welcome thought but for the ache in her heart. How could she be banished?

The realization still stung deep within, and she could not bring herself to fully accept it. Surely Xerxes would come to his senses and change his mind on the morrow. But Omid had told her of the decree that ran with her and away from her, carried by messengers throughout the kingdom. Her banishment was permanent and complete. She would never see her husband's face again.

As the last of her things were packed and readied in carts, the news had come from Omid that she would live in the palace in Persepolis. When Xerxes came to winter there, she would move to a place he would have built for her in the far reaches of the kingdom. She would not return to Susa again.

Persepolis held a large, beautiful palace, perhaps nicer than the one in Susa, but apparently this arrangement was the king's temporary answer to the dilemma he faced on where to send her. It would take time to secure proper lodging. That he had not suggested she be imprisoned or executed had made the blow easier to bear. Her son would live, and she with him. And it was a kindness that Omid and her maids had been sent to accompany her. A kindness to her, though probably not to them.

Perhaps Xerxes did care for her—though his actions this night made her doubt. His fine talk, his compliments, his favor . . . fleeting things, all of them.

A deep sigh escaped as she shifted Gazsi to a more comfortable position. She closed her eyes. Perhaps if she could just pretend tonight had not happened . . . She would awaken in her bed, or the king would call for her any moment now and she would attend him and rest beside him . . .

She'd made the right decision, hadn't she? If she had gone with his eunuchs and allowed Xerxes to display her beauty to his men, what might that have meant once she arrived to an unruly, drunken crowd? Would the king have asked her to remove her royal robe? How much of her beauty did he want her to display?

Once Xerxes sobered, he would regret this entire evening.

Of that she had no doubt. She knew him too well. Had been his friend before he wore the crown and his only lover for years. Would he really put Amestris in her place as queen? The woman had given him two sons, so undoubtedly one of them would follow his father to the throne. But would Xerxes care for Amestris as he had for her?

She shook her head, unable to imagine it. The Xerxes she knew would not, could not, love Amestris the way he loved her. He might allow her position to be elevated, but he would not care for her in the same way. He could not. He had told her so more than once, and she'd seen the truth in his eyes.

He had also promised to protect and keep her, and she now saw how well he kept his word. She looked through a slit in the curtain at the moon shining down on her and brushed a tear from her cheek. Persepolis was a long walk for her litter bearers. Far enough from the king that even if he changed his mind, he could not act quickly to undo what he had done.

Amestris sought out Memucan late, long after the king and the rest of the men had dispersed. She was not likely to receive a summons from Xerxes this night, and she was eager to hear all that had happened. If Biztha had returned to tell her, she could have gone to her rooms and let Memucan be. The news of the eunuchs' execution had come as a blow. She had never expected Xerxes to kill his messengers simply because his wife refused him. But then one never knew where the king's thoughts and his temper might take him.

She turned a corner in the hall and emerged into the passage that led to the king's gardens. A shadowy figure approached, and she breathed easier once he spoke.

"I thought you would give me until tomorrow to ask for details," Memucan said, his words slightly slurred.

"You're drunk." She made a disgusted sound. "You should have remained clearheaded. What if things had gone differently?"

"But they did not, now did they?" His sharp tone made her step back. "I had to drink. One does not ignore the food and wine of the king while sitting in the king's presence."

"No, of course not." She lowered her voice, hoping he detected a softening in her tone. "Please, tell me everything."

"I am sure you already know as much as you need to know. I made your suggestion to the king, he acted on it, and Vashti refused. Now she is on her way out of Susa, and we have no acting queen."

"He did not name a successor then?" She would have heard if Xerxes had named her, but she needed to hear Memucan tell her just the same.

"No, he did not. He was too busy writing the edict. I doubt he has fully comprehended what he has done or that he will never see Vashti again." Memucan rubbed a hand over the stubble along his jaw.

"When he is sober, we must convince him that I am the best choice." She searched his face. He wouldn't back out on her now, would he?

"I am tired, Amestris. I did what you asked. What happens next is not my decision. If the king asks my opinion, I will suggest you, of course. But after tonight, I believe it will be in my best interest to stay clear of him for some time. He will not be pleased with the man who suggested Vashti appear before him, because without that desire, she would still be here. And like it or not, my dear 'queen,' the king loved

Vashti. He will not soon get over her." He rubbed his eyes as if trying to keep them open.

"Where did they send her?" If she knew, she could find a way to be rid of Vashti for good. That would help Xerxes to forget her. And there were always those who were willing to do anything for gold.

"I don't know." Memucan eyed her with suspicion. "Why do you care?"

"Surely someone knows."

"Someone surely does. The king must. Perhaps his closest servants do, but I'm in no mood to ask. And I believe the king did not wish her whereabouts to be known. Even if you ask, I doubt you will find your answer." He turned and started to walk away.

"Wait!" Amestris moved closer to him but stopped short of clutching his arm.

He whirled about. "What now?"

How dare he growl at her? She was his superior! But she dare not push him. Not when he was still filled with too much wine. He might speak to the wrong person, and her part in this could put her life in jeopardy. She could not risk it.

"Nothing. Thank you. I just wanted to thank you for what you did. When I am queen, I will make sure you are richly rewarded." She smiled, though she wondered if he could sense her insincerity. She had no certainty that she would ever reign in Vashti's place. Her son might be Xerxes' heir, but mothers did not rise with the same favor until their sons ruled.

"I hope you get what you want, Amestris. It is hard to grasp at the wind." Memucan walked away then, and she stood looking after him for a long time, wondering why he should think her ambitions were as fleeting as the wind.

CHAPTER *Ten*

The room spun and that telltale sick feeling grew within Xerxes, despite the fact that he'd passed out and slept for hours. He was getting too old to consume so much wine. What was it about being around his men that caused him to lower himself to the ways of a common man? He drank from intricately carved golden goblets, each different from the next, and consumed the finest wines in all of Persia. In the entire known world, for that matter. Was he so weak that he could not hold a few goblets of wine and not feel ill the next day?

How else did a man feel merry if not for the consumption of fine food and drink? He forced his head from the pillow but slumped back and closed his eyes to still the whirling room. He must get hold of himself. Vashti would know how to help. He must call for her to come at once and work her skilled fingers along his temples and shoulders. She would ease the suffering simply by her presence.

He courted a smile at the thought, until a vivid memory assaulted him. Swift images moved through his mind. A summons. A refusal. A command against his eunuchs. Biztha? Harbona? His guards had marched them away, their heads covered.

He sat abruptly and leaned over the side of the bed, losing what remained in his stomach onto the rich carpet beneath his raised bed. Servants moved about like silent rodents, wiping his mouth, cleaning the mess, settling him among the cushions of the bed.

All the while his mind cried out to stop the memories. Was he dreaming?

"Vashti!" He heard his voice through cracked lips, a whisper barely audible. No one approached him.

"Vashti!" he called again, louder this time.

Footsteps drew close, slowly, cautiously.

"My lord? May I help you with something?" The voice sounded strange. Not one of his attending eunuchs.

He forced his eyes to open and focus on the man. "Send for Vashti. I want Vashti now!" Would he never be free of the incompetence surrounding him? What was so incredibly hard about sending for his wife? Everyone knew that he needed her when the wine overtook him.

The servant cleared his throat, and Xerxes searched his face. The man would not meet his gaze.

"Look at me," he commanded despite his pounding head. "Tell me why no one in the palace seems capable of sending for my wife. Is this such a difficult task that I have to ask twice?"

The servant clasped his hands around his belt and twisted the fabric in nervous hands. "My lord king. May you live forever."

Yes, yes, stop the pleasantries. A sense of foreboding filled him at the man's downcast look.

"I fear the king has been ill and forgotten the events that transpired last evening."

The sick feeling returned to his gut, and he feared he would embarrass himself once more. "Tell me everything." Why couldn't he remember? But a part of him sensed that he could if he would allow the memories to fully surface.

"Last evening," the man said, his voice quavering, "the king celebrated the final night of the feast with his men. In the course of time, when the king's heart grew merry with wine, he commanded Queen Vashti to appear before him, wearing the royal crown in order to display her beauty to the crowd. The king sent the seven eunuchs to bring Vashti to him, but the queen refused to come. This angered the king, and he ordered the execution of the eunuchs and banished the queen from ever entering his presence again. She was sent to Persepolis under cover of darkness until a suitable home could be built for her. The king then wrote a decree that cannot be revoked, commanding all men to rule their own households, and messengers were dispatched throughout the entire kingdom. My lord." He stopped, his breath coming fast as though he feared his fate would be that of the eunuchs.

"I did this?"

"Yes, my lord. It is written in the laws of the Medes and Persians and cannot be revoked." The man's face paled as Xerxes stared at him.

Memories of Memucan's suggestions and his willing compliance, his wrath that Vashti refused him, his rash decisions, suddenly came flooding back. Why had she refused to come? Yet deep down he knew that the fault lay with him. He should never have put her in such a compromising position. She was trying to protect his honor and keep him from humiliating them both. Vashti had always been his confidante and the wiser one. And he had sent her away, never to return.

What a fool you are, Xerxes! How could you do such a thing? A deep sense of grief and loss filled him, and he wondered if he had the strength to ever rise from his bed and rule his kingdom again. He was a complete and utter fool for sending her away, and worse, for banishing her forever.

The thought turned the spinning room into an inner sense of spiraling downward until he wondered if he would ever climb out of his sudden depression.

"I've lost her then," he said, not wanting a response.

The man merely nodded and stepped back from the bed.

Xerxes turned on his side, gingerly so as not to awaken the sick feeling or deepen the pounding of his head. But it was no use. He would not sleep again, though sleep was all he longed to do. He had lost his life's true love, and he had no one to blame but himself.

Weeks passed, and Xerxes made every attempt to push thoughts of Vashti from his mind. War loomed on the horizon, and he expected his fighting men to gather outside Susa by month's end. The distraction was perfect, for his muddled thoughts could make no sense of his actions that day. He had tried desperately to recall each moment, to give himself a reason to point the blame at someone else. Surely the suggestion had not been his alone. Memucan stood behind this. Memucan and the other seven nobles. Perhaps some of his wives. Or his mother.

His constant frustration came to a head a week before he was to head to war.

"My lord, the soldiers have begun to arrive and are setting up camp outside of the city," Memucan said. "Is there anything we can do to help you, my lord, to prepare for your personal needs?" He had seemed unduly subdued since Vashti's loss, and Xerxes studied this advisor and relative of Amestris.

"You can tell me, Memucan, why I sent my favorite wife into exile and had my eunuchs executed for her actions. I am at a loss to understand why I, king of kings, would do something so utterly foolish when Vashti was not breaking any laws. In fact, it was I who would have humiliated both her and myself, but she stopped me from doing so." He gripped his staff, his knuckles whitening, and his gaze swept the room, stopping to pierce each of his nobles with a withering look. "Perhaps one of my other nobles can tell me why such a thing as banishing her came from your mouth to my ear." He glared at Memucan. The man's idea to banish his queen was one thing he managed to recall quite clearly.

"My lord," Memucan said, his voice lacking his normal confidence, "we had all been drinking wine for a week. I fear none of us were thinking through things as we should."

"And yet it is only I who suffered loss. My queen and I. Tell me, Memucan, did my mother or one of my wives put you up to the suggestion?" He wouldn't doubt for a moment if his mother or Amestris had plotted to remove Vashti from his presence. His mother had often made it clear that he deserved better than a foreigner for a wife.

"My lord, forgive me. The idea was something we thought of in our drunken stupor. We did not realize the consequences." Memucan was clearly trembling now, and Xerxes pondered why. The man obviously feared the same fate he had given the eunuchs. With good reason, no doubt.

But he could not execute a relative of his wife. He could, however, depose the man from his authority. Yes, that was what he needed to do. To replace Memucan with someone worthier. Someone who did not grovel or whine or listen to the king's wives at the expense of the king's happiness.

"I have no doubt you are guilty of something, Memucan." He lifted his gaze to take in the other nobles. "The whole lot of you are guilty of something, or I would not be sitting here today, heading to war, without my favorite wife to comfort me!" His shouted words rang in the silent hall. "Therefore, I decree this day that you, Memucan, will no longer sit with my advisors or enter my court without my summons. You and the other six nobles are dismissed from my service. I will find a better man to replace the entire worthless lot of you." He clapped his hands on his final word, and his guards appeared and escorted the nobles from his audience chamber. The room stood silent.

Was there no one he could trust?

Doubt filled him as he descended the stairs from his throne and returned to his chambers. He would work with his new servants, the ones he had chosen to replace his seven eunuchs, and ready himself for war. Perhaps by the time he returned, he would have discovered a worthy man capable of advising him and have put Vashti from his mind. He would come home and her presence would no longer linger in the corners of every room.

On his last night at the palace, he told three of his servants, "Make sure the palace is cleaned, aired, and treated with whatever you must do to remove all memory of Vashti. When

I return, I had better not find a single trace of her life here."

The next day, dressed in his military garb and surrounded by bodyguards, he mounted his horse and left for battle.

But as his horse passed through Susa's gates, he wondered how he would ever remove her from his heart.

PART TWO

After these things, when the anger of King Ahasuerus [Xerxes] had abated, he remembered Vashti and what she had done and what had been decreed against her. Then the king's young men who attended him said, "Let beautiful young virgins be sought out for the king. And let the king appoint officers in all the provinces of his kingdom to gather all the beautiful young virgins to the harem in Susa the citadel, under custody of Hegai, the king's eunuch, who is in charge of the women. Let their cosmetics be given them. And let the young woman who pleases the king be queen instead of Vashti." This pleased the king, and he did so.

Esther 2:1–4 ESV

CHAPTER Eleven

Four Years Later

Hadassah knelt at Levia's bedside and placed a cool cloth on her head. The woman moaned but did not open her eyes. *Oh Ima, why can you not get well?*

Levia had contracted a fever weeks ago, right in the midst of their planning for Mordecai to approach Gad's father. It was past time for Mordecai to see Hadassah wed, and Gad was a match she readily agreed to. Once the betrothal was sealed and announced to their small Hebrew community, the wedding plans could begin.

But Levia had taken ill before Mordecai could make the visit, and instead of improving, each day she had grown weaker. Though the fever had left, her body did not seem capable of gaining strength.

"Hadassah?" Levia's voice sounded faint.

Hadassah leaned close. "I'm here, Ima." She moved the

cloth and brushed tendrils of hair from the older woman's forehead.

Silence fell between them again, and Hadassah studied her ima, searching for signs of slowed breathing. Levia had taken to speaking in single words, calling a name or mumbling something others could not understand. Attempts to pour a little broth into her mouth only worked part of the time.

Please, Levia. Mordecai needs you. I need you.

But she couldn't say the words aloud. What if Levia's time on earth was nearing its end? What would Mordecai do without her?

Hadassah dipped the cloth in the tepid water again and placed it over Levia's forehead. Levia shivered as though the water brought a chill. She blinked and met Hadassah's worried gaze.

Levia glanced beyond her for a brief moment, then looked again at Hadassah. "Mordecai?"

"He has gone to work at the palace. You have been sleeping so long, and there was nothing he could do here." Hadassah secretly wondered if Mordecai worked to escape impending loss. Levia had not noticed his absence until now.

"He will be home soon?"

Hadassah's heart lifted. It was the most Levia had said in weeks.

"Yes, yes. Shall I fetch you some porridge to eat? You need to regain your strength." Hadassah stood, then grasped Levia's cool hand.

Levia nodded. "Help me to sit up."

Hadassah rearranged the pillows behind her, then hurried to retrieve some leftover porridge she'd kept warm in a clay bowl near the oven. Mordecai had built them a new oven when Levia took ill, venting it through an open window in the cooking area.

She returned to Levia's side, pleased to see her alert and waiting. "You've been ill for weeks. This should help." Hadassah offered her a small piece of bread dipped in the thin barley porridge.

Levia took a bite, then another, but after the third swallow, she stopped. "That's enough for now." She offered Hadassah a smile, albeit a sad one.

"A little more later then. Soon you will be on your feet again." Hadassah would believe for both of them because the alternative was something she could not accept.

"Yes. When Mordecai returns."

"Shall I fetch him?" She suddenly needed to do something outside of the walls of this house, where she had stayed during Levia's illness. "Will you be all right without me for a few minutes? It won't take me long."

Levia nodded. "Yes. That would be good. I will wait." This time her smile held warmth.

Bolstered by the assurance that her ima was indeed on the mend, Hadassah donned her scarf and hurried down the cobbled street, past the market square, toward the city gate where Mordecai worked for the king. Even in the king's absence, there was work to be done, though Hadassah could not imagine what her abba did with his time.

She approached the gate from the city's interior and asked the guard to allow her to speak with her abba. Moments later, Mordecai hurried down the steps to greet her.

"Is it Levia? Is she . . . ?"

"She is awake and asking for you." Hadassah beamed, joy filling her. Soon she would be betrothed, once Levia made a full recovery. If it were proper, she would run to Gad's house and tell him so. But returning home with Mordecai must come first.

Mordecai turned and spoke to one of the guards, then walked with her toward the house. "She is better then."

"She seems to be. She ate a few bites of bread and porridge. We spoke and she smiled." Hadassah glanced at this wise man who had been her father for as long as she had known. What thoughts went through his mind? Should she mention the betrothal now that Levia was on the mend?

They turned the corner to their street and hurried along the path to the house. Mordecai burst through the door and rushed to the back room where Levia had lain for weeks. Hadassah remained in the sitting area, allowing him to spend time with his wife alone. The sound of muffled voices drifted to her as she sat, picked up her spindle, and worked the wool into thread.

At last Mordecai joined her. "She sleeps," he said, looking slightly dazed.

"She is still weak." Hadassah stopped the spindle and stood. "I drew you away from work too soon. Let me begin the evening meal while you rest." She hurried to the cooking room and searched the jars for the few remaining vegetables she had picked earlier that week, poured lentils and barley into a pot of bubbling water, and added cumin and salt and rosemary. The bread would not be warm since she had baked it in the morning, but she had spent all of her time caring for Levia. Most nights Mordecai's daughters-in-law brought them something to eat.

Hadassah finished and took the meal to Mordecai, who had fallen asleep among the cushions. He rarely slept long at night, so she hesitated to wake him.

He saved her the decision by opening his eyes. "You are ready?"

"Yes."

He took the bread and stew from her hands, blessed it, and offered some to her. They ate in silence. At last Hadassah set some of the softest pieces of bread aside, dipped them in the stew, and stood. "I will take this to Levia. Perhaps she has awakened."

Mordecai set his food aside and shook his head. He stood and took the food from her hands. "I will do it."

Hadassah complied but still followed him into the room.

"Levia? We have brought your favorite lentil stew." Mordecai spoke as if to a small child. Did he think his wife could not understand his normal tone?

Hadassah came around the other side of the bed and noted the shadow over Levia's face. Dusk had fallen, so she lit the lamp.

"Levia?" Mordecai called again, louder this time.

Hadassah joined him and held the lamp near Levia's face.

Mordecai sucked in a breath, the food slipping from his hands. Hadassah felt her face pale at the gray pallor of Levia's skin.

Mordecai leaned over his wife to listen for breath. He took her hand, but it remained limp in his. "She's cold," he said, his words lifeless. He touched his wife's face but drew back.

"Is she . . . gone?" Hadassah knew the answer, but she could not believe that Levia had been here only moments ago, eating and speaking with them, and then suddenly had gone to Sheol.

Mordecai released Levia's hand and sank to his knees at

her side, his voice a loud cry. He rocked back and forth and laid his head beside Levia's body, weeping.

Hadassah's tears came freely, but she could not keen as others did who mourned their dead. She set the lamp in the niche in the wall and backed out of the room. She must tell Mordecai's sons, and the women must prepare the body for burial. This much she knew. And she could manage to do what she knew.

The trip to the burial cave was long, as Mordecai did not wish to bury his dead within the walls of a foreign city. Never mind that they could not travel to Israel. The caves outside of Susa would do. Levia would rest with Hadassah's parents and grandparents, who had come into captivity more than seventy years before.

Hadassah stood beside her friend Jola, silent tears streaming down her face. Mordecai, his head covered in ashes and his robe torn, stumbled as he walked behind his sons, who carried the bier with Levia's body wrapped in linens.

"I must go to him," Hadassah said, glancing at Jola, then inclined her head toward Mordecai.

Jola nodded and followed. They came alongside Mordecai, and Hadassah grasped his arm. Mordecai gripped her hand and gave her a grateful look. He had wept in the privacy of their home, but here he staggered like a drunken man, his cheeks stained, his voice silent.

"It will be all right, Abba." Hadassah bent close to whisper the words. By his look she knew he did not believe her.

The cave drew near, and Hadassah's cousins set the body on the ground before they heaved the stone from the entrance. Fresh tears filled Hadassah's eyes as they carried Levia's lifeless body to rest inside. Mordecai broke free of Hadassah's grip and followed his sons into the cave. Bitter wails echoed from inside the walls.

Hadassah stood, unable to move. Jola slipped her arm around Hadassah's waist. Behind them the small Hebrew community wept. Was Gad among the mourners? But now was not the time to think about weddings or betrothals. Not until the time of mourning had passed.

Many moments later, Mordecai and his sons emerged from the cave. Mordecai looked out over the crowd, squinting against the sun's setting glare. "Levia was a good woman." His voice broke, and his Adam's apple moved hard in his attempt to swallow. "She did much to help our community, and no better wife or mother exists in all Israel or Persia." He paused, and though Hadassah thought the praise too much considering the other women in the crowd, she knew no one would fault him for saying such things on this day.

"We must never forget her," he said. "May God receive her spirit."

Hadassah's cousins moved the huge boulder in place, the squeal of stone on stone drowning out Mordecai's quiet weeping.

Hadassah again went to his side and helped him turn to walk back to the city. She glanced at the group of men and women, spotting Gad with his parents. A troubled look on his face made Hadassah blink. Was he sharing her grief? Or was there some other cause for his concern?

She briefly searched for some sign of acknowledgment of her in his obviously distracted look, but finding none, she turned back to Mordecai and focused on each step in front of her. If Levia were here she would ask her why a man might avoid meeting a woman's gaze or seem preoccupied with something other than the loss to their community, to her family. His future betrothed's family.

Had Levia's death created a change in plans for Gad and his family? Could not Mordecai seek a future for her without Levia's help? He would not keep Hadassah with him indefinitely. Her thoughts whirled, and guilt filled her for thinking about herself when she was still mourning the loss of her adopted ima. Yet a part of her worried. Nothing had gone right since talk of the betrothal began. Levia had taken ill soon after they'd begun their discussion of marriage.

Were Gad's parents superstitious enough to think Levia's death was a curse on Mordecai's family? Nothing had yet been sealed between them. Hadassah wasn't officially promised to him. So there was no reason they would think such thoughts.

How foolish you are, Hadassah, she chided herself. She trudged slowly beside Mordecai through the gates of Susa, which shut behind them just as the sun set. There was a time for everything, and this was the time to mourn. Not to worry about a future she could not control.

CHAPTER *Twelve*

Three Weeks Later

Mordecai paused at the threshold of his house, still troubled every time he entered the place he had lived with Levia for their entire married life. The scent of onions and cumin and freshly baked bread greeted him. He crossed into the room, met by Hadassah's warm smile.

"Welcome home," she said, kissing his cheek. "The meal is almost ready."

He removed his sandals and sank onto one of the low couches. For the first few weeks his sons and daughters-in-law had joined them for each evening meal, but for the past week, it had been only himself and Hadassah, and the house seemed empty. He watched her move into the cooking area and soon return with a clay pot steaming with his favorite stew. She had already set bread and bowls on a rug on the floor.

"You should be working for a husband, not for me," he

said, looking intently into her beautiful dark eyes. He needed to see her safely married. Hadn't Levia told him he should have done so over a year ago? Why had he waited? Now he would be forced to handle all of the awkward arrangements on his own without his faithful wife to guide him. But arrange them he must. He wasn't sure why, but he felt a sense of urgency he had not known before. Perhaps he should go even this night.

"How was your day?" Hadassah's cheery tone interrupted his musings. "I heard the women talking at the well. There is news that the king might soon return. Are they right?"

Mordecai held up a hand to stay her questions, blessed the food, and then broke off a piece of bread. "Yes, the rumors are true. Runners have spotted his retinue less than a day's journey from Susa. And on the heels of their news, Xerxes' own messengers came ahead of him to announce his coming. The palace is in an uproar as servants clean and prepare everything to his liking."

"He's been gone a long time." Hadassah took a bite, then looked to him as if expecting an answer.

"Four years and a lost war. I can guarantee that he will not be returning in a good mood." Mordecai sipped from his cup, then focused on eating.

"It's too bad that he could not conquer the Greeks. They are so small a country. The king certainly had the advantage of men." Hadassah smiled at his surprised look. "I listen when you speak." She shrugged.

He gave her a curious look. "You know also, then, that the Greeks were strategic in their planning and outmaneuvered the king. He had fully intended on subduing them, and with Vashti gone, I fear we will face the brunt of his frustration.

Or he will hide away in his rooms and we will continue on as if we had no ruler."

"Surely his advisors have kept peace in Susa in his absence." Hadassah set her bread aside.

"Peace, yes. But all of the focus was on keeping contact with the warriors, supplying their needs. Now, without the war, the city will go back to normal—assuming they remember what normal looked like." Mordecai finished his last bite and leaned back while Hadassah cleared away the leftovers.

She joined him moments later. "What will the king do without Vashti?" She picked up her spindle and he watched her work.

"I imagine Amestris will take her place. Or the king will look for a new wife." He glanced toward the room where Levia had breathed her last. A new wife could never replace the one a man had loved and lost.

"I suppose after four years he might be over the grief of losing the queen." Hadassah tied off a piece of thread and attached a new bundle of wool to the spindle.

"Does one ever get over such loss?" Mordecai spoke to himself, not expecting her to answer. She was a child. What did she know of love? And yet one look at her and he knew she was more than ready to marry. Why did he still hesitate to approach Gad's father?

"Have you given any thought to my betrothal, Abba?"

Her pet name for him always made him feel warm inside. She was his daughter, blood or not. And he needed to do right by her. He closed his eyes for a brief moment, seeing five-year-old Hadassah clinging to his hand or sitting on his knee. Now she should be giving him grandchildren to do the same.

"I have. Some. I will speak to Gad's father after the Sabbath. Does that please you?" He searched her face, struck by her beauty. When had she grown into such an appealing woman?

"What a wonderful plan!" She laid aside her work and came over to kiss his cheek. "I will prepare a special Sabbath meal to celebrate."

Mordecai chuckled at her exuberance. "Perhaps you should wait to hear the man's answer, my daughter."

Hadassah smiled, showing even white teeth. "How can he refuse you? You are a trusted scribe at the king's gate. Of course they will agree."

"If they agree, it will be because you are Hadassah, the most desirable maid in Susa." He patted her hand.

She blushed and went back to her work. "I hope they will agree," she said, her look suddenly solemn.

He puzzled over her change in expression but decided perhaps it was just a woman's jittery ways. Still, he must settle the matter with Gad's father before much more time passed. Hadassah needed to be safely wed. Why he even considered her unsafe was something he did not allow himself to explore.

Hadassah sang as she worked the next morning, anticipating the Sabbath and all that would follow afterward. In three more days she would know whether or not Gad found her acceptable.

She looked about the room and decided she needed to make a trip to the market, for there was little left on the shelf to complete a meal and the garden offered little that she had not already picked. Next year she would plant more. Even as

Gad's wife, she would make certain that Mordecai was cared for. Surely Gad's family would understand.

She lifted a basket from its place beside the door, which she latched behind her. Jola's house crossed her path, so she stopped to invite her friend to join her.

"It's good to see you out of that house for a change," Jola said, tucking her basket beneath her arm. "I was beginning to wonder if we would ever see you again."

Hadassah smiled at her friend, ignoring the way the words sounded, considering their recent loss. Hadassah and Levia would have made this trip daily if she were still here, but until now Hadassah could not bring herself to venture out alone. Of course, she would soon need to think of life in a different way, and she could not mourn Levia's loss forever, no matter how much she missed her.

"I know you were in mourning." Jola's slender fingers touched Hadassah's arm. "I did not mean to speak insensitively."

"It is nothing." Hadassah looked ahead as they took a bend in the road. "I ran out of food to prepare meals for Abba, and truthfully, I was growing anxious to see you and the people in our community. I don't enjoy being so alone."

"Well, I'm glad you are back." They fell into a comfortable step. "Besides, I have been going out of my mind wanting to tell you the news!" Jola twirled in a little dance. "I'm betrothed!"

Hadassah's heart lifted and she laughed. "Betrothed? Who is the man blessed to have my closest friend? When is the wedding? And why didn't you invite me to the betrothal?" She pouted and Jola laughed.

"I didn't expect it. Everything happened so fast, and with

Levia's illness and everything . . ." Her voice trailed off. "At first I thought there had been a mistake because Gad had always favored you, so when his father approached mine . . ." She paused. "His father said that they had chosen me."

Hadassah's breath caught, and she felt as if her heart had stopped beating. Gad and Jola? But what of her? Heat crept up her neck. She glanced beyond Jola, knowing she could not betray her feelings even to her friend. "His father said that?" The words seemed incredulous given the talks she and Gad had shared on occasion during their childhood and at certain feasts.

Jola nodded. "They came before Levia took ill. I . . . my father didn't know you liked Gad, and he accepted before I could tell him." She looked at the dust beneath their feet. "I didn't mean to hurt you, Hadassah."

Hadassah heard the sincerity in her friend's words. It was the father's place to secure a husband for his daughters, and normally when a girl grew to marriageable age, the father of an eligible young man sought out her father. Gad's father could have come to Mordecai as easily as he had gone to Jola's father. *No wonder Gad did not meet my gaze at the funeral procession.* Had his eyes wandered to Jola when Hadassah thought he was gazing into the distance?

She glanced at her friend, then looked away. Jola was shorter than Hadassah, but her features were pleasing to the eye. Had Gad been drawn to Jola's beauty or her personality? Or did he simply know her better? After all, Mordecai's family did not join the community of Hebrews nearly as often as Jola's did.

She shook herself, not pleased with her train of thought. "I am happy for you. Obviously you are who Gad wants or his father would not have asked."

"But . . . I'm sorry you did not know. I wanted you to be happy for me—I did not want to tell you this way."

"How else might you have told me? I was in mourning. You did nothing wrong." Hadassah picked up her pace, and they moved again toward the market. "And I am happy for you. Truly." She touched Jola's arm and looked deeply into her eyes. "Abba will find another suitable man, or perhaps that man will find him. I cannot do anything but trust Adonai with my future. It is not like we can control these things."

Jola's downcast expression did not abate. "No, we cannot."

Hadassah touched her friend's shoulder. "There is no need to continue to fret. I will forgive you for not inviting me to the betrothal, but you simply must let me be part of your maids at your wedding."

Jola brightened, smiling at last. "You were the first person I intended to ask."

"Good. Now tell me all about the betrothal. And perhaps help me pick a good cheese for Abba." Hadassah joined Jola in laughter, and the two continued their trip, perusing the shops and filling their baskets.

Hadassah pushed thoughts of Gad aside as she left Jola at her house and continued down the lane to her own home. A sick feeling filled her at the thought of breaking the news to Mordecai.

As she chopped vegetables for their evening stew, she could not make her heart comprehend what had happened. She'd thought she and Gad had an understanding. She could not shake the feeling of betrayal, but she knew she could not let Mordecai know of her hurt. She must be strong for him. He was all she had.

CHAPTER Thirteen

Xerxes rode through the streets of Susa to the shouts and fanfare he might have expected had he been a conquering king. No doubt his servants had ordered the display of affection and support, but despite the shouts of "Long live the king!" and "To the king of kings, may he live forever!" he could not muster a smile or even a wave of greeting.

He stood tall in the saddle and maneuvered his mount through the palace gates, relieved when the crowds were at last behind him. He rode to the stables and dismounted, handed the reins to a servant, and hurried to the cooler interior of his rooms. Guards flanked him, servants saluted him, but he ignored them all.

He stopped at the door to his private chambers, recalling the last days he had spent here. Four years and the place looked no different, yet it seemed utterly foreign. Empty. Lifeless. This was the place he had shared with Vashti more often than any other wife, and he could not bear the thought of entering.

"I want new quarters arranged for me this very night." His command brought sharp gasps from a few of his servants. He turned about and glared at them. "Do you find my command too taxing?"

"No, my lord. That is . . . where would you like us to move your things?" one servant sputtered.

"I do not want *these* things. I want *new* things. A new bed, chairs, tables, everything! I never want to see these chambers again. Do you understand?" He felt heat crawl up his neck and wondered if he was being foolish. He had imagined crawling into his bed and remaining there for days. But now, after looking upon the furniture where Vashti had sat, the bed where they had shared their love, the table where they had shared many meals . . . he couldn't bear it. What had he done to deserve such incompetent advisors?

"I am sure the king's servants can find new rooms with new furnishings in short order," a voice said from the end of the hall. The man moved closer and bowed before the king. "Your Majesty. As I was your humble servant throughout the campaign, if you will allow me, I will make sure your eunuchs have you settled in the finest rooms in the palace before nightfall. If Your Majesty likes, might I suggest a brief respite in the gardens where the cooking staff has prepared refreshments for my lord. You will have complete privacy should you so desire it." He bowed again.

"Haman," Xerxes said. "I thought you only a military man. But I see you are a man of many abilities."

"It pleases me to serve you, my lord. I have no other desire than to serve my king."

"And I am pleased to accept your service. If you can deliver on your promise before nightfall, I will promote you to one of my advisors." Xerxes studied the man's reaction, pleased to see nothing but a humble nod.

"I will do better than my best, my lord." He bowed again, then commanded the servants to follow him while Xerxes' guards walked with him to his private gardens. Haman's sudden appearance was not surprising, as the man had been around nearly every turn during the Greek campaign, always meeting a need before the king expressed it.

He will go far in my service if he can keep his promises. Xerxes tucked the man's name into the back of his mind and felt the slightest hope he'd had since entering Susa. A new advisor would be a welcome change.

A week later, Xerxes woke in his new chambers, at last beginning to get used to the difference. The bed and other furnishings were new, the view from the window was better than his old one, and the tapestries and adornments were still simple yet somehow more elegant, as Vashti would have said.

But despite the change, despite the feeling that he had returned to a new life, his heart still ached in a place no one could reach. He missed Vashti. Even deposing Memucan, which he had done against Amestris's adamant pleas, had not taken away that loss.

And his best efforts could not shake the feeling that struck him afresh each morning. Defeated, he thought briefly of sending for one of his concubines but quickly dismissed the thought.

A servant approached as he rose and offered him his day

robe. He slipped his arms through it and tied the belt, then walked to the window, where a table stood laden with food to break his fast.

He had no appetite for food, but he sat and picked at the bread and cheese. When he had finished the last sip of pomegranate juice, another servant approached to clear the food away.

"Tell me," Xerxes said to the man, "how do the servants see me? What are they speaking about when they know I cannot hear?"

The man set the utensils down, his expression wary. "I do not pay attention to gossips, my lord. I do not think I can answer the question to the king's satisfaction."

"But you could tell me what you think of me." Why he pressed the young man—too young, barely into his manhood—he couldn't say, but somehow Xerxes needed a distraction. Surely someone could tell him what was wrong with him!

"I think, my lord," the man said, unable to hold the king's gaze, "that my lord king is unhappy. That since the queen's departure, he misses the queen and isn't sure what he should do."

"Observant of you." Xerxes studied the man for a lengthy breath. "Do you have a solution for your king?"

The servant cleared his throat, but his gaze did not waver from studying something he found interesting near his feet. "Perhaps . . . let beautiful young virgins be sought out for the king. And let the king appoint officers in all the provinces of his kingdom to gather the virgins to the harem in Susa the citadel, under custody of Hegai. Let their cosmetics be given them. And let the young woman who pleases the king be queen instead of Vashti."

Xerxes stared at the servant, then let his gaze rest on the other young men who circled the room, waiting to jump at his smallest command or whim of desire. Had they discussed this among themselves? Surely one servant did not come up with this plan alone.

"This is a good plan," he said at last, looking from one servant to the next. "And since you probably all had a hand in coming up with this idea, I will allow you to speak to Haman and my other advisors to set this into motion immediately."

The first servant smiled and bowed. "It will be as you say, my lord."

Xerxes dismissed him along with the rest. Only his guards remained outside the door. But the silence, for once, did not oppress him. Suddenly he had a new goal. A new mission. To find a young virgin to replace Vashti. A queen of greater beauty and finer worth than his first love. An impossible task, but he would enjoy the process of seeking her.

Mordecai saw the edict nailed to the post at the king's gate and read it with increasing alarm.

> *All beautiful virgins of marriageable age are to report to the palace in Susa, to Hegai, the eunuch in charge of the king's harem. The virgin who pleases the king will become queen in Vashti's place.*

All virgins? He hurried down the steps and half ran, half walked the entire length of the journey home. Hadassah! What had he done? He should have found a husband for her. Especially once Gad's father had betrothed him to Jola.

He should have sought out every Jew in Susa until he found a suitable mate for his girl.

Was there still time? If he hid her from the king's men, who would surely search the city to make sure every virgin was accounted for, could he betroth her to someone before she was found?

His side hurt as he ran, so he slowed his pace and dragged in air. Would the king honor a Jewish betrothal? He could not rush a wedding. Could he? What man would wish to wed so soon? Everyone would talk and assume the worst of Hadassah.

But what would they think of her if she ended up in the harem of the king? He placed a hand to his forehead and muttered frustrated words. Why had he waited so long? He could not blame Levia's death on this, for Levia had begged him to begin the search a year ago. *Foolish Mordecai. This is your doing—your punishment for keeping her too long.* Levia wouldn't have condemned him quite as harshly as his own thoughts did, but she would have worried and nagged him. She might have kept him from waiting until it was too late!

He turned a corner and saw the lights coming from the surrounding houses. Hadassah would have the evening meal ready and would greet him with joy. And he would greet her with the worst news of her life.

What should he do? He glanced heavenward, but no inspiration came from the place where Adonai dwelt. If he had been a faithful Jew, he would have taken his family to Jerusalem with the rest and worked to rebuild the temple. But no. He had stayed in Susa to serve a pagan king.

And now he would lose his last treasure to that king, to be lost among thousands of women who would never again see their families. All because he had waited too long. All because the king was a selfish pagan.

He did not allow himself to dwell on that overmuch. He must work instead to find a way out, perhaps take Hadassah even now out of Persia.

His thoughts churned. He should tell her. But he wasn't sure he dared.

CHAPTER Fourteen

Hadassah moved from the cooking area of the inner court into the house, where she could observe her neighbors from the window. She had baked, chopped, weeded the garden, spun thread, worked the shuttle, and woven in silence, never able to shake the restlessness that filled her every waking moment.

This was not supposed to be her life. *She* was the one who was supposed to be betrothed to Gad. Not Jola. Not her best friend.

Levia was not supposed to be in the grave. Her parents were not supposed to have died before she could know them. And she most definitely was not supposed to be Mordecai's only solace.

Where were her cousins and their wives? Why did they not come to visit more often? But she knew the answer. They had work and families, and Mordecai had assured them he was fine. Don't trouble themselves. But she disagreed. He needed them now more than ever. She could not be all that he had. She could not replace Levia.

And now what was to become of her? She turned from the window and paced the sitting room. Mordecai would be home soon. The evening meal was nearly ready, but she was torn with how to approach the subject that had remained closed between them. She had told him of Gad and Jola's betrothal in order to spare him the trouble of seeking out Gad's father, but nothing else had been said beyond that basic information. And Hadassah grew more concerned with each passing day.

Footsteps outside the door startled her. She whirled about to see Mordecai enter the house.

"You are early." She met his gaze, noting the furrowed brow. "Is something wrong?" His expression sent a feeling of dread to her middle.

He looked at her for a lengthy moment, then bent to untie his sandals and closed the door behind him. He moved to the window and closed the shutters, then walked through the house, making sure every window and door was latched as though night had already fallen.

Hadassah followed him to each room. "You are scaring me, Abba. What is going on?"

He turned and released a deep sigh. "Come." He took her arm and led her to the sitting room, to a couch opposite him. She sat on the edge. He sank into the cushion, elbows on his knees.

"There is news," he said at last, his eyes never leaving her face as though he were memorizing each feature. "You are too beautiful." His voice was suddenly distant.

Hadassah blinked. "The news is that I am too beautiful?

Are you trying to hide me away from the rest of the city?" She nearly laughed at his outrageous behavior.

Mordecai shook his head and then bowed as though praying. He looked up again and took her hands. "The king has sent messengers throughout the kingdom. An edict has been written and posted on the doors of the king's gates and in other prominent places throughout the city." He swallowed.

"What does the edict say?"

"The king is sending men throughout the kingdom to gather beautiful virgins and bring them to Susa in order for them to enter the king's harem. The king will pick a new queen from among them to replace Vashti." He let out a rushed breath.

"Beautiful virgins." Hadassah repeated his words, her tone dull. "And I am too beautiful."

"Yes. Unless I can find a Jewish man to wed you immediately." Mordecai met her gaze with an imploring look. "Surely there is someone among our people who would be suitable for you. Under the circumstances, the man would understand. You are a worthy woman and will make some man a fine wife. I am only sorry that I did not try to find someone for you sooner."

Hadassah held back the hurt that he should have consulted Gad's father a year ago, back when she and Gad were friendly at feasts and she thought he cared for her. Obviously he cared for Jola more.

"Are you not going to say something, my child? I have failed you, but we could make this right. Just give me a name of someone to ask. I fear I have not kept up with all of the young men of marriageable age as Levia would have done. But we must find someone swiftly lest the king's men see you and take you against your will."

Hadassah looked at her hands still clasped in Mordecai's. She pulled them free and stood, pacing again. She turned at last. "I should get the food. We must eat before the stew burns." Though it was too early for the evening meal, she hurried to the cooking area and returned with the bread and lentil stew. She retrieved clay cups and plates and a jug of goat's milk and placed it all before Mordecai.

He blessed the food and they ate in silence. Hadassah's mind whirled. What was she supposed to say to him? There were no eligible men among their people whom she found acceptable. Gad had been the only one she'd cared for. Her mind blanked as to whom she might mention to Mordecai.

"I do not know, Abba," she said at last. "I only know that most young men my age are already betrothed or wed. There may be a few younger. We don't meet together often, so I have not met many of them. I admit I have spent most of my time with Levia, my cousins' wives, and Jola."

Mordecai looked stricken. "I must go to meet with the men of our people and ask them myself then. If they have virgin daughters, there is no doubt they will be seeking young men as well. Perhaps we can all come together and secretly wed all of you to whatever men are available, preferably to a man who is not already married, for I do not wish to see you in the role of a secondary wife. I must go out tonight and see to this before it is too late." He took a swig from his cup and stood.

Hadassah stared at him. "But . . ."

Mordecai shook his head. "No. This is the right thing to do. Do not try to dissuade me, Daughter. I must see that you are safe."

"If the king's men discover the hasty timing of my marriage, will that not bode poorly for you?" She had heard the king could be ruthless, and she did not want to discover that anger aimed against one she loved. The only one she truly had left.

"They will not find out. And once you are wed, you are no longer a virgin, so they will not want you. Do not worry about me." He donned his sandals and hurried out into the night.

Hadassah stared after him, worry niggling her insides. She cleared away the food, lit a lamp, and sat with her spinning, silently praying. *Adonai, I do not know what is best right now. But I want to marry a man who will love me. Like I thought Gad might be capable of doing. I want what Levia and Mordecai had. If I do not ask too much, please guide Mordecai in his choosing. And please keep the king's men from finding me before he can do what he seeks to do.*

She worked long into the night, watching the door, her fear mounting. If he had good news, he would have returned quickly. If something had happened to him, what would she do?

Mordecai left the last house in the Jewish quarter, his shoulders sagging. Defeat settled over him, and he wondered if his feet would keep moving toward home. What was he going to tell Hadassah? That all of the young men her age had made commitments to others? That the only choices were to be second wife to an older man or to wait for a child to reach adulthood?

He shouldn't be surprised at the responses. Their community in Susa was small, and her beauty was actually a deterrent to some fathers. Too many were aware of the king's roving desires, and even if she was married, a beautiful woman could be taken and her husband killed. Had not their ancestors

Abraham and Isaac feared the same thing? So they had lied to the kings of their day and told them that their wives were really their sisters.

Hadassah's beauty would work against her with her own people. Should he look to the pagan people of Susa among whom they lived? A weighted feeling settled within him, and he stopped outside of his door, dreading the reaction he would get once he opened it.

Light flickered behind the closed shutters, barely visible but enough to tell him that Hadassah had waited up for him. He needed to do something to better block the light. If the guards came at night, he would not want to appear as though they were awake. Not that sleep would stop them. But if they didn't see Hadassah, they wouldn't know of her beauty, and he could keep her hidden and safe until he could find a way to take her out of Persia.

Yes. That idea, which had floated in his thoughts since he read the edict, now bloomed and pushed out every other possibility. He could not keep her safe here. He could not see her married, so he must take her away. They could seek help from some of the men and go by cover of night. Or perhaps they could join a caravan and disguise themselves until they were safely out of Susa.

Safe. The word played over and over in his mind. If she landed in the king's harem, Mordecai could not protect her there. He would lose all control over her future. And she could end up alone and barren with no life but to entertain herself with whatever the king's concubines did to fill their time.

One night with the king would ruin her.

He stood still, staring at his front door, letting that thought sink deep into his being. She would take some convincing to leave, of course. But he would make his case, and she would obey as she always did. He shook himself. It was Levia who had always needed convincing, not Hadassah. Hadassah simply did what he asked of her. She would see reason and help him to plan. She would stay secluded until they could enact their escape.

He drew in a deep breath and strengthened his resolve, then opened the door and met Hadassah's relieved look. "You are back at last."

"Yes." He quickly closed the door, removed his sandals, and sat opposite her.

"Tell me." She laid the spindle aside. "Things did not go well, did they?"

He shook his head. "No, they did not. Every eligible young man is already betrothed. You could become second wife to an older man or wait for a child to reach manhood. Our community is too small. There may be some Jews in other areas of the kingdom, but here we have no one."

"Perhaps we should travel to some of those other areas then." She leaned forward. "You could find an excuse to go on an errand for the king—perhaps he would allow you to be one of those who seeks virgins for his harem—and I could go veiled as your wife. When we visit Hebrew communities we could make inquiries. Surely there is someone who would want me."

Her tone made his heart ache. How he wished he could comfort her. "That is one possibility. Another is for us to disguise ourselves and join a caravan leaving Susa. Once we are out of Persian territory, we could make our way to Jerusalem. Perhaps there are families there, but at least you would be out of the king's reach."

Hadassah slowly nodded. "The king would not send to Jerusalem for virgins, would he?"

Suddenly Mordecai was not as certain as he had been at the start. "No. He would not." He hoped his words were true. Thus far the king had let the Israelites in Jerusalem be.

"But what of my idea to find a husband in other parts of the king's realm?" Hadassah twisted the sash at her waist. "I think we will find more Jews in Persia than in Israel."

She was right, of course. But he hesitated, his thoughts churning. "It is too risky," he said, taking her hand. "If even one Jew saw you unveiled, they would be able to tell you are not my wife because of your youth." Though old men did wed young women, it was a risk to look at Hadassah and think her married to a man clearly old enough to be her father. "Besides, if they are loyal to Persia, they might start asking questions."

"But you would be the king's emissary. Who would question you?" She sounded so urgent.

"The king does not send out men alone. They go in pairs or groups. And while women might accompany them to protect the virgins, we risk too much. You could be discovered." And yet, she would surely be discovered here. Were his objections wise?

"I cannot stay within the walls of this house until the danger is past, Abba. People know me. Who will go to the market for our food?"

"I will," he said, his words coming out harsher than he intended.

"You cannot work at the king's gate and take care of the home and the food and the clothing by yourself." She crossed her arms, her jaw set.

"Your cousins' wives will help me."

Hadassah gave a disgruntled sigh. "They are busy, Abba. They will not have time to do all that I do. And what of me? Am I to sit in a dark house for weeks, perhaps months? It is not possible."

Mordecai stood and took to wearing a path in the floor with his pacing. Other than the sound of his footsteps, silence fell between them. At last he sank back onto the couch. "I cannot leave Susa without drawing suspicion. Not with the king at home in his palace. And I cannot hide you forever. In this you are right."

"What then shall we do?" Genuine worry filled Hadassah's tone.

"Do not leave the house without a head covering. Only virgins walk about uncovered, so let them assume you are wed. Do not go to the market alone. Take one of your cousins' wives with you. Stay close to the house as often as possible. The more you can avoid the streets, the better." Mordecai closed his eyes, defeated. "I will do my best to keep you safe, Hadassah, but I fear that unless Adonai watches over you, even these measures will not help."

"So there is no hope of your plans to travel to Jerusalem?" A hint of despair filled her voice.

"It is not impossible. But it will take time. I will watch for a caravan, and if you stay close to the house, there is a chance we can flee. If the right things fall into place, we can leave soon. I will ask your cousins' wives to purchase items we will need. But remember—if you must go out, pretend you are wed. If a palace official speaks to you, talk of your husband. Perhaps they will believe you have one."

"So you would have me lie to protect myself."

"It is no more than Abraham did to protect himself in Egypt."

She nodded, though skepticism filled her gaze. "I've never liked lying," she said softly.

"I know," he said. "I would not ask it of you if the situation was not dire."

She acknowledged his words with a slight nod and then stood. "We should get some sleep." She tucked the wool and spindle into a basket and walked to her room, leaving him feeling like a failure as a father, and never more desperate in his life.

CHAPTER *Fifteen*

A week passed and Hadassah dressed as Levia once did, though she wore the veil to partially cover her face as well as her hair. Somehow pretending she was wed didn't seem right. Could she not trust the God of her fathers to keep her from the king's men? But she did not know Him as she knew Mordecai. And obeying Mordecai seemed wiser than trusting in one she could not see. Mordecai knew the king far better than she did. Her adopted father would not advise her falsely. Their discussion of the subject had been a daily concern, even after they had exhausted their options the week before.

If only Gad had wanted her sooner. Had wanted her at all. The sting of rejection still hit her when she saw Jola or considered the man she had thought would be hers. The last time she had looked upon his face was at Levia's burial, and hadn't she known even then, before Jola had broken the news? Levia had assured her there would be a swarm of young men begging for her hand. Why then had none wanted her when she needed one of them most?

She examined her apparel and picked up her basket. She had waited as long as she could to visit the market. With Jola along, they would appear as two married women, for now that Jola was betrothed, she could wear the veil. No guards would look their way twice.

But as she walked the short distance to Jola's home, she knew Jola's mother would inquire about the veil. Though Hadassah could explain about the king's edict, her lie could put Jola's entire family in danger. She simply could not lie to the woman. She ducked into the courtyard, looked this way and that, and pulled the veil from her head, then knocked on the door. Jola's mother answered and welcomed Hadassah into the house.

"Is Jola ready?"

Jola appeared, head covered, basket in hand. The two girls left the house, and when they had walked just out of sight of Jola's mother, Hadassah quickly pulled the veil over her head and face.

Jola turned to face her. "What is this?" She pointed to the veil. "Do you . . . are you betrothed now as well?" A smile lit her face. "Who is he? And so quickly? Is it because of the king's edict?"

Hadassah hushed her friend with a gentle hand to her mouth. "Shh." She turned toward the market, her gaze darting in every direction. When the area appeared free of the king's men, she leaned closer to Jola. "Abba asked me to wear it lest I stand out and the king's men take me to the palace."

Jola stared at her. "He asked you to lie to protect yourself?"

"Please, keep your voice down."

Jola clamped her mouth shut. “Forgive me,” she whispered. “It is a wise plan, and you can trust me to keep your secret.”

“Thank you.” As Hadassah turned again to walk to the market, two of the king’s men stood a short distance away, looking intently in her direction.

Hadassah stopped.

“Keep walking,” Jola said. “Don’t act guilty.”

Hadassah nodded and moved her basket to the other hand. “So how is your family?” She spoke to cover her feeling of panic.

“Ima and I spend much time spinning and weaving.”

They passed the king’s men, and Hadassah fought the feeling that everything in her life was spiraling out of control, though nothing had happened. The men had not spoken a word. Yet Hadassah dare not breathe a sigh of relief.

She and Jola continued talking of trivial matters until the market came into sight. Hadassah at last drew in a breath and released it, but she did not look behind her. She pulled Jola closer. “Can you see? Have they gone?”

Hadassah released her grip, and Jola moved in a position opposite her, pretending to look at a round of cheese. She met Hadassah’s gaze and slowly shook her head. “I don’t think Gad would like this flavor.” She took Hadassah’s arm, and Hadassah had to force her feet not to run fast and far. They moved together to another booth.

“Are they following us?” Hadassah could barely breathe.

Jola’s expression did not change. “It appears that the fabric booth has moved to another area. Come.” But her words told Hadassah that her worst fears were about to come true. *Please, Adonai, spare me for Abba’s sake.*

They walked past the baker and jeweler and perfumer, and still Jola's eyes revealed they were being followed. They stopped at the fabric booth, though neither of them had come for cloth.

The merchant attempted to sell them a few items, and Jola purchased some colored thread, but Hadassah's heart raced so fast she struggled to remember the items she needed. She must focus.

As they left the merchant to seek a seller of fig cakes and pressed raisins, the king's men approached them. "Please, if you will," one said, catching Jola's attention, "come over here and speak with us."

Jola exchanged a look with Hadassah. "Can you not speak with us here? Our husbands would not wish us to speak with strange men."

"So both of you are wed?"

Jola nodded, and Hadassah felt her cheeks heat.

"And yet one of you came out of your house unveiled." The man looked at Hadassah. "Why would a married woman leave her home unveiled, only to veil herself once she was out of sight of the house?"

Hadassah swallowed hard. How could they have possibly seen her? But these were the king's men. They could hide anywhere with the king's permission. Mordecai was right. There was no way to keep her safe in Susa.

"She was in a hurry. I should have waited for her to be ready," Jola said, but Hadassah could tell the men did not believe her.

"So if we ask the woman who answered the door if this was true, since it is clear you do not both live with her, she will tell us this same story?" The man sneered. "I know virgins are not all rushing to enter the king's harem, but you do not realize the privilege you miss by trying to stay away."

"Forgive me, my lord," Hadassah said. "My friend is right. I was not ready and we were in a hurry."

"So both of you are married? You can take us to your husbands then." The one speaking lifted a brow, his expression skeptical.

"Our husbands work in the fields. It would be hard to find exactly where they are working." Hadassah tasted the lie but reasoned that she was obeying Mordecai. God forgive her.

"We can easily wait for them to return," the man said.

The girls exchanged another look.

"Unless you are not speaking the truth." The man had a gleam in his eyes, though he made no attempt to move closer to them.

"We speak the truth," Jola said, her words rushed.

Fear spiked in Hadassah's heart as she slowly nodded in agreement. The only man she could claim as husband was her father, for there was no one else who would lie for her.

The men studied them for a lengthy moment. "All right. You may go. But next time, keep your veil in place."

Hadassah watched as they turned and left, looking about the market, probably hoping to catch some other unsuspecting virgin.

She breathed another relieved sigh. "Let's get out of here."

"Don't you want to get what you came for? They won't bother us again." Jola led her toward the vegetable stand, and Hadassah purchased the items she'd been in need of for a week.

They walked slowly toward Jola's house, leaving the market behind them. "I will be more careful next time," Hadassah said softly as they approached Jola's courtyard.

"Yes. As will I." Jola bid her farewell, and Hadassah hurried home.

As she turned the corner of her street, she nearly bumped into Gad, who was obviously headed to Jola's house. "Gad." She found it hard to swallow.

"Hadassah. Is that you beneath the veils?" His smile was congenial but casual.

"Yes." She looked this way and that. "It is good to see you, but I must go." She turned to flee toward her house as she caught movement up the street beyond Gad. More of the king's men?

"Wait," Gad said, making her turn back to him. "Who can I congratulate on your betrothal? I had not heard the news."

She swallowed hard. Saw the men coming closer. They were dressed as Persians, but she could not see the king's insignia on their tunics. "No one," she whispered. "Now I really must go."

She turned again and hurried her steps, but the sound of the men approaching grew louder. Would they follow her into her house? They stopped suddenly, and she heard male voices behind her. She wagered a glance and felt her heart sink as she saw Gad talking to the men. He pointed in her direction.

He had told them. He must have. She half ran toward her house, heart pounding. She reached the courtyard and rushed to the door, but a voice called to her.

"Stop, in the name of the king. Turn around."

Hadassah could not move. Sweat trickled down her back, and the feeling of betrayal from a man she thought she'd loved cut like a flint knife straight to her middle. *Oh, let me die.* How could she face Mordecai after this? He would kill Gad if he knew.

She could not tell him. For Jola's sake.

"I said, turn around."

This time she slowly complied. Two different servants of the king stood before her.

"Are you a virgin?" one asked.

She could lie. She did not know for sure what Gad had told them.

"That man told us you are not married," the other one said.

Should she believe him?

"I think you should talk to my father," she said at last.

"Who is your father?"

"He is Mordecai, and he works at the king's gate."

"What is your name?"

She and Mordecai had discussed what to do if she ever faced this situation. "Do not tell them you are Jewish," he had said. "And tell them your name is Esther. It is the Persian version of Hadassah."

"What is your name?" the man asked again.

"Esther," she said, nearly choking on the name. "I am the daughter of Abihail. My cousin Mordecai is my adopted father."

"Let us find your father then," one of the men said, "so we can confirm what we already know is true. And you can bid him farewell."

Head held high, Hadassah followed after the men toward the king's gate. Mordecai was not going to be happy to see her.

Hadassah listened as the king's men called Mordecai to come out from the king's gate. "Is this your daughter?" one asked.

Mordecai looked at her, and she read the warning in his gaze. "Yes. This is my Esther."

"She is a virgin, is she not?"

Mordecai faced the man. "She is not yet betrothed, no."

"So she is a virgin," the man repeated, as though he wanted proof.

"She is a virgin." Mordecai's voice sounded strange, as if the words were forced through his throat.

"You will please come with us then."

Mordecai stepped through the gate and took Hadassah's arm.

"Lead us to your house so your daughter can gather her things. By order of the king, she is to be placed in the care of Hegai, the eunuch in charge of the king's harem."

Mordecai walked ahead of the men, still holding Hadassah's arm. The streets felt foreign instead of familiar, her heart pounding as though she were walking to her death. She sensed the sorrow coming from Mordecai, though he said nothing until they reached the house. He commanded the king's men to wait outside, then followed Hadassah to her room.

"Gather just your clothing. They will provide you with cosmetics. They will probably give you new clothes as well, but at least you will have something familiar." He drew closer and whispered in her ear, "Remember what I told you. Never speak of your heritage. You are Esther now, a Persian star, and you will shine like the dawn in the king's palace." He took her chin in his hand. "I am sorry that I did not do more to protect you sooner."

She touched his cheek. "There is no need to fear, Abba. Perhaps this is God's plan for me. In any case, it was my fault, not yours."

He lifted a brow and gave her a curious look.

"I removed my veil at Jola's house lest her mother ask questions I could not truthfully answer. The men must have been hiding, because I did not see them but they saw me. I should have been more careful." A tear slipped down her cheek. She could not tell him that those men had let her go and that Gad's words had condemned her. Hadn't they?

"There, there. It was an honest mistake. You are an honest girl, my Esther. But you must not let your honesty reveal your heritage." His voice lowered despite the shuttered windows. "Now hurry, for the king's men will not wait long before they come through the door and take you by force. Better to go willingly. Tell them you were afraid if you must, but do not reveal that you would ever purposely disobey the king's orders."

She nodded, then quickly tossed a few tunics and her best robe into a basket, along with her favorite scarf and a ring that had belonged to her mother. She looked over the room, her spirits dimming as she realized she would never live in this house again. Never sleep in her bed. Never cook for Mordecai or share his home.

She was not leaving with the joy of a bridegroom's shout or the songs of a wedding feast. She was leaving to join thousands of other young women to spend one night with a ruthless king who was old enough to be her father. One night. Would it come sooner or later? And what would she do with the rest of her life lived alone in a palace?

She moved in a daze through the sitting room to the door where the king's men waited, but Mordecai stopped her with a hand on her shoulder. She felt his arms come around her in a warm embrace such as she had not known since childhood.

Tears tightened her throat, and she saw a sheen in Mordecai's eyes as he pulled back to study her face.

"I don't want to go," she whispered. "I need you."

"And I you," he said, nearly choking on the words.

"I will never forget you. If they let me, I will call for you."

"I will check on you daily, and you will be always in my prayers."

She could not speak. She clung to him and wet his shoulder with her tears.

He patted her back and held her tight. "I love you, my Hadassah," he spoke softly into her ear.

She gulped, forcing back the urge to weep uncontrollably. She straightened and smiled, swiping her cheeks. Mordecai cupped her cheek.

"I love you, Abba." She searched his face, memorizing each line. How soon would she see him again? Would she ever see him again?

Guards knocked on the door, startling them. Resignation filled Mordecai's dark eyes, and Hadassah released her grip on his arms and turned again toward the door. "I suppose we must go."

"Yes," he said. He touched the small of her back as though offering his support.

They followed the guards to the palace gates, where she was ushered into the harem. Where he could not follow.

CHAPTER Sixteen

Amestris paced the palace halls, attempting to hold her temper in check. Nothing had gone the way she had planned. Memucan had failed her, and now he was as useless to her as Vashti was to Xerxes. There was some small measure of comfort in that thought—that her husband should suffer as much as she suffered.

But there should be no suffering for either one of them. If he had simply named her queen in Vashti's place, there would be no need for this "beauty" search. What a completely and utterly foolish idea!

She had borne the king's heir and more besides. He had no need of more women. He had a harem full of them already. What purpose could there possibly be to flood Susa with thousands of young stargazed women who thought they stood even a remote chance of becoming queen in Vashti's place? Ludicrous!

She must do something to make sure he chose the most

pliable woman, someone she could control and train. It would not be the same as assuming full leadership, but if she held the reins of the young filly, she would control the girl and, by extension, the king.

The thought did little to lighten her bitter mood, but she moved toward the harem just the same. A line of young women waited to enter their rooms. Where did Hegai think he could possibly fit all of them?

Normally she did not travel to this area of the palace. At least Xerxes had given her rooms of her own. Rooms she did not have to share with his concubines. His mother would not have allowed him to do less, for which Amestris felt the slightest bit of gratitude. She didn't care overmuch for Atossa, but at least the woman had been useful in this. And she would make sure her mother-in-law did more for her in days to come when it came time for Xerxes to name a co-regent.

Whoever he named queen must never bear his child. Amestris rubbed suddenly sweaty hands over her royal robe. Was there some potion she could slip into the girl's food or drink to prevent a child? She must consult her physicians. Surely there was a way, though it seemed as impossible as her other attempts to gain control.

She pushed the thought temporarily aside and moved closer to the area where Hegai inspected the newest group of virgins. Amestris swallowed the acrid taste of jealousy as she glimpsed women younger and more beautiful than she had ever been. Much as she hated to admit such a thing, Xerxes' young servants had concocted an ingenious plan. This "contest" would keep the king happily distracted and in a good mood for years. Even with his insatiable lust, he would not call for a woman every night, and it would take a year before any of them were pampered and bathed and oiled enough to make them pleasing to his tastes.

She had endured the same treatments the year she prepared for her wedding to the man. But their love had always been overshadowed by his love for Vashti. Amestris always felt that Xerxes was performing a duty with her, not truly caring about anything she said or did. His interest only changed when she announced another pregnancy, but even then, Vashti took first place. She had ruled his heart like no other, and if these young virgins thought for a moment that they might take her place or win his love, they were sorely mistaken.

But let them discover that sorry truth on their own. She would befriend them only to control. She would do nothing to help them when they came to her, confused at Xerxes' inattention. A slow smile thinned her lips as she stepped closer, still hidden by a large marble pillar, to hear Hegai's words.

"Your name, please?"

A young beauty with smooth, flowing dark hair and the darkest, widest eyes Amestris had ever seen stood before the king's eunuch. "Esther, my lord. Daughter of Abihail. Adopted by Mordecai, son of Jair." The girl's voice carried a cultured lilt. She must come from wealth or privilege. Whatever was she doing caught up in this . . . mess?

"Mordecai. He sits at the king's gate."

"Yes, my lord. He is my adoptive father, as both of my parents are dead." Esther spoke matter-of-factly, as though the news was not recent

Perhaps she was not so privileged after all. Just fortunate to be beautiful. A shame.

"Your age?" Hegai's scribe jotted notes on clay as the questions were answered.

"Fifteen, my lord."

Stop calling him "my lord"! He is a eunuch! Amestris clenched her jaw against her building frustration.

Hegai looked the girl up and down. "You will wait over there." He pointed to a spot not far from him, then continued with the rest of the group.

What purpose could he have with Esther? Amestris waited, stepping farther into the shadows.

Another group of women approached, but Hegai put his underling in charge of taking their names and information. He moved away from the entrance area and walked closer to Esther. Amestris could not hear from this vantage point, but dare she move closer? She did not want Hegai becoming aware of her interest in these girls. She would need a good reason for being here, and at the moment she had none.

She watched a little longer and saw Hegai call seven young maids to Esther's side, then personally lead the girl to another part of the harem. So Hegai liked this one. He could not have been more obvious about that.

Good. Perhaps her job of finding the next queen wouldn't be as hard as she thought. She could just watch Hegai to see whom else he favored. There must be more virgins who had caught his eye, young women who had been given a special place in the palace.

She headed back to her rooms, pondering how to go about gathering more information and what she might do once she had it.

Esther looked at the ornate surroundings, struck by the enormity of the palace. Marble pillars spread down halls that seemed to extend forever. Mosaic tiles created detailed patterns of blue, red, gold, and white, and finely woven tapestries hung from limestone walls.

Hegai stood taller than Mordecai, but his girth was wider and his hair completely missing from his head. Esther did her best not to stare at his size, for she sensed kindness in his eyes. She followed him, along with seven young maids, down those long, winding halls toward a set of rooms that were bigger than Mordecai's entire house.

When they reached the door, Hegai opened it and turned to her. "Esther, I want you to meet Shirin, Hettie, Jazmin, Rosana, Parisa, Mahin, and Zareen. Each one of them will be devoted to you alone." He pointed at her.

Esther smiled at each girl, heat filling her face. Shirin was not much younger than Esther herself. Were all of the virgins given such treatment? But she did not question Hegai. Instead, she followed him into the suite of rooms and listened intently as he pointed to various side rooms and articles of use within each one.

"You will have your own private bathing pool." He moved past the area with a deep and wide hole where steam rose off the water, which was heated from an underground source. "And over here is the bed where your maids will apply special oils and perfumes. Each young woman undergoes these beauty treatments for an entire year before they meet the king."

Esther nodded, taking in the narrow bed where pots of oils and ointments and flasks of perfume stood along one wall. On a low table were smaller alabaster caskets of cosmetics and the tools to apply them. She would not need her personal combs, and once Hegai showed her a room filled with garments of various colors and designs, she realized that her tunics and even her best robe would never measure up to the glamour here.

"You will be given jewels, and when the time comes to spend your night with the king, you will be allowed to choose whatever you want to take with you." He clasped his hands in front of him. "Once you leave here, you will move to the concubines' quarters. You will not return to this place, but it is yours for the next year. I suggest you make the best use of your time here."

Esther nodded again, her head spinning with too much information. She glanced about her, then looked back at Hegai.

"Do you have any questions?" His tone softened as his hands fell to his sides, and she sensed again the kindness she'd first seen in him.

"No. Nothing. That is, I can think of nothing yet to ask." She laughed lightly. "This is all so . . . exotic." She moved her hand in an arc over the living quarters. "I have never seen anything like these rooms."

"You will see far more before your year is up." He stroked his bare chin. "You will take your meals with the other girls in a dining hall, but if you have any particular foods you would like to have, simply let me know. I will check on you often."

Esther tilted her head, debating whether or not to give him the dietary laws she had followed all of her life. He would wonder about her background if she said too much. Could she word the request in such a way so as not to draw attention?

"I can tell you want to say something." He quirked a brow.

"It is only . . . I am used to a minimal diet where I come from. We ate from the garden and ate many lentils and nuts and raisins and dates. And bread, of course." She searched his face. "We rarely ate meat—sometimes goat or lamb—but in the city we could not keep flocks or herds or afford to purchase much from the butchers."

"Well, you can have your fill of meat here," he said, smiling. "There is no lack of what the king has to offer."

Esther hesitated and swallowed, then took a chance in spite of the warnings in her head to remain silent. "I simply fear that too drastic a change in my diet might make me ill. It is not that I am ungrateful for whatever the king has to offer."

Hegai regarded her. "I hadn't considered that, but you are wise to think of it. I will make sure your diet consists only of things you are used to. It would not bode well for me if you became ill."

"Thank you, my lord." She bowed her head.

He cleared his throat. "It is just Hegai. I am simply a eunuch, not a lord or nobleman."

"Thank you, Hegai." She bowed her head again. "I appreciate all you have done for me."

"It is my pleasure."

At that moment the seven maids joined her, all talking at once.

"That is my excuse to leave you now." He winked and turned on his heel, leaving the rooms. Her rooms. With seven maids. What was she supposed to do with seven girls to attend her?

CHAPTER Seventeen

Mordecai left his house before dawn, no longer able to abide the feeling that he was utterly alone. He could spend time with his sons, but their homes were too small to add a room for him, and he couldn't bear to become a burden to his daughters-in-law or grandchildren.

He had not counted on losing both Levia and Hadassah in such a short time. Why? He glanced heavenward and rubbed a hand over his head. Surely this was the fault of his hesitance. He should have gone with those who had traveled to Jerusalem years ago when his sons were young and Hadassah a babe in arms.

But the loss of Hadassah's parents and his work at the king's gate had caused him to wait. Hadassah was too young, he had reasoned. His work too important. Ha! No work was so important that a man should risk losing his family over it.

Hadassah would not be in the king's palace now if he had simply left when doing so was easy. Instead, he had counted himself among friends with the Jews who had stayed in Susa, and he'd felt safe enough to remain. No harm had come to them in the seventy years they had been captives. What could possibly go wrong now that they were able to return to their homeland if they so desired?

Before the king's edict they had been free. But since that notice had appeared on the post of the king's gate, he knew that leaving would have drawn attention to Hadassah. If only she had remained in the house and never gone out.

Mordecai walked toward the rising sun and soon reached the area outside of the king's harem—a place where family and friends could come to hear news of their loved ones who now belonged to the king. He wandered about the narrow section of mosaic tiles and peered through the latticed windows. Only one of them afforded a view of anything inside, and if one were fortunate, they might see a servant passing by. Mordecai waited, hoping one of the eunuchs would speak with him.

His pulse quickened as the door opened, and Hegai stepped into the garden area opposite the walkway. A small crowd had gathered and now drew close.

"I will take a few questions. That is all." Hegai stood straight, towering over those gathered before him.

"How is my daughter Mara?" one desperate woman cried.

"And mine. Her name is Teita."

More cries from mothers shouting the names of their daughters filled the small court.

Mordecai felt out of place, as if it were foolish for a father to ask after his daughter. Even worse for a cousin to care what happened to a much younger cousin.

"*You're her true father.*" Levia's reminder sang in his thoughts, and he raised his voice above the cackle of females.

"My daughter is Esther. Is she well?" At his commanding tone, silence descended.

Hegai looked in his direction. "Esther is your daughter?"

"Yes. My adopted daughter. Her parents died when she was very young. Is she well?" A surge of hope filled him that Hegai seemed to recognize her name.

"Esther is quite well. And you are Mordecai, who works at the king's gate." Hegai looked him over as if he were trying to read his thoughts.

"Yes, yes. Please, is there anything you can tell me?" He hated the urgency in his tone, but he felt a sudden desperation to know.

Hegai rubbed a hand over his clean-shaven chin. "Esther is well placed in rooms with seven maids and will be well cared for. Expect her to be in this area for the next year." He addressed the crowd then. "All of the girls will be in this area of the harem for a year of beauty treatments before they meet the king. You need not fear. All of them will be treated with kindness and respect."

A murmur of female voices filled the court once again, and Mordecai nodded at Hegai and mouthed his thanks, then turned to hurry toward the king's gate to work. It wasn't much. And yet—seven maids? Had all of the girls received such a gift? A maid was a sign of wealth, but seven?

He glanced heavenward again. *Forgive me.* He should never have doubted that Adonai would not forsake Hadassah in this place. Seven maids! Surely God himself had smiled on his girl and would look after her.

But Mordecai would return to the harem court to make sure just the same.

Esther awoke to the singing of birds in the garden trees outside of her rooms. She blinked and stretched, still unused to the luxury of her surroundings despite the six months that had already passed. Oil of myrrh treatments had been completed the night before. Today she would begin a regimen of other ointments and perfumes.

So much fuss simply to spend one night in a king's bed. She no longer blushed at the thought, for Hegai's underlings had taught her many things a virgin would not normally know. Ways to entice a man and things to expect of him—things he might request of her.

At first her cheeks had heated hotter than the setting sun at the thought of things she might be asked to say or do, but no longer. Was the king truly so simple as to want only one thing from his queen? Would he not also wish to know her? To know her mind and what she thought? A queen should not simply be an object of beauty or desire. But from what she had heard of the man, she knew she could not expect anything from him.

"Are you ready to rise, my lady?" Mahin asked as she reached for Esther's covers and pulled them to the foot of the bed.

"Of course." She smiled at her maid, grateful for the girl's delightful sense of humor, even if she would have preferred to stay abed a little longer. She had learned quickly to keep her complaints to herself. There was no use being disagreeable to servants who were simply trying to please their masters.

"Rosana is waiting with your clothes, and Hettie and Parisa will escort you to the dining hall. After you break your fast, we will begin lessons in court etiquette and give you your first bath in oil of frankincense."

"Thank you, Mahin." She allowed the girl to help her rise, and after she attended to her personal needs, Esther practiced walking with measured, graceful steps toward the small chamber reserved for her many garments. To have an entire room just for clothing still seemed surreal to her, especially in those moments when she recalled Mordecai and the home she'd shared with him and Levia. How was he doing without her?

"Mahin?" She turned around at the threshold of the garment room.

"Yes, my lady?" The girl paused from stripping the bed of linens, which would soon be replaced with fresh ones.

"Would you please either check with Hegai or go to the harem court and see how my father, Mordecai, fares? I know he visits daily, but I do not always hear how he is doing." A sudden feeling of nostalgia and longing filled her. She missed her home. She missed her family. She missed Jola. Had she married Gad in the months Esther had been shut up in these rooms? She fought a sense of sorrow that life would never be the same again.

"I will be happy to check on him for you." Mahin dropped the sheets and hurried to do Esther's bidding.

How strange it seemed to have at least one of seven women at her side every moment of the day. Restlessness filled her. She was never left to herself or even allowed time to think. Even at night, the maids slept on pallets nearby.

She shook the thoughts aside and moved into the area where Rosana helped her dress. A pale blue length of fabric was draped over one shoulder, reaching from head to foot, and a dark green fabric covered her other shoulder. Both lengths of soft linen were tied at the waist with a golden sash. Golden sandals were fitted to her feet, and her hair was brushed and styled. Even her cosmetics were applied before she could walk the halls to the banquet room, though only the other contestants would be in attendance.

At last she moved between Hettie and Parisa toward the rooms where she could finally eat. She passed tables piled with sweet pastries, nutmeats, cheeses, and fruit of all kinds, and came at last to the table Hegai had set aside for her. Her meal held simpler fare, though she ate many of the same things as her fellow virgins. She avoided the sweeter choices in favor of the fresh fruit and cheese and bread. How she wished she could send some of the food she didn't need to Mordecai. Was he getting enough to eat? Were her cousins' wives taking care to see that he wasn't always alone?

After the meal she met Mahin midway to her rooms and smiled her greeting.

"I have news of your father," the maid said.

Esther slowed her pace. "Tell me," she said as they moved through the winding halls.

"He is well. Hegai said he asks after you often and stops near the court daily. He said Mordecai worries too much and that he reassures him you are fine. And Hegai said that if you would like to see him, you could be at the door when he visits the families and look through the latticework, as long as you stay out of sight. It is the best he can offer you." Mahin blew out a breath as if she had been holding the words too long.

"I would love to see him again, even if he cannot see me. Thank you, Mahin." Esther hugged the girl, who hugged her back like a sister might, then quickly released her and turned away as if she had done something wrong.

Esther sighed. She would never grow used to these strange customs of maids and servants fearing her. She wanted to be treated as everyone else. To be accepted and even loved.

"I will visit tomorrow then." She entered her rooms and followed Zareen to the treatment room. Another day of oils and massages and lessons in how to move and speak and even hold a cup of wine in her hand. Nothing in her previous life had prepared her for this. But she was determined to learn well.

Esther stood near the appointed window the following morning and watched, anxious. Her heart skipped a beat at the sight of Mordecai pacing, waiting to speak with Hegai. *Oh Abba!* How she longed to walk through the door and fall into his arms. To be his Hadassah again and let this whole ordeal end.

She strained to hear as Hegai at last spoke to Mordecai. The eunuch must have indicated that Esther was watching, for Mordecai looked in her direction. The clear view of his bearded face, the haggard lines along his brow, only increased Esther's homesickness. He needed her. She could see it in his eyes, but there was nothing she could do or say to let him know she was all right. *Was* she all right?

The thoughts lingered with her the next day, making it even harder to be graceful and kind. *Why, Adonai?* Why was she here? What purpose could there possibly be to live her life in a king's harem, a wife yet not a wife to a notoriously womanizing man who could have her killed or call her to his bed on a whim? In her six months at the palace, she had yet to see the king even from a distance and had no idea what he looked like up close. From the street as an onlooker in a crowd of people, she had glimpsed the man in his military garb, but his face lay hidden behind a helmet.

What if she could not bear to look at him without wincing? He could have massive scars from the wars in which he had fought. He could be big and brutish and mean. What if he hated her?

She swallowed the fear and pushed back the anxious thoughts. This would do her no good. She could not change her circumstances. She could not pray her way out of this—*if* God even heard her from this foreign land. Did He? Or was He only with the people who had returned to Jerusalem?

Why did she think for a single moment that God cared for a lonely young woman in a foreign palace in a foreign land?

The doubts and confusion followed her throughout the day. Even Mahin's humor could not pull her from the nearness of tears.

"What's wrong, mistress?" Jazmin asked when the last of the beauty treatments ended for the day. "You're usually cheerful and smiling. Has someone offended you? I will report them to Hegai, and he will see to it that you are no longer troubled."

Esther looked at her maid. "No, no. Do not tell him of my struggle. I am simply homesick today, that is all. It is nothing. Truly. It will pass with a good night's sleep."

Jazmin nodded, her look one of understanding. "I remember when they first brought me here. I cried for days after they left, but my parents could not afford to feed me, and, well . . . they had little choice. The king needed servants and I would be cared for." She touched the fabric of her clothes. "I am well fed and dressed and have good work to do. It was the best decision they could have made. One day soon, you will see, this isn't as bad as it seems now."

Esther looked beyond Jazmin through the open windows. A walk in the gardens would cheer her. And the girl was right. At least Esther would be cared for as the wife of the king, whereas her maids would never marry. Perhaps her status wasn't quite as bad as she thought.

"I think I would like to step outside for a little while." She moved to the door that separated her rooms from the gardens. Jazmin followed at a discreet distance. Her maids were certainly persistent in protecting her.

The night breeze cooled her flushed skin, and she lifted her head to the setting sun. The scent of the almond trees mingled with the headier lavender and roses, calming her. The sun dipped slowly, setting off a wild array of pinks and oranges, and a splay of yellow that pointed toward the clouds brought a song to Esther's soul.

Perhaps Adonai had not abandoned her in this place. Could she have a purpose even as one in hundreds or a thousand in a harem? Would God grant her favor in the king's eyes and allow her to know him—to see him more than one night?

She pondered the thought. Did she want to know the king more than one night would allow? What was he like, truly? In that moment she decided it was time she discovered the man behind the crown. She had six months left to try to learn all she could of Xerxes, the king who had lost the war with Greece, who had deposed his favorite wife, and who could not seem to make a wise decision. Surely there was more to him than the gossips proclaimed.

Whatever it took, she must discover a way to find out.

CHAPTER Eighteen

Esther finally summoned her courage two months later and requested an audience with Hegai. He came to her rooms one morning and sent her maids away, leaving them alone.

"You have questions?" Hegai sat across from her, his gaze probing, as if he could read her very thoughts.

"Yes," she said, deciding the man had too much to do for her to waste his time in hesitation. "I wish to better understand the king. I have never seen him or met him, and I do not wish to enter his chambers in four months without some knowledge of who he is."

Hegai's jaw clenched, and he looked about despite the closed doors and the privacy they shared. "You know what every other virgin knows. I am sure your maids have told you enough."

She studied him. "Is it wrong of me to ask to know more than the gossips say? I know nothing of his character, of his personality. What does he enjoy? Does he laugh easily? Is he a man of quick temper? What goals does he have for the kingdom?"

Hegai smiled, his shoulders relaxing. "Ah, I see. You ask intelligent questions, but I fear I do not know the answers to any of them. These are things the wife of the king might one day ask, and things perhaps his advisors understand, but I daresay that King Xerxes is a private man. He does not share such things with his servants."

"And yet, from what I understand, it was his servants who recognized his sorrow over Vashti and suggested this contest. Is that not correct?" Esther twisted the belt at her waist.

"It is correct." Hegai leaned forward, elbows on his knees. "Esther, I like you. I think you hold much potential to please the king." He lowered his voice. "I can see that you are sincere in your desire to understand the king, so I will tell you what I do know."

She waited expectantly.

"The king married Vashti when they were both young. He was not yet reigning as king at the time, and she remained his only wife for many years. They had one son, but he was born before Xerxes took the throne. His mother did not like Vashti, from what I understand, so she picked Amestris to be his wife after his coronation. Amestris has borne the king two sons, and her firstborn will be his heir."

"Vashti's son went with her into exile," Esther said, and Hegai nodded.

"Yes. And Amestris wanted to be named queen in her place. She is a rival to watch closely. Be careful who you trust, Esther, even here, because I have seen Amestris enter these quarters though she does not belong here, and she likely has spies among the maids."

Esther lifted a brow, alarm shooting through her.

Hegai interpreted her look with a raised hand. "You need not fear the women in your service. I handpicked each one, and they are loyal to me alone. But you must still be careful not to speak of personal things or ask questions about the king to the other contestants or other servants. Don't even speak of them to your maids if others can hear. Even if Amestris means the virgins no harm, others might. There are always people in the king's house who want to harm him. This is why he speaks very little about his personal thoughts or desires."

Esther leaned back on the plush couch, processing this new information. Why hadn't Hegai told her this sooner? Perhaps her own reticence to speak had caused him to feel no need to warn her. Hadn't she kept her feelings and thoughts close to her heart? Mordecai had warned her to keep her heritage safe, and she had done much more. She had told very little even to her maids.

"This is all new to me, Hegai. I understand from my father that things can go on here that might not bode well for me or the king or others in the palace. But I never thought there might be danger from one of the king's wives or even the servants. I do not believe I have met Amestris. Is this something I should do? Would it not be wise to know who to watch out for?"

Hegai straightened and once again glanced about the room. "The next time I see her moving through these halls, I will find you and point her out to you. Once you have moved to the king's harem under Shaashgaz, you will see all of the king's wives and concubines and undoubtedly the king's mother from time to time. I have no doubt Amestris stops in to flaunt her privileged place to the other women the king never sees."

Esther fought the sadness his words evoked. "It seems so strange to know that I will only have one night with him, and that he will likely never call for me again. How do those women live without anything to do?"

Hegai laughed. "Oh, my child. They have plenty to do. They create beautiful tapestries and mosaics that end up in rooms in this palace or the one in Persepolis. They care for their children if they have them. Even though their servants carry out most of their duties, they are allowed to work on whatever projects please them."

Esther smiled simply because she could think of no other appropriate reaction. "That is good to know."

Hegai stood, and Esther stood with him. "I have no more information to give you regarding the king himself, but if you will take my advice and learn from me these next four months, I will do all I can to help you learn to please him. Who knows? Perhaps you will win his heart. In the meantime, I will speak with my servants and we will try to discover the answers to at least some of your questions. But leave those things to me. Do not ask anyone but me."

"I will do whatever you say," Esther promised, walking with him to the door.

"Good." He regarded her. "If I were to choose, I think you would make a perfect queen."

He left her then, her thoughts reeling. Until that moment, she had never considered the possibility that she could actually win the king's heart and become Persia's next queen. She was too young. Too inexperienced. Too Jewish. Jewish maidens did not become Persian queens.

But Hegai did not know that. And perhaps her youth and beauty would be enough to entice the king. Still, she sensed she would have to learn more than simple obedience or exotic moves in his bed to win his heart. She would need to actually care for him. And she had no idea how to care for a man she had never met.

Mordecai climbed the steps at the king's gate and took his place in the room where he recorded cases that were brought to the city officials, who then determined whether they should be brought before the king. The large room ran the width and breadth of the gate, which was more like another building than a normal entrance one would place in front of a courtyard.

Mordecai had worked in this location for more years than he could count, and normally he found the work interesting. No two cases were ever the same, and in the early years Darius, the previous king, would hear many of them himself. While Darius kept a tight rein on his kingdom and secluded himself in his chambers with few courtiers and many guards, he trusted his guards to protect him and seemed to enjoy passing judgment on those needing someone to judge between them.

But Xerxes was not at all like his father, and since his return from Greece he had grown more secluded, almost paranoid. He had gone so far as to issue a decree that no one was to enter his presence uninvited. Few men other than his closest advisors and his guards were allowed to see his face. Should anyone violate his orders, they would be immediately killed, unless the king was in a generous mood and held forth his golden scepter.

Xerxes had worsened in recent days. To approach him meant risking his swift wrath. Mordecai shivered at the memory of a few who had tried to approach the king uninvited and without the proper humility.

Since then, very few cases came before Xerxes as they had in the earlier years of his reign. In the years when Vashti remained his queen.

Would a new queen make a difference in the man?

Mordecai dipped his reed into the ink and listened as the first group approached the city elders. He recorded the important details—their names, the reason for their complaint, and the date. Midmorning, one of the eunuchs would carry the list to an advisor, who would then approach the king.

How many men would be sent away disappointed? How many cases would the elders simply rule upon, deeming them not critical enough for the king's ears?

"How does your daughter fare today, Mordecai?" Teresh, one of the king's eunuchs who often relayed information between the officials and the advisors, asked as he approached.

Mordecai looked up and offered the man a slight smile. "She is well. Thank you." He looked again at his work, in no mood for frivolous talk.

"Good. Good. I hope she does well." Teresh walked away before Mordecai could respond.

Strange man. Mordecai did not trust any of the Persians or other people groups who worked for the king. The thought made him pause. When had he trusted anyone but himself or his sons? Levia. He used to trust Levia. And Hadassah. Even his sons' wives were too new to the family to share his thoughts with. And he rarely entered into conversations with the men in the Jewish community except on those occasional Sabbaths when he joined them.

You have no friends, Mordecai. A pitiful thought. As he listened to the complaints and recorded them by rote, he pondered the realization. Levia had been his life. His children his joy. To lose Levia and Hadassah in the same year had been too much. He had closed himself in. Kept himself distant from others when he probably needed their company now more than ever.

He needed to change. Somehow he needed to reach out to his community, spend more time with his family, and stop worrying so much about Hadassah. He could not change what had happened to her, and if she was lonely or being mistreated or threatened in some way, it was beyond his control. He could not even step inside the halls of the king's harem, and that was not likely to change once she became one of the king's wives. Though he supposed it was a question worth asking the next time Hegai came out to converse with him.

None of the other mothers or fathers came to the harem courtyard daily like he did. No one else carried his sense of guilt. Or fear. And sometimes no one came to speak to him. Why bother when he was the only one visiting?

He looked heavenward. *Perhaps tomorrow, Adonai?* The prayer could not hurt, though he had to admit he had not been as attentive to prayer or the Scriptures as he should have been in recent months. Years even. When had he lost his love of his God? When had he cared more for the things of this life than pleasing Adonai?

Had God taken Hadassah because of his failure? Because of his disobedience to the law? Had he made a grave mistake in telling Hadassah to keep her heritage a secret? For a lengthy moment he felt his chest burn with the wondering. What good could it have done to try to keep her safe? Only God could keep her safe in that place of intrigue. In the room alone with the king.

And yet God was the one person he had not bothered asking to do so.

CHAPTER Nineteen

Esther walked the halls of the king's harem, Shirin at her side. "Where are we going?" Esther asked once they had passed the quarters of the other virgins. She had taken Hegai's words to heart and rarely spoke of anything other than simple things in the company of the other women.

"To the king's library." Shirin shrugged as if the reason for this visit should be obvious. "Hegai said you wished to know more of the king's exploits. One of the king's scribes is going to read to you from a scroll. Whatever you wish to learn is yours to choose."

"Thank you." Esther hid her surprise at Hegai's quick answer to her request. Word had come to her the week after their talk that Xerxes had gone to Persepolis to oversee building projects there. Besides completing the palace of his father, Darius, he was building a Gate of All Nations. Would he also seek out Vashti there? Rumors floated throughout the harem that the king had secretly sent her there, but would he go against the law of the Medes and Persians and allow her into his presence? There would be no need for this contest if he accepted Vashti back into his life.

She shook the thought aside as they entered a small room filled with scrolls from the ornate ceiling to the mosaic floor. A scribe sat at a wide desk, and chairs were positioned in various places along the walls. All thoughts of Vashti vanished at the sight of so many scrolls containing annals of the kings of Persia. How had Hegai managed to gain her entrance here?

"Mistress Esther, is it?" The scribe rose and welcomed her into the room. Shirin followed but remained behind her.

"Yes, my lord." She bowed, and the scribe chuckled.

"You have no need to bow to servants, mistress. Only the king is to be so revered, or those he assigns the highest ranking in his kingdom. His wives and concubines are not to trouble themselves with mere servants like myself." He bowed to her instead, and she smiled, masking her discomfort.

"Now," he said, taking his seat again after directing her to choose a seat along one of the walls, "tell me what it is you would like to learn of the king."

"Read to me of his conquests in battle. Of his victories." She wasn't all that interested in war but sensed that the more she knew of the way of kings, the better. And kingdoms and war seemed to go hand in hand.

The scribe raised a brow, his expression one of surprise. "No other wife of the king has ever asked such a thing." He went to the wall and pulled a scroll from the stack. "Are you sure you would not rather read of his history, his childhood, his family? Women are more often concerned with these things."

She lifted her chin to better gaze into his eyes. "I would

like to learn all, but if we have time for only one visit, I would like to learn what the king enjoys best. Would that not be his victories in war?"

The scribe studied her a moment. "Xerxes is a king who has gone to war because war is expected. He warred with Greece because his father, Darius, had the desire but died before he could carry out his wishes. He has put down rebellions in Babylon and Egypt, but he does not go to war by choice, mistress. Even now he is building in Persepolis. He is a king of peace more than war."

Esther folded her hands in her lap, her mind whirling with this new information. "Then I would like to hear whatever you think is best for me to understand the king."

The scribe touched his bare chin and turned to look over the scrolls. He pulled a different one from its slot and unrolled it on the desk.

As he read to her, Esther listened, trying to memorize the names of Xerxes' family, his building projects, and his decrees, one of which caused a sinking feeling in her middle. Apparently at some point in his past, he stopped trusting his closest advisors, and no one was allowed into his presence without permission, on pain of death. Perhaps her future husband—was she to consider him that?—trusted no one but himself.

She pondered the thought as she returned to her rooms with Shirin. "Yet he has many advisors," she said aloud before she could stop herself.

"Yes, mistress, the king always seeks advice, sometimes even from his servants." Shirin spoke softly as they approached the rooms of the virgins on their way to her apartments.

"I see." Esther picked up her pace, suddenly needing to escape these halls and rest in the cool of her rooms.

Of course he trusted people. Probably more often than he wanted to. If he did not, he would not ask advice and she would not be in this predicament. Unless perhaps the king had no confidence in his own judgments.

She stopped short at the threshold and looked at Shirin but kept her thoughts to herself. As Shirin left her to the care of Parisa and Rosana, she wondered if the king was a man ruled by fear of failure. Perhaps he trusted those closest to him because he could not trust himself.

Xerxes rode his horse through the streets of Persepolis, surrounded by guards, with Haman and two of his nobles, Carshena and Shethar, at his side. He stopped at the Gate of All Nations and examined the four stone columns rising toward the sky, then moved to each of the three doorways. Workmen heaved a cart carrying a massive bull toward the western entrance, the second of the pair that would guard the door. The gate was impressive, but not nearly as impressive as the Apadana, the great audience halls with numerous columns that rose to the height of nearly twelve men.

He reined in his steed and cantered toward the south entrance that led to the construction on the great hall. He motioned for Haman to draw up beside him. A guard moved to allow the man closer access.

"Make a note that I want this hall finished before I choose my new queen. Give them six months. If I have not found a queen by then, at least the hall will be ready." He looked over the unfinished work with pride of ownership, but he chafed at realizing how much there was left to do.

"My lord, if you are willing to hire more workmen, I am

certain that we can have this project finished in time. One column alone can take months to move into place." Haman spoke candidly, yet his voice carried his typically humble tone. He rested a hand on his horse's neck and glanced at Xerxes.

Xerxes watched the men, their bare backs dripping with sweat as they worked. They had many columns to set in place, the floor to lay down, and the roof to put on, not to mention the many inner touches, the golden interlays, the tapestries, the throne, and the benches for people to wait for an audience with him.

But he wanted to bring his new bride here. The hall in Susa would suffice, as it matched this one in magnificence, but somehow he thought bringing her here would wipe out his memories of Vashti. He should never have sent Vashti to Persepolis. Even now, he debated the idea of having his servants seek her out and move her to another town. The temptation to avoid a city he loved was too great, the temptation to find her too strong.

Curse Memucan and his ideas! He should never have put Vashti in that position or listened to his foolish advisor. Why could he not make a simple decision without allowing others to insert their opinions?

Haman spoke, interrupting his internal tirade. "Shall I order more men to work on this project, my lord? Or would you halt work on the Gate of All Nations to finish this first?"

Xerxes regarded the man, wondering whether he should listen to yet another advisor's advice. Realistically, he would not finish with the virgins for another year unless he found one he wanted sooner rather than later. He had already wasted six months on his concubines while he waited for the virgins, none of whom were the least bit interesting. None of them were like Vashti. Or her opposite, which might be better.

"Hire more men. Tell them to increase the pace, but not at the expense of the work. The work comes first. They must make this excellent, a place to make their king proud to live in and nations awed to visit." He turned and rode in the opposite direction, up a hill toward the palace there. "We will return to Susa tomorrow," he said to Haman. "Make sure everything is ready."

He rode forward with his guards, leaving his advisors behind. The visit here had been worthwhile, but he could not shake the restlessness that called him back to Susa. Why he imagined that city a better place than this, he could not say. Susa held all of the memories of his failures. But it also held the hope of a brighter future. One he was anxious to begin.

CHAPTER Twenty

The chill of midspring caused Esther to burrow deeper into the covers and relish this, her last day in the hall of virgins. Her maids milled in silence about the room, one fanning a small fire in a brick oven, another setting food at a table near the fire, a third off in another room preparing a bath.

"You are awake," Mahin said, smiling down at her. "I see you wish you were not. Did we make too much noise, mistress?"

Esther poked her head above the warm blankets. "I was just enjoying the warmth and the feeling of the bed on my last morning here."

Mahin looked away, and Esther caught a glimpse of tears in her eyes. "We will miss you." Her voice sounded hoarse.

Esther sat up, the covers forgotten. "You have no need of that. You will surely go with me to the king's harem for his wives."

Mahin shook her head. "I do not know whether Hegai can

spare us. And I do not know if you are allowed to keep us. Most virgins do not take their maids with them."

Esther pondered the girl's words as Parisa held open a thick robe for her and Rosana led her to sit and eat. She would not be joining the other virgins in the dining hall today. Nothing would be the same today or after this day, and the thought brought tension to her middle and caused a sense of anxiety and excitement to mingle within her. She looked at her maids, all of them avoiding her gaze.

"Well, this will never do," she said, smiling at them. "If I have anything to say about it, if any request is given to me, I will ask for all of you. And if I am refused, you must obey your next mistress willingly. It does no good to compare one with another, as you may come to hate me or her, depending on whom you like better."

Mahin laughed and the others giggled. "The very thought that we could ever hate you." Mahin laughed harder, a delightful sound. "You are the most gracious of them all. Everyone loves you, mistress. Do you not realize this?"

She shook her head. "I have not given the matter any thought."

"Well, they do. Especially Hegai. He favors you best," Zareen said.

Esther fingered a date, embarrassed by the praise. "I am glad," she said softly. She looked overlong at each piece of furniture, each article of clothing, each woman in her care, each item of food set before her, in an attempt to extend the moments and place them solidly in her memory. At last she stood and walked to the window to gaze on the gardens that had brought her much peace in her year here.

A knock at the door caused her to turn. Hettie hurried to

answer it. Hegai stood tall in the arch of the door and moved inside, his girth and height seeming to fill the room.

She walked closer. "Hegai. Thank you for coming." Her maids stood back as if they did not know what to do. Or perhaps they waited for his instructions for her.

"This is your day, Esther. You may choose whatever you like to take to the king. Remember, this is your last day to occupy these rooms. So take what means the most to you." He looked at her with an expression of fatherly affection.

Esther studied him, her heart aching, already missing him. "I would like you to pick for me, Hegai. I trust you. You know the king better than I, whereas I only know what I have been told, some of which is not likely to be completely true. I would take my mother's ring, but other than that, I ask you to choose, please."

Hegai smiled, his mouth slightly tilted to one side and his eyes lit with a boyish enthusiasm. "Thank you, Esther." He looked at her maids. "After you have bathed and oiled her with the faintest hint of frankincense, use no other perfume. Apply only the lightest of the cosmetics. She is beautiful without them, so let us not mar her beauty." He studied her. "Dress her in a simple white, semi-sheer tunic. The king will enjoy the ability to see her well. But cover the tunic with a pale blue robe trimmed in purple."

Parisa hurried to the garment room and returned with clothing that matched Hegai's description. "Do these suffice, my lord?"

Hegai took the tunic and robe and nodded. "Soft and beautiful. Yes. This is perfect. Tie the robe with a purple sash. Place a golden pendant around her neck and hang golden earrings from her ears. Let me see her choice of sandals."

Parisa hurried back to the room after laying the garments flat on the bed, which had already been stripped of its linens. She returned with an armful of sandals and set them on a chair.

Hegai bent to examine them and pulled a pair of intricately carved leather devoid of jewels from the pile. "You will go as a virgin with hints of wealth to show off your character and your beauty. You may wear your mother's ring, but do not wear bracelets. The less distraction you give him, the better. The king, you shall see, likes simple pleasures, despite the ornate designs you find throughout the palace."

"And my hair?" Esther's head spun with his quick choices. She sensed by his look that Hegai had planned this for some time, probably in the hopes that she would ask for his help. She breathed a silent prayer of thanks to Adonai, for she knew she could never have decided on her own.

Hegai rubbed his chin and had her turn about. Her long, dark hair fell to the middle of her back. To wear it down would be scandalous. Her heart beat faster at the thought, for she had no idea what Hegai would suggest or what the king would desire.

"Wear it up. Hold it in place with combs that are easily removed. The king will enjoy removing them." His frank comment made heat fill her cheeks, despite her training. To think that this night all of her training would come to fruition caused repeated bouts of anxiety to fill her. Could Hegai see the rapid pounding of her heart beneath her robe?

"Parisa, you do her hair. You have a knack for setting the combs just right."

Parisa nodded. "Yes, my lord."

"All right then." Hegai looked her over once more. "I will leave you to enjoy your last day here, but be ready to come with me before the sun sets. The king often enjoys watching it glow, and perhaps he would enjoy sharing that with you."

Esther simply nodded as Hegai turned and walked out as quickly as he had come. Her maids all began to talk at once, and Esther moved as one in a dream, or perhaps as a lamb to the slaughter, if she thought overmuch on what was really about to take place. This day would go too fast. She told herself over and over again that she was ready.

Hegai again appeared at Esther's door hours later as the sun began its descent over Persia. Her heart had beat like a steady drum all day, but now as she saw the smile and approving nod of Hegai and the giddy excitement of her maids who stood surrounding her, it slowed to a normal rhythm. What had been done was done. What would be would be. She had only to control her emotions, her actions, and her words. The rest was up to God. Did He care about her situation in this foreign place?

The walk down the long, winding palace halls seemed to stretch on and on, to the point that even her maids fell silent, the only noise Hegai's heavy footfalls. When they reached the hall leading to the king's chambers, Hegai dismissed her maids and pointed to a door several paces away. "From here you must go alone." He regarded her with gentle affection. "Do all that has been taught to you. Remember my advice, and treat the king as graciously as you have everyone else within the palace. Do this and you will find the experience a good one."

He bowed to her, and she fought to keep tears at bay. Would she ever see him again? Once she entered the second harem she would be under the care of a different eunuch. The temptation to hug him filled her, but she knew if she mussed her gown, he would be troubled and anxious. So she simply leaned forward and kissed his cheek.

"Thank you, Hegai. I will never forget you or all you have done for me." She moved on at his parting nod, her heart once again picking up its pace. She reminded herself to move slowly, with grace. Guards stood on either side of the door, but they did not look her way. Was she supposed to knock?

Before she could think of what to do next, the door opened and a servant ushered her into the room. Hegai must have timed her entrance with the servant. She stepped across the threshold and glanced about the room. Hegai had been right. The king's tastes were simple, not elegant as the rest of the palace was.

"Welcome." A man who could only be the king stepped toward her. His straight brown hair fell to his shoulders, and his light brown beard was cropped short. Green eyes focused on her, making her breath catch. He was older than she but still bore a handsome, well-muscled frame beneath his unadorned purple robe. No crown graced his head. Nevertheless, she bowed low at his approach.

"Tell me your name," he said.

He took her hand, and she straightened. "Esther, my lord."

He studied her for a lengthy moment, his smile casual. "Come. Share a meal with me." He led her to a table near a window that allowed him a wide view of the city he ruled. "Sit." He motioned to a cushioned stool, where she gingerly sat, watching him.

Golden plates were piled high with food, and smaller golden bowls sat at each setting. Wine sparkled in golden goblets with intricate designs as though waiting for them to taste its richness.

"Are you hungry?" He tilted his head to better look at her.

"Not overmuch. But I could eat a few things." In truth, she had lost her appetite soon after the morning meal. Anticipation and a hint of dread had replaced her need for food.

"I am not surprised." He broke off a piece of bread and filled the bowl with nuts and fruit. "You are likely worried what to expect from me." He said it so matter-of-factly that she looked up and searched his gaze.

"I have been curious about you since the day they brought me here." She smiled. "And yet no one seemed to be able to tell me the things I wished to know."

He laughed. "You have likely been listening to the gossips."

"And learning about the wars you have won and the grand structures you are building. But that does not tell me about you, oh king." She told her heart to slow lest she speak too fast and say too much.

"What would you like to know?" He popped a grape into his mouth.

"I would like to hear you tell of the things you care about. Tell me whatever you would like to tell." She toyed with the bread he had given her, then took a small bite.

He picked up his cup and sipped but did not hold it long. For the remainder of the meal, and afterward in the sitting room, he talked about becoming king, the wars with everyone but Greece, and his pride in the buildings he was in the process of constructing. He did not mention his other wives or children, and Esther did not ask.

"You already seem to know and understand these things," he said when he finished.

"I was allowed to visit the king's library, where a scribe read to me some of your exploits and the history written in the annals of kings. I hope this does not displease you." She silently hoped she had not revealed something that might get Hegai in trouble.

The king smiled. "I am amazed that you had interest. I have no issue against you gaining such knowledge. No other wife has ever cared what I do."

She searched his gaze. "I would think it very odd not to care what my husband enjoys or gives his time to do. Your words surprise me."

He rose and took her hand in his. "And you surprise me, Esther." He moved his hand to the small of her back and led her into an adjoining room, his private sleeping quarters.

Esther told herself to remain calm, but she felt her body tense at the sight of the large canopied bed. This was why she had come. She could not run or deny him what was rightfully his. Or not rightfully his, but he was the king, after all. She drew in a slow breath.

"Are you afraid?" He turned her to face him. "I see it in your eyes."

She lowered her gaze for a brief moment, then looked up. "I fear, my lord, that this brings to mind my upbringing that says not to lie with a man without the benefit of marriage, of a covenant between us. I know this is not the same, for I already belong to you."

"Yes, you do," he said, but there was no anger in his tone.

Esther again lowered her head, suddenly ashamed that she had been so forthright. "Forgive me, my lord."

She felt the gentle pressure of his fingers lift her chin. He looked deeply into her eyes as if he were reading a scroll. "All of the women who are called to these chambers come willing to please me. They do whatever I ask them to do, and this is part of it." He gestured toward the bed.

"Yes, my lord. I know that it is."

"You do not need to fear me, Esther."

She simply nodded.

"But you do."

She smoothed her gown. "I will do whatever you ask of me, my lord."

"You remind me of Vashti," he said, his tone low, husky. "And yet you are nothing like her." A deep sigh escaped him. "You draw out a need within me to protect you, though you are willing to do whatever I ask. You delight me, Esther." His slight smile seemed to need her affirmation.

"Thank you, my lord. I find myself grateful for your kindness to me."

Silence passed between them as he studied her. She could not decide whether she should look into his eyes or at her feet, and she longed to fidget with her sash.

"Remove your robe," he said at last. He took a step back from her as she did as he asked. "Now turn around slowly."

Heat filled her cheeks, and she prayed he did not notice as he looked at her through the sheer tunic. She expected the king to step forward and take her into his arms at any moment, but when she faced him again, he simply stood watching her. At last he stepped closer, bent to pick up her robe, and held the arms open for her.

She put her arms through the sleeves, her mind whirling. He took the sash and tied it around her waist, his breath so close it fanned her face. Would he kiss her? Did he find her unpleasing? Was he sending her away without the benefit of becoming his wife?

He took her hand again and walked her back to his sitting room. He led her to a couch filled with cushions, one he had occupied as they talked after the meal. Confusion swirled within her as he knelt in front of her. Her heart picked up its earlier unsettling rhythm, and she did not miss the ardent desire in his gaze.

He lifted her hand to his lips and kissed each finger. When he came to her mother's ring, he paused. "Tell me about this ring. It is not like the jewels I provide my women."

"It belonged to my mother. She died when I was a baby."

The comment brought a look of approval to his eyes. He smiled. "Esther. You have made me feel things tonight that I have not felt in a very long time. A sense that I must protect you at all costs has arisen within me." He paused as if searching for the right words. "I have the strongest desire to take you to my bed, and yet I cannot. Not yet."

She gave him a quizzical look, not sure whether to fear or hope.

"I want you, Esther. But I also want you to be happy, and this is a life you did not choose. So I will give you a choice. You can either marry me at week's end and take Vashti's place as queen of Persia . . . or you may go back to your father and marry a man of your desire. You are young and I am old in comparison. And I am not likely to ever make such an offer to anyone again. This is completely out of character for me." He laughed lightly. "My advisors would think me mad."

"You would offer me this and never take me to your bed?"

The idea seemed incredulous since she had spent the past year preparing for that very thing.

He nodded. “It is as though the gods will not allow me to touch you outside of marriage. I do not understand it, but you give me a feeling that we could truly be of one heart and soul. I do not wish to mar that with rushing what you would normally expect from a husband.”

“You wish to be my husband?”

“Must I say it again?”

She shook her head. “No, my lord. I am just astonished. Forgive me. I would not wish to make the king repeat his words.”

He kissed her fingers once more. The action stirred something within her, and she found that despite their age difference, she could not refuse him. Gad had been lost to her long ago, and there was no other man in her village she would want or who would want her, now that everyone would assume she had spent a night with the king.

She wondered if his request bordered on desire alone or if he could feel the emotion between them. Did he love her? So soon?

“I would be most honored to marry you, my king.”

At the king’s loud shout, she jumped. He stood and pulled her to her feet and into his arms, then twirled her about like a dancer. Laughter bubbled from deep within him, and she joined him. He set her on her feet once more and bent to kiss her cheek. “You cannot imagine how much I want you,” he whispered in her ear. “But I will wait until week’s end. In the meantime, you will return to Hegai and prepare for our wedding.”

She smiled into his eyes, igniting a look she interpreted

as love. She returned his look, hoping he could sense her feelings without words.

"You may address me as Xerxes," he said softly.

She touched his cheek, for she sensed the offer was a great gift. "Thank you . . . Xerxes. It is a strong name, fit for a great king."

He laughed again, giddy as a young boy, and twirled her about the room. Then he led her to the door and called for his servants.

"We have a new queen!" he announced. "Call all of my servants and bring Hegai. We have a week to prepare a wedding feast like no other for the new queen of Persia."

PART THREE

And the king loved Esther more than any of the other young women. He was so delighted with her that he set the royal crown on her head and declared her queen instead of Vashti. To celebrate the occasion, he gave a great banquet in Esther's honor for all his nobles and officials, declaring a public holiday for the provinces and giving generous gifts to everyone.

Even after all the young women had been transferred to the second harem and Mordecai had become a palace official, Esther continued to keep her family background and nationality a secret. She was still following Mordecai's directions, just as she did when she lived in his home.

Esther 2:17–20

CHAPTER *Twenty-one*

The day of the wedding had Esther out of bed with the dawn. She stretched for the last time—truly the last time—in the bed she had occupied for a year, and went through all of the routines she had gone through hundreds of times before. This time it was not Hegai who saw to her gown, but Xerxes' own mother, Atossa.

The week had flown by, with servants scurrying like chased rats through the palace halls, sewing and baking and decorating the banquet hall in gold and purple and more hanging lamps than she had ever seen. Mordecai had even been elevated to a palace official, and during the rush of preparations all of the virgins who were still waiting to visit the king were transferred to his other harem. None had been given the choice he had offered to her, to return home. They might never see his face, but they belonged to him.

Esther stepped into the gardens one last time and gazed at the pink hues of dawn with the billowy white clouds. *Thank*

You. She knew that somehow God saw. He understood her emotions, and He had placed her in the king's life for a reason. She searched the heavens, but there was no answer to be drawn there. If God still spoke as He had long ago, she did not hear Him. No prophet had spoken during their exile, though she had heard tales of Daniel and Ezra, who seemed to have God's ear.

Do You see me? For her, a mere woman, to expect an answer seemed futile. And yet, had not God spoken to Rebekah and Deborah and others of long ago? Could He not speak to her before she entered into marriage with a pagan, uncircumcised king?

She waited, listening. A slight breeze kissed her cheeks and birds twittered their greeting as she at last moved back into her rooms, where her maids frantically accosted her.

"Where have you been?"

"We need to get started. You cannot be late for your wedding."

"You're marrying the king!"

Esther listened to the same delighted chatter and giggles she'd heard all week and simply smiled, then allowed them to bathe and pamper and feed and at last finally dress her. They set jewels in her ears, at her throat, and on her arms and finally placed golden sandals on her feet. They did her hair with jewels and combs and declared her ready.

"Let me look at you," Hegai said from the doorway.

She turned for a last glimpse of her mentor, her friend. "Do I please you?" She smiled as she turned in a circle.

"It is impossible for you to not please me, my queen." He bowed. "If you will come with me now, your father is waiting to escort you to the banquet hall."

Esther's heart beat hard at the realization that she would at last have access to Mordecai in a way she'd only hoped to have again. She walked with Hegai and her maids to the bend in the hall where Mordecai waited, and took his arm as they walked the rest of the way to the banquet.

"You are ravishing, my daughter," Mordecai said for her ears alone.

"Thank you, Abba." She offered him a bright smile. "This is so much more than I ever expected."

"It is exactly as I believed possible . . . hoped would happen. You are blessed, Ha—Esther." He coughed at the near mistake of using her true name, but she merely laughed lightly to cover the sound.

"They have given you a position as a palace official. I am glad." They drew close to the banquet doors now.

"I will still work at the city gate, but I will also have an office in the palace, working between the two." He patted her arm. "You should know that the king asked me to place my seal on a document of marriage for your sake. He did not need to do so since you already belong to him, but he seemed to think this would please you."

She stopped. Looked at him and briefly touched his cheek. "Thank you for doing as he asked. His gesture makes me even more aware that God has allowed this for a purpose."

"Perhaps you will do much good for the people." He walked them to the doors, where guards waited to announce her presence.

She glanced back and saw that Hegai and her maids had disappeared, probably finding another way to watch and help with the festivities. She had requested her maids follow her into her marriage, and Xerxes had readily agreed. Hegai could deny her nothing. She only wished she could have kept him as her eunuch.

"It is time," Mordecai said, releasing her hand.

"Yes." She drew in a breath as the doors opened and the trumpets announced her arrival.

Servants took her from Mordecai's side and escorted her to a seat near the king's throne. Mordecai was seated at a table with the king's nobles. The king's throne remained vacant, but Esther knew that he would appear last.

Her nerves betrayed her as a slight shiver worked through her. All eyes were on her until the louder trumpets blared and the king followed his flag bearers into the hall. Her breath caught at the finery he wore, an ornate robe with purple trimmed in gold, fit for the monarch he was. How could he have possibly found her desirable? She was Hadassah, a simple Jewish girl. But he did not know that.

He took his seat upon the gilded throne and extended the scepter to her, bidding her to rise. She stood and walked gracefully up the steps, then took the throne placed there for her to sit beside him.

He rose from his seat once she was settled, and a guard brought a royal crown resting in an alabaster box. Xerxes lifted it out and placed it on her head. "Now, my sweet girl, you are officially my wife and my queen." His whispered words spoken with intensity matched the passion in his green eyes. He was indeed handsome.

As he took her hand to lift her to her feet, he turned them to face the crowd. "Behold, today Persia has a new queen! Queen Esther!" His voice boomed in the hall, which quickly erupted in cheers.

Xerxes smiled at the effect of his words. Once the noise

quieted, he led her to a table where the two of them ate, facing the people who also indulged in the king's plenteous feast.

"Tonight cannot come soon enough," he said, leaning close to her ear. He lifted his cup and offered her a drink from it.

She sipped and smiled into his eyes. "No, it cannot," she said, cheered at the ardent fire in his gaze. For a moment, she wondered if he would whisk her away from the feast before it could end, but he was a gracious host and allowed the celebration to last long into the night.

When at last most of the guests were besotted with wine, he took her hand and they walked together, surrounded by guards, toward his suite of rooms. "Are you afraid?" he asked as they crossed the threshold, the question he had asked her a week ago.

She looked at him and gave him a slow, sultry smile. "No longer, my lord."

He laughed. "How you delight me, Esther my queen." He removed her crown and placed it on a table, then slowly undid the belt at her waist and set the garment over a chair. He moved her up the step where the canopied bed sat, its curtains opened to show flower petals on the pillows and sheets made of the softest silk.

He bent low to kiss her, pulling the combs and jewels from her hair. She waited, spellbound, uncertain. But at last she reached for his robe and pulled it from his shoulders. Servants should hang up such a rich garment, but he did not allow her to carefully drape it anywhere. She dropped it where they stood.

He lifted her in his arms and set her among the flower petals, then sat beside her and took her face in his hands. His kiss deepened, and she felt her heart race as his finger traced her chin, her neck, and stopped at the pulse at her throat. "You are beautiful. My most favored one."

He closed the curtains before she could say a word in response.

CHAPTER Twenty-two

Xerxes gazed at Esther as she slept, marveling at the way her expression held such peace, her dark hair splayed over the pristine white cushion beneath her head. He had found not a single flaw in her and had quickly concluded that she surpassed even Vashti in beauty.

He released a deep, contented sigh as he shifted slightly on one elbow. Esther stirred and opened her eyes to meet his gaze. Her smile, slow and appreciative, caused a greater sense of protectiveness to rise within him. Did she love him? Could she love him? Without doubt he loved her. She had pleased him like no other.

"You are awake," he said, surprised at the huskiness in his voice. What was this new feeling of exuberant joy? He was not one to grow flustered like this. Never like this. But Esther . . . he could not stop the need to touch his lips to hers.

"I find you have tempted me beyond reason," he said when he felt confident that his voice would not again betray him.

She wrapped both arms around his neck and pulled him closer. "I am glad," she whispered against his ear. "If I were not a temptation, you might not find me pleasing." She kissed him, this time not waiting for him to take the lead as she had the night before.

He laughed when she pulled away, and they both caught their breath. "How bold my queen has become!" He drew her closer. "It is a good thing that I am king. We can take a week, a month, however long we wish, to be together." He brushed a length of hair behind her ear. "Does that please you, my love?"

She cupped his stubbled cheek. "Very much, my king."

"I will know we have made progress when you call me Xerxes without fear." He sat up and helped her to rise. "Let us see what they have set for us to break our fast."

They soon settled at a large table near the window, where he had fed her the night he thought he could claim her as he had every other concubine. But that night had changed him forever.

"Today I will show you the rooms that will be yours as queen. They are not yet ready, so you will stay with me until they are. Does this please you?" He could send her to the second harem, but then Amestris would lord it over her that she had separate apartments while Esther, his queen, did not. He would not allow Amestris to gloat over this woman. Not now. Not ever.

"That would please me very much . . . Xerxes. I am anxious to see what you have prepared for me, but I am grateful for every moment we can spend together." She took a date and kissed it before offering it to him.

He bit into it and then bent to kiss her again. This woman

never ceased to amaze him. How bold she had become for one so young, and yet so graceful and even obedient. Not like Amestris or Vashti. She captured his imagination in ways he did not understand.

"Tell me, my love, more about yourself. I know nothing of your past other than that your parents are dead and Mordecai adopted you." He leaned one elbow on the table and gazed into her eyes.

Esther picked a piece of goat cheese from her plate and held it in her fingers. She looked at him, her dark eyes somber. "My past is filled with joy and sadness. I do not wish to sadden you, my lord."

He took her hand. "I want to know you, Esther. Whatever saddens you matters to me. Whatever brings you joy, better still." Had he ever asked such questions of Vashti? What had happened to make him so enamored with this woman?

She searched his gaze and squeezed his hand. "All right. As you know, my father died before I was born, and my mother shortly after my birth. Mordecai, my cousin, was married to Levia and they had three sons, so adding me as their daughter seemed not only right but a perfect fit to their family. Mordecai has been the only father I have ever known. Levia was like a mother to me."

"Was?" He caught the slight change in her expression as she spoke of the woman.

"She passed on shortly before I was brought to the palace."

"So Mordecai lost you and his wife close together."

"Yes. Though he still has his sons, they are married with children, so he lives alone now. This is why I try to look out for him when it is possible . . . if it is possible." Her eyes held a glint of wariness.

"Of course it is possible. Your father will never need to fear in my kingdom. He will be under my protection for your sake." She set the cheese aside, and he took both of her hands in his. "You are close to these cousins, Mordecai's children?"

She shrugged. "Yes, we were as children. But they are much older. I did not see them often."

He nodded. He would have to make sure her family was cared for and protected.

"Are you ready to visit those rooms?" He pulled her to her feet.

"I would like to change my clothes first. Unless we should walk about the palace in our night robes." She laughed, a delightful sound.

He joined her. Somehow the way she spoke never embarrassed him, even if he should have thought of her suggestion first. "Wear that blue and purple robe I like. The one trimmed in gold."

"The one I wore the first time? With the same tunic?" Her cheeks held the most becoming blush of color.

He drew her close and kissed her forehead. "Yes. What else did you think we were going to do during our wedding week . . . or month?"

Her smile turned coy. "I will do my best, my king."

He chuckled. She was toying with him, and he loved her for it even more. She had bewitched him, this dark-eyed beauty with no parents and no lineage. His mother was probably apoplectic by now, considering how upset she had been that Vashti was not a full-blooded Persian. And now he had placed a woman with no obvious past in Vashti's place, above his mother's pick of a pure-blooded Persian.

He moved to his dressing chamber, smiling as he went. Anything he could do to thwart the plans of his mother and Amestris suited him just fine. And Esther was the perfect person for that role.

Amestris paced Atossa's chambers while her sons, Darius II and Artaxerxes, played quietly in an adjacent chamber, watched over by one of their maids.

"You are going to wear out the rug, my dear. Please, sit." Atossa crossed one leg over the other and folded her hands over her knees. "I know this marriage upsets you, but stop fretting. Xerxes will grow tired of the girl in time, and your sons are still heirs to the throne. Don't let a simple peasant girl destroy all that we have built."

Amestris sat opposite her mother-in-law, but she could not stop fidgeting. She twisted the rings on her fingers. "He should never have held that contest. And I should have done more to stop it. To stop Hegai from helping Esther." She stood again, unable to sit. "Did you see that he didn't even have her cover her face at the banquet? She willingly allowed herself to be dressed in such a way that everyone could see her beauty—exactly what he had asked of Vashti, which she rightly refused—and this unknown nobody allows the world to gaze on her face? If she were of Persian birth, she would know the customs. She would have insisted on a screen to separate her from the guests. Xerxes should not have allowed the people to see his bride." She slumped into the chair again. "Instead, he displayed her for all to see, even placing the crown on her head? Himself? It's an outrage!" Her voice rose on the last syllable.

Atossa held up a hand for quiet. "You're going to alarm the servants. Hush now, my dear."

"You agree with him?" Amestris's eyes widened. Did her mother-in-law actually *like* the girl?

Atossa shook her head. "No, of course not. But Xerxes has never been the same since Vashti's loss. I should have known that he could never follow through with a law that would take her from him without consequence. He loved her from his youth."

"And what am I? Just an added necessity to give him sons born after he wore the crown?" She glanced toward the chamber where the boys made fighting noises as if they were in battle with an enemy. Perhaps they were. At least that's how she felt.

"If Esther bears a child, what then?" The thought had caused her to lose more than one night's sleep.

Atossa lifted one shoulder in a slight shrug. "So she bears him children. It will not affect Darius's claim to the throne. He is the heir. Artaxerxes is the second if something ever happens to his brother. You have nothing to fear."

"I have everything to fear. *I* should be queen. I always should have been queen. Instead I have to contend with *her*." She could not bear to say the girl's name aloud. Star. Her husband had fallen in love with a beautiful young girl with a celestial name, so how was she supposed to compete with that?

"You have nothing to fear, Amestris." Atossa seemed to be growing weary of the conversation. "In time my son will find his new wife less than attractive. Or he will discover something about her he cannot abide. Or he will find a different concubine to fill his appetite for all things new. He is rarely satisfied for long."

Amestris released a frustrated sigh. This visit had profited her nothing. Atossa was no help. She had come hoping for suggestions, for ways to unseat Esther from Xerxes' grasp and take her place. But she did not know how to do that. She had spent plenty of time with him, long enough to conceive his children, but he had rarely spoken to her since Vashti's loss. He had flatly refused her suggestions that she would make him proud as queen in Vashti's place.

Perhaps she had acted too soon when she'd made that plea with him. What if he had figured out that she had conspired with Memucan to rid him of Vashti? She felt the color drain from her face. He had deposed Memucan but allowed her to stay. Why couldn't she be satisfied with that?

But it wasn't enough. It was never enough. And the longer she thought on it, even after she left Atossa and took her boys back to her apartments, she knew she could not continue to live this way. Xerxes had done her wrong by ignoring her wishes. He had no business placing a young woman with no royal heritage on the throne that rightfully belonged to her.

Anger brewed within her chest, a fire burning hot. Whatever love she'd had for Xerxes had fled long ago. But she had never considered herself capable of hating him.

Did she hate him? Hate was such a strong feeling.

As the sun set over Susa and she lay alone upon her bed, she did not see the opulence around her or the privileges she held over most of the king's women. She only saw him looking at Esther instead of her. Crowning Esther queen in her place. Loving Esther as he should have loved her.

Someday she would find a way to make him pay for what he had done to her, to her sons. Kings were not immune to disasters. And once Darius was old enough to rule in his place—or sooner if she had her way—she would destroy the things Xerxes held so dear. Perhaps even take his life.

That thought made her sit straight up in bed. No. She was not one to go *that* far. But the seed remained planted in her mind as sleep eluded her for yet another miserable night.

CHAPTER Twenty-three

"Would you like to take a trip with me tomorrow?" Xerxes searched every facet of Esther's beautiful face and could not withhold a smile. She was perfect in every way. How was it possible that a woman could hold such qualities? And yet in their first month together he had not seen a single flaw.

"Where would we go?" She smiled at the servant who cleared the utensils and plates from the table where they still sat. Hands clasped in her lap, she gave him her full attention.

"I would take you to Persepolis to see the building projects going on there. They are simply magnificent, and I want to see their progress. You could come with me and my retinue." She would need her retinue as well, which could make for a large company and some inconvenience, but if he brought her, it couldn't be helped.

"I would love to accompany you!" She clapped her hands

like a little girl, then leaned forward to kiss his cheek. "Thank you for asking me."

He grinned, feeling as young as he once did in Vashti's presence. Esther brought back the joys of youth, and he felt a sense of deep gratitude and satisfaction that he had listened to his servants when they suggested the contest that had brought her to him. He would not admit to her his deep need, nor how well she fulfilled that in him, but he felt it just the same.

"Good. I will have my guards set the plans in motion. You may bring your maids and any other servants you require, as the trip will take us away from Susa for a week. Tell them to pack whatever you need." He studied her another moment before rising. "Would you like to bring your father?" He would not dream of bringing his mother or other wives, but he suspected that Esther held a special bond with Mordecai.

She smoothed her gown and glanced beyond him as though something out the window had caught her eye. When her gaze met his, she smiled. "I would be honored to bring my father along, but only if he will not be a hindrance or cause a problem for you, my husband."

He stood and took her hands in his, pulling her close. "He will only cause a problem if he tries to advise me in how to be a good husband or comes between us in any way." He kissed her thoroughly, then released her with a deep sigh.

She laughed, the sound filled with delight. "I would not let him! And he would never attempt such a thing. He would simply enjoy seeing the great work you are doing. And it will give him something to brag about to his friends." She stroked his cheek. "Fathers love to brag, you see."

He wouldn't know, for Darius had rarely spoken in ways that made Xerxes feel confident or assured that he could handle the kingdom in his father's stead. Was that why he always needed the advice of others to make decisions? Was he so weak a man that he could not choose to do things in his own kingdom without help?

He shoved the thoughts aside. At least Esther had a father who took pride in her. He hoped that one day Mordecai might look on him the same. "He is certainly welcome to join us. Tell your servants to be ready by morning. Today you and I will spend the day touring the many gardens of Susa while the servants prepare."

She wrapped her arms about his neck and kissed his cheek once more. "Thank you," she whispered. "I will hurry."

He walked her to the door, and guards walked her to her rooms while he called his servants to make arrangements. This was a good decision.

The next day Esther sat in a curtained litter atop a camel while Xerxes rode a horse, surrounded by his guards and Carshena, Admatha, and Haman. His servants trailed behind, and Mordecai rode in Esther's company. Esther's maids rode in groups on the backs of camels, and other servants rode in carts with the supplies.

The trip took longer than she expected, the road bumpy at times with numerous bends, but at least it was warm enough that the rainy season had not turned the earth to mud. Wintering in Persepolis was sought before the rains began because of the terrain.

Still, with the sun shining down on them, she had not expected to spend the day, curtained off from the sights around her. She peered from between the fine linen curtains and watched the beauty of the countryside slip past. How much better it would have been to ride beside her husband and share the experience with him. But he seemed caught up in conversation with Haman and Carshena, though occasionally he drew closer to her and said a few words to Mordecai.

She sensed that this was the future of her life, despite his desire to have her near. No doubt he truly wanted to show her the building projects. But he was also anxious to return to his life as king, to talk often with his advisors, to do the work he was accustomed to. She was his wife, but queen or not, this closeness could not last. He had so many other duties, so many wives to deal with. He could not put them off forever.

This trip was his way of sharing his life with her, but as they made camp that night, she sensed the reality of her future yet again when she stood some distance off, waiting as servants prepared her tent. She glimpsed Xerxes near the fire talking intently with Haman.

"He seems to favor that man," Mordecai said from behind her.

She turned and greeted him with a smile. "Abba. I'm so glad you came." She took his hand, and together they walked away from the tents where her maids slept and other servants milled about. Two guards followed her at a discreet distance.

"I am grateful to be invited. I have always wanted to see Persepolis. I hear that the buildings his father began are indeed magnificent. I can only imagine the works that have risen under his direction. Your husband has a great interest in designing great structures." Mordecai glanced heavenward, looked quickly behind them, then stepped slightly closer. "You have kept what I entrusted to you, yes?"

He meant her heritage, of course. "Yes, Abba. All is well."

She shifted her gaze from him to the camp, where her husband still sat with Haman. "Why does he inquire advice of only one man when he brought three with him?"

Mordecai rubbed his bearded chin, and she caught his concerned expression in the light of the moon. He lowered his voice so only she could hear. "I suspect that Haman endeared himself to the king during the war with Greece. No one had heard of him until they returned from that disastrous war."

Esther simply nodded. To say more about the war was to risk being overheard. She had never asked about Greece, and she did not intend to start now. "The king seems to like him."

"Yes." Mordecai touched her shoulder. "Be careful," he whispered.

She raised a brow, wishing he would explain himself, but even here with the distance of land and trees, guards stood too close. "I will."

They walked toward her readied tent in silence, and he bid her good night. She had hoped Xerxes would share his tent with her, but as the night waned and he did not come, she knew at yet another level that her life was changing. Only a month of wedded bliss? She was not sure she was going to like the changes.

The following day they arrived in Persepolis. Esther walked with her maids along the main thoroughfare, taking in the magnificence of the grand buildings Xerxes' father had begun to build. The great palace remained in the distance, a shining jewel among the other marvels of architecture.

The sound of horses' hooves clapping the stone pavement

drew her attention. Her maids scooted to the edge of the road as the king's black steed strutted like a proud prince and stopped at her side.

"Come," Xerxes said, offering his hand to her.

She gave him a dubious look but placed her hand in his larger one. He lifted her with ease and settled her in front of him, one hand resting on her middle to steady her. His touch did anything but!

He leaned close. "Do not fear. I have never dropped anyone yet."

She laughed, her tension easing but a little. "Let us hope this is not the first time!"

His delighted chuckle and kiss against her left ear caused her pulse to race in time to the pawing feet of the horse. "Just lean into me. I'll protect you."

She drew in a breath and did as he asked. In the next moment, he clucked his tongue and loosened the reins. The steed began a gentle walk, almost musical in its swaying rhythm. The wide palace stairs were built to hold the weight of a horse and rider, and the steed carried them up, stopping at each step before moving on.

"Look around," he whispered against her ear. She slowly turned her head. The horse moved up another step.

"The view grows grander the higher we go," she said, awe tingeing her voice. The marble beneath them shone bright like the rays of the sun. "It's stunning." She drew in a breath and released it at the top.

Xerxes maneuvered the horse around to face the street. The view of the surrounding hills and the colorful array of flowers streaming down the sides like a woman's hair undone left Esther without words. She could not tell her husband, but God's beauty had outdone his great building project.

"If you think this is grand," he said, interrupting her musing, "wait until you see the Gate of All Nations." He leaned close, his hand possessive against her ribs. "Ah, my love, I have still so much to show you."

She felt his heart beating against her back, his desire for her stirring her. "I look forward to you showing it to me." She turned to look back at him and kissed his cheek.

He laughed outright. "How you beguile me, my Persian star. Are you ready to take the steps down again?"

She nodded. "If you are ready to lead me."

He smiled as he turned to take her through columned palace halls and then guided the horse back down the grand steps. They reached the street, and the horse trotted toward the Gate of All Nations.

"The roof was not in place the last time I visited, but as you can see"—he pointed as they approached the gate—"the four bell-topped columns are completed and the roof is nearly finished." Xerxes took her hand and squeezed, then motioned toward one of the massive bulls at the western entrance. "Is it not grand?"

"It is grand indeed," she said, her breath catching at the gleaming sight. She had never seen the bronze oxen that held up the bronze basin of Solomon's temple, but Mordecai had spent time explaining much of her heritage to her. She could not help but make the comparison in her mind now. Surely Solomon's work far outshone the carvings of pagan artisans. Yet she could not deny the beauty in the work. Perhaps God had gifted the Persians as He had the Jews.

"So what do you think of all I have shown you? I know

it is not finished, but the work is wonderful, is it not?" He kicked the horse's sides as they slowly made their way back to the camp.

She leaned into him. "You are a talented man, my husband. No greater king could have built the things you have built, for no greater king lives." As Solomon no longer lived, truly no greater king existed during this time in history.

She felt the pressure of his hand against her middle as the wind whipped her face. He leaned close to her ear. "Tonight we will not rest outside in tents. The rooms I inhabit are ready in the palace. Join me in my rooms tonight. You will find the palace at Persepolis equally as grand as the one in Susa."

She smiled. Perhaps her life was not set to change quite as quickly as she had feared. "I will be honored to see it, especially if you are the one to show me."

Her comment garnered a lingering kiss and a look that said more than words could say, and she knew she had won him again. Perhaps she could keep him from his men for the rest of the trip and begin the next phase of her marriage another day.

CHAPTER Twenty-four

Amestris fumed up and down Susa's palace halls. Susa's *empty* palace halls. Never mind the servants and many other women Xerxes claimed as his who remained at their work or in their rooms. Or that Atossa had not journeyed with her son. The king had left Susa and taken *her* with him to Persepolis. Barely married a month and he felt compelled by some strange magic to take a child bride to visit his winter palace and to show her his building projects? Unthinkable!

"You're just upset that he didn't take you, Amestris," Atossa had said the day they left. "And by the time you stop fretting, they will have already returned. It's not like he took enough with him to stay an entire season. He likes to see how the projects are coming, so he took a trip."

The words still burned in her heart as she neared the forbidden royal audience chamber, where guards stood at attention despite the absence of the king. She recognized two from the times she had been alone with the king in his chambers.

"May we help you, my queen?" Bigthan said, bowing at the waist.

Amestris looked them up and down. "Don't you normally stand guard at the king's private quarters? What are you doing here?" She caught the look of discontent that passed between them. "Don't fear. You can tell me."

Teresh rubbed a hand over his jaw, his gaze wary. "The king is away. We were told to stand guard here, as he has no need of a guard when he is not in residence."

Amestris studied the man. "I would think that the king would want his private quarters protected more than his audience chamber." She allowed the slightest hint of derision to drip from her tone.

"Apparently not, my queen," Bigthan said. "Nor were we asked to guard him on his journey." He clamped his mouth shut, as though he had said more than he intended.

Amestris's heart beat faster, her mind whirling with plans. And the exhilaration of healthy fear. These men could be useful to her if she placed the right words in their hearing and allowed them to come to their own conclusions. They could help her be rid of her nemesis.

"I imagine the new queen may have had something to do with the king's choice of guards. Women have a powerful effect on the king." She tilted her head and offered them an understanding frown. "If *I* had gone with him, I most certainly would have included both of you."

Teresh's face brightened. "Oh, my queen, we have no doubt of your kindness. We would have done everything to protect you." He nodded and fidgeted as though he suddenly could not stand still.

"But forgive me, my queen," Bigthan interrupted. "I don't think the new queen made the decision. For some reason the king has taken a liking to Haman the Agagite. I think he made the suggestion of which guards to take with them."

Amestris stroked her chin, processing this new information. So much could be deduced from so few words. For one, it was obvious that at least Bigthan favored Esther. He would be no help in getting rid of her. Second, Haman could be either a threat or an ally, but right now he stood in the way of what she wanted. Perhaps the suggestion to harm Esther was not as plausible as she first thought. Word could get back to Esther and Amestris could be ruined. Though it would be her word against two simple guards.

She released a deep sigh. "Ah well, I am sorry you were left behind. I, too, would have gone, but I am fairly certain the king wanted Esther alone. I understand they are newly wed, but some of his decisions of late . . ." She let the sentence hang in the cool air.

"He has made many poor ones," Teresh said, frowning. "Since he returned from the war with Greece, he has been harsh with the servants, and"—he leaned closer—"he has changed our wages three times. He has spent so much on feasting and war that the servants and guards are like slaves here."

Amestris hid a smile. So they were angry with Xerxes. Good. If she could simply get them to transfer that anger to Esther . . . but Esther had not treated them as Xerxes had. Amestris would not be able to persuade them to hate Esther any more than they might hate her.

"Perhaps something can be done once the king returns."

She smiled at each of them. "I'm sure you can come up with a plan to persuade the king to change his ways."

"He wouldn't listen to us." Bigthan tightened his grip on his sword. She understood the need for the men to carry them, but the sight unnerved her.

"You are quite sure of this? Surely the king can be a reasonable man." But he was not. If he was reasonable, he would have named her queen.

"No one dares to speak to him, my queen. Unless he speaks to us. Even then, we simply answer yes and hurry to do his bidding. He does not invite conversation." Teresh shifted from foot to foot, still fidgeting.

"And yet his servants suggested the beauty contest." Amestris raised a brow. "Do you mean to tell me that Xerxes will allow his servants to speak but not his guards? Or is he just displeased with the two of you?" She was fueling their anger, but she didn't care.

The two men looked at each other, then faced her again. "We don't know," Bigthan said, his mouth a firm line.

"But I have seen him speak to other guards. The ones he took with him." Teresh met her gaze. "It seems he is not happy with us."

"And why would that be?" She lowered her voice and offered a sympathetic smile. "You have done nothing to upset him, have you?"

Both men shook their heads. "Nothing, my queen," Teresh said.

She held their gazes. "I see. Then it is just Xerxes being ornery and making foolish decisions as usual." She crossed her arms. "When my son Darius takes the throne, I will make sure you are better respected. Even though he is young, I am training him to treat those who serve us far better than his father does. If his father passes on while he is yet a child, I most certainly will guide him to treat men of your stature with respect and dignity." She nodded at each one, pleased with the awe she caught in their gazes. "Good day to you both."

She turned and walked to her rooms, her step light. She might not have achieved her goal of planting distrust and worse toward Esther, but she had fueled anger toward the king himself. Perhaps in the end that would prove to be the better choice.

Esther woke with the dawn and stepped into the gardens Xerxes had built for her, adjacent to her spacious rooms. They had been in Susa again for several weeks, and she had seen little of the king since their return. Though he had called for her several times a week, the change she had seen coming was now becoming routine.

She stopped to inspect some of the blossoms on the almond trees and watched the butterflies flap tiny wings from the bushes to the skies. Oh, to have such freedom. Like a bird, they were not confined to the king's palaces or a specific set of rooms. If she thought on it overmuch, she had to admit that in her new life she felt more like a bird caged than one set free. And she missed her family. Not Mordecai, for she saw him often, but her cousins, their wives, the children. Especially the children. How long it had been since she had chased Isha through the house and taught the children of Noah!

She walked past the almond trees, forcing her mind to ponder the beauty around her. Gratitude was a better choice than lonely complaints. She could not change her circumstances.

She was here, and Adonai must have a purpose for her even now. But how was she supposed to serve the king when she saw him so infrequently? What was a queen to do that might help the people of Susa or surrounding cities? She did not want to be the hostess at a feast, though she understood this was part of her role as queen. She simply saw no use in reveling and feasting, the very thing that had set in motion all that had happened to bring her here. And caused Xerxes much loss. There must be more productive things she could do—things that would help those in her husband's kingdom. Perhaps if she got the chance again, she would ask him.

Without a child to raise or feasts to plan, what was she to do with her time? She fingered the soft petals of a red poppy, then turned and headed back toward her rooms as the pink hues of dawn dissipated into the blues of the morning sky.

Perhaps she could visit Mordecai if he was not at the king's gate today. Or perhaps she should visit the other wives in the harem and get to know them. Maybe her maids would have a suggestion. Suddenly it was Hegai whose advice she wanted, but she knew she could not call him from his duties or return to her former place to find him. Hathach was the eunuch in charge of her care now, though she did not yet trust him as she had Hegai. In time.

Mahin met her as she stepped into her rooms. "There you are, my lady." She bowed, as all of them did now that she was queen.

"Yes. I'm here." She walked toward the table where food awaited her.

"You have a visitor," Mahin said, coming up behind her. "Your father is here."

Esther stopped and faced her maid. "Let him in then."

She would invite him to join her. But why was he here so early? Why was he here at all?

She met him in her sitting room. "What's wrong?"

He looked about him. "I need to speak with you privately."

She called Mahin. "Have everyone leave us." She gave the girl a pointed look.

When the room had cleared even of the guards, who no doubt stood just outside, she motioned for him to speak. "What happened?"

He cleared his throat and clasped his hands in his lap. "There is a plot to kill the king."

A little gasp escaped before she could stop it. "What?"

"I overheard two guards talking about it when I served at the king's gate this morning. I was early, so they no doubt thought they were alone." He met her gaze. "Bigthan and Teresh are plotting to kill the king when he is asleep. I could hear the anger seeping from their tones."

"Bigthan and Teresh guard the king's private quarters." She had met them many times. They had seemed pleasant enough. Why on earth would they want to harm Xerxes? What would she do if they succeeded? "They must be stopped."

"Exactly why I came to you. You must go and tell the king so their plan will be thwarted."

The very thought of approaching the king sent her heart pumping. "Of course. I will go at once." Though she wondered if he would receive her willingly. She called loudly for her maids to return. "Help me to dress. Quickly now." All seven maids rushed to do her bidding.

Mordecai stood. "I will wait outside and walk with you."

"I will be only a moment." She dare not waste more time than that.

CHAPTER Twenty-five

Esther's heart raced. She hurried beside Mordecai with guards before and behind all the way to the king's private quarters. Bigthan and Teresh stood up ahead, guarding the door as they always did.

A boulder-sized knot settled in her middle. She slowed, glancing at Mordecai. "I did not expect them to be here."

"Nor did I," he said. They were standing at the end of the long hall to the king's rooms, well out of the guards' earshot. "They were at the king's gate earlier, but apparently they had reason to return to their duties."

Esther's fear mingled with indecision. The door to the king's rooms soon opened and Amestris emerged, head high. She wore the clothes of her royal status, as though she, too, had been to see the king rather than simply coming from spending a night with him.

Esther moved to the side of the hall and waited for her to pass. The woman barely gave her a nod as her guards escorted her back toward her rooms. Esther watched her go, but the moment she was out of sight, she bid Mordecai to wait for her, gathered her courage, and moved forward. She nodded at Bigthan and Teresh, then knocked on the door.

A servant opened and bid her to enter.

"This seems to be my day for visits from my wives," Xerxes said. He rose from the couch where he had clearly been lounging and pulled her into his arms. "I have missed you."

"And I you." She smiled and kissed his cheek.

He led her to sit beside him. She followed with a quick glance behind her.

"Is something troubling you, my love?" He took her hand and stroked her palm.

The feelings he evoked momentarily distracted her. She shook herself. "I have news," she whispered against his ear. "For your ears alone."

He lifted a brow. "Serious news?"

She nodded. He stood again and led her to the gardens outside of his rooms, away from his guards.

"Keep them at a distance." She indicated the guards that followed them.

His look held confusion, but he held up a hand to keep them at bay. "What is this serious news you have to tell me? Are you expecting a child?"

She smiled. "I wish my news were such a happy occasion, my lord. But I would not have pulled you away from your men for that." She clasped her hands in front of her. "I fear you are in danger. My father, Mordecai, overheard your guards Bigthan and Teresh, the ones who stand guard at your private quarters, plotting to assassinate you."

Xerxes stared at her, searching her face as if he wasn't sure he should believe her. "I just reinstalled them there . . ." His voice trailed off. "Amestris seemed to think them worthy men, and I had no reason to disagree with her, though I am nearly always willing to find such a reason."

"I might have agreed with her until this news from my father. He heard it himself early this morning. They were at the king's gate, and Mordecai does not believe they noticed him there." She took his hand. "I thought you should know immediately."

He seemed briefly dazed but a moment later roused himself, intertwined their fingers, and walked back to his rooms. "We will investigate the matter quietly. Tell no one what you have told me. And send me Mordecai."

"Yes, my lord. He is waiting in the hall outside." Esther smiled again. "I thought you might like to question him yourself."

His look held approval. "You thought well."

"Thank you." She moved to the door and left to find Mordecai. But she couldn't stop the chill that swept through her as she passed Bigthan and Teresh on her way. She silently prayed they would not act before Xerxes could fully investigate.

Xerxes paced his chamber, his nerves on edge, his anger rising. How dare these men even think to harm him? Had they planned to murder him in his sleep? The very thought that the people he had entrusted with his life could prove to be so treacherous galled him. Why had Amestris thought them trustworthy? Could Esther be wrong? Or Amestris? Or was he surrounded by complete incompetence?

But no. He knew Esther too well. She would not have come to him if it were not important. A knock startled him, and he moved to the window as the servant allowed Mordecai to enter.

He faced his father-in-law and motioned him closer. "Esther tells me you have news for me."

Mordecai glanced at the door, seemingly satisfied to see it closed. "Yes. This morning I went early to the king's gate, and Bigthan and Teresh were there. They did not see me, but I could hear their conversation clearly. They have grown quite angry with the king regarding their wages and what they perceive as mistreatment. They spoke of ways they might kill you as you slept."

So his fears were true. "What ways had they in mind?"

Mordecai cleared his throat and glanced once more at the door. "They mentioned a dagger or sword or drugging your wine with poison."

"They have given this much thought." Xerxes rubbed his chin, his anger barely controlled.

"It would seem so, yes." Mordecai took a step back and clasped his hands behind his back.

"Did anyone else hear them? That you know of?" How else was he supposed to investigate this?

"No one that I know of, my lord. I might suggest talking to their friends. Perhaps other guards heard them speak in anger against you." Mordecai gave a slight bow.

"A wise thought," Xerxes said, turning to walk Mordecai back to the door. "I will let you know what we discover."

Once Mordecai left, Xerxes called Haman to him and had Bigthan and Teresh put under watch. The rest of the day, guards were questioned and servants interrogated. By nightfall, all of Susa knew of the men's crimes. Bigthan and Teresh screamed in agony on two sharp impaling stakes at the city gate for all to see.

As the sun set over the city and the screams of the men grew silent, Xerxes called his scribe to him. "Record this incident in *The Book of the History of King Xerxes' Reign*. And give the credit for the discovery of this plot to Mordecai, Queen Esther's father."

Amestris sat alone in her rooms and kept even the shutters drawn. News of Bigthan and Teresh's plot and subsequent execution had spread quickly throughout the palace, even the city, and she had not slept for fear that Xerxes' investigation would somehow come back to her.

But as the weeks slowly passed and she risked being seen outside of her rooms with no consequences, her confidence grew. Apparently neither man had incriminated her or mentioned their conversation, for no one approached or even questioned her. Not even the king had called for her to ask why she had desired to have them remain as his personal guards. Was the man so completely foolish? Too bad they had not been able to carry out their plans. She could even now be ruling as Darius's guardian. People would bow to her instead of Esther or Xerxes. Even Haman had gained more popularity with the king of late than she had.

Was it time for her to make a new ally? How much could Haman be trusted, and did she dare make him her acquaintance—even friend? He had a wife and many sons, she'd heard, so at the very least she could befriend his wife.

Stop and think, Amestris. It's much too soon to continue plotting and scheming again. Let it rest.

But no matter how often she tried to talk herself out of letting things remain as they were, she could not stop hating her husband and his new queen. Atossa had promised her that Xerxes would love her more than Vashti.

Nothing had gone the way it was supposed to. None of her dreams, her schemes, her plans had done her one bit of good. But she could not stop trying. She had to ensure that her sons remained Xerxes' only heirs. Perhaps she could begin a rumor to get him to stop asking for Esther, to keep her from bearing his child.

But even that thought seemed impossible. How was she supposed to convince her husband that not seeing Esther was a good thing—especially since it was Esther's father who had saved his life?

You are pathetic, Amestris.

She wished she didn't believe that.

CHAPTER Twenty-six

Amestris woke early several weeks later, irritable and determined. Bigthan and Teresh were dead. Vashti banished. Esther queen. And all of it was her mother-in-law's fault. If Atossa had not promised Amestris that Xerxes would raise her to the highest level in his harem to be queen over all of his women, even Vashti, she would never have married the man.

She stomped through her suite and banged on the door of her sleeping maids' room. "Get up, you lazy slaves." She imagined Atossa telling her to keep her voice down—she would wake the household. But she didn't care.

Two bleary-eyed young maidens appeared, blinking at her in the barest light of dawn.

"Get dressed," Amestris barked. "And ready my sons. We are going to see their grandmother." She would have left the boys behind, but she fully intended to remind Atossa that she deserved more than she had ever been given. Her sons deserved better. "Help me dress," she added as she moved to her dressing room.

What she would say to her mother-in-law remained to be seen, but she simply must do something. Sitting here in these rooms, watching the days drift by, hearing the rumors, knowing her husband favored nearly every person over her, made her want to scream at the heavens. But screaming would only bring her the wrong kind of attention. Screaming was meant for dying men like Bigthan and Teresh.

She shuddered at the memory and searched her many gowns for one that appealed to her. One of her maids helped her to put it on, and another had begun to adorn her hair when a knock sounded at her outer door.

She looked at her eunuch standing guard nearby. "Who would be up so early?" And why come to her here?

Another eunuch answered the knock, and Amestris met one of Atossa's servants just inside the door. She did not invite the man inside, though by the look on his face, she wondered if sitting would be the wiser choice.

"What news do you bring? Has Atossa sent you? Has something happened to the king?" How fortuitous that would be! But she set her mouth in a grim line lest she reveal her thoughts and searched the man's troubled face.

"I'm afraid the queen mother has taken ill. She is feverish and calling for you," the man said.

Amestris felt as though someone had struck her. Atossa ill? "I will come at once." She looked at her maids. "Keep the boys here." She dare not risk exposing them to illness.

She followed the servant, her guards at her sides, her mind churning. Obviously her complaints would have to wait until Atossa recovered. But how had she grown ill so quickly?

Hadn't she seemed the picture of health at last evening's meal? Had someone poisoned her food? A shiver worked through Amestris. One could never be too careful.

But there would be no reason for someone to kill the king's mother. She must have encountered an illness some other way.

The hall took several turns before Amestris stood at the great doors leading to the queen mother's chambers. She entered without knocking as the guard stood outside.

"Take me to her." Amestris kept her voice low at the somber mood in the room.

A servant stopped her at the threshold. "She is gravely ill, my queen. Perhaps it is wise not to get too close to her."

Amestris nodded, then slowly moved past the servant. She approached the end of the bed. Atossa's breathing was shallow, her face drenched in sweat.

"Someone put a cool cloth on her forehead." Amestris glared at one of the servants, who hurried to do her bidding. Did these people know nothing about caring for the sick?

She waited a moment for them to make Atossa more comfortable, then forced herself to take a good look at her mother-in-law. Her pallor held a grayish cast, and her breathing did not come with ease.

"Atossa?" Amestris spoke softly, but the woman's eyes were closed, and she made no attempt to respond. "Atossa?" She spoke louder this time. Still no response. She looked to the nearest servant. "I was told she asked for me."

The woman nodded. "She did, my queen. She speaks on and off, but it seems as though she is dreaming when she does so. She spoke your name. We thought that meant she wanted to see you."

"She can hardly see me if she doesn't open her eyes." Amestris's patience felt stretched thin, and her skin grew clammy in the heated room. No windows were open and the lights were dim. The place carried the scent of coming death.

Impossible! Atossa could not have grown ill so quickly. Xerxes would surely punish his mother's entire staff if she died suddenly.

Amestris glanced again at Atossa's prone body. *You can't die. We have too much to do yet.*

But she could not say the words, or anything else that she would not want servants to overhear. She needed fresh air and to leave this oppressive place.

"Has anyone told the king?" Xerxes should be here, not her. Atossa must have spoken her name in a fit of delirium. It was her son she needed.

"Messengers are on their way to him now. We did not wish to wake him too soon," one eunuch said.

Incompetent servants, all of them! "He would want to be awakened if his mother is dying, you fools." Amestris strode from the bedchamber with one last glance at Atossa. She would walk toward Xerxes' rooms. Let him think that she cared that he be informed about his mother's health—that Atossa's servants did little to help her. Perhaps she would gain some favor in his eyes during this dreadful hour of need.

Xerxes heard the servant's words but struggled to process their meaning. "My mother is ill?"

"Yes, my lord. She grew suddenly ill in the night. She is feverish and says things in her sleep, but she will not awaken. We thought you should know."

Esther touched his arm, reminding him of her presence. "I'm sorry to hear this, my lord. Shall I call for your manservant to dress you to visit her right away?"

He nodded simply because he suspected she could tell that he felt wooden and suddenly lost as to what to do.

Esther slid from the bed and wrapped her robe about her, then directed his servants to dress him and give him nourishment and a quick cup of cold goat's milk. Then she kissed his cheek, and he hurried to his mother's rooms.

How could this have happened? His mother was young and should live many more years. His heart picked up its pace as he moved with the sudden urge to see her. He stopped short as he met Amestris in the hall close to his mother's rooms.

"My lord." She bowed low. "I see you have heard. I thought to come to you myself, as the servants seemed not to know which way to turn."

He stared at her. How was it that she knew about his mother before he did? But he shoved that thought aside. If only he had thought to bring Esther with him. He would brush right past this woman, who grew more dislikable with each passing day, and avoid her oily charm.

"There is no need, Amestris. My mother's servants have already told me what I need to know. You may leave us now." He did move past her then, triumph in his heart at the shocked look on her face. But as he entered his mother's rooms, saw the dark interior, smelled the odor of impending death—or had she already passed—he felt lost again, like a young boy abandoned.

He hurried to her chambers, where a servant told him what he already knew. He stepped closer and knelt at her side.

"Maman?" He spoke close to her ear, but she only stirred. She did not wake. "Maman, come back to me."

She did not seem to hear him, and her breathing grew labored.

He took her hand. Though she appeared feverish, her fingers were cold to his touch. He wrapped both hands around her frail one and laid his head on the bed. How long he stayed with her, he could not tell, for the room was too dark to see the sun moving across the sky. But his knees began to cramp, and as he shifted to stand, the sound of death caught in her throat. She gave a hoarse gurgle, until at last she breathed no more.

Xerxes stood over her, tears filling his eyes. There was so much he would have said. So much more he wanted to hear her say.

He turned abruptly. He could not bear this grief. Not here. Not now. *Oh Maman!* He glanced back at her still form. She had been guiding and controlling him most of his life. But she had loved him, and he knew at some deep level that no one else in his kingdom cared for him like she had.

CHAPTER Twenty-seven

Four Years Later

Esther leaned on one elbow and studied Xerxes as he slept. His body twitched now and then, as though his dreams were troubled. Her brow furrowed as concern weighted her heart. How she longed to touch his forehead, to wipe the cares of the world from his mind, but she dared not wake him.

The predawn gray hues of early morn filtered in patches along the mosaic-tiled floor of the room, just visible beneath the curtain of the bed coverings. She had missed this time with him. But in the past four years, he had not called for her as often as he used to. Amestris had managed to steal him away from her, and his wandering eyes had caused him to call on some of the other women of the harem.

She saw him perhaps twice a month, and it never seemed like enough. Did he love her?

He shifted position, his arm brushing hers, startling him awake. He blinked several times, rubbing sleep from his eyes.

Dawn's pink light now peeked through the curtain, and Esther smiled down at him. "You are awake."

He made a grumbling noise in his throat, cleared it, then looked at her. "I suppose I am. And what a beautiful sight to awaken to, my love." He shifted to face her, his dark hair showing signs of gray. He touched her cheek. "The gods surely blessed me the day they sent me you."

Her cheeks heated at the compliment. Xerxes was not one to say such things often, and with his inattention of late, she had wondered. How hard it was to be wed to a king! Why had her life come to this? But she smiled again and kissed his cheek. "Thank you, my lord."

They rose and settled to break their fast, Esther's mind whirling with thoughts she could not say. Would he call for her again soon? Why did he suddenly find it so important to spend time with Amestris?

"I've invited Haman to bring his wife to a banquet tonight," he said, interrupting her musings. "Zeresh and Amestris have become friends, and I thought it would be good for you to meet her as well. Haman is going to go far in service to the kingdom, and I think it wise for my favorite wife to know his family." He cupped her chin and held it, searching her gaze.

"Haman, my lord?" Esther returned his scrutiny, struggling to understand. Years ago it had been Mordecai's information that had saved the king's life. "Has Haman done something to please you? I would be honored to hear it." She hoped he sensed honesty in her tone and not the concern that nagged her whenever Haman came up in conversations with Mordecai. The man's obvious desire for power troubled her. How far would he take such desire? Might he also consider an assassination plot against the king?

Xerxes released his grip and tilted his head. "You truly want to know? These things are political. They will surely bore you, my love."

"Not at all, my husband. Anything that interests you holds interest for me as well. I do not know Haman well enough to understand his position in the kingdom." She offered him a slice of goat cheese and took one for herself, settling back to listen.

Xerxes chuckled, swallowed the cheese, and took a swig of water from a sweating goblet. "All right, my dear wife. I will tell you why I am soon going to promote Haman to the highest position in the land. Though you must promise me not to tell his wife or even your servants. Everyone will know when the time is right."

Esther nodded. "I will not speak a word of it."

Xerxes seemed satisfied with her comment and proceeded to tell her all of the ways that Haman had helped him during the war, given advice on the building projects, and transformed the palace to wipe out all memory of Vashti, though Esther wondered if anything could wipe her husband's first love from his mind.

"He has done much for you," she said when he had finished. Yet none of what he said seemed to warrant such a high position—second only to the king. Surely there was a better reason, but Xerxes did not seem to have one. Perhaps Haman just made him feel as though he had found someone he could trust, leaving him free to do whatever he pleased. Was that the true source of the king's desire to have a man at his right hand?

"Does something trouble you, my love?" Xerxes asked, taking her hand. "Your brow is furrowed as though you find my choice displeasing."

"Oh no, my lord," she quickly said, forcing her tense shoulders to relax. "I suppose I am simply nervous about meeting Haman's wife, considering how much the man has meant to you and your kingdom. I hope I do not displease her."

Xerxes leaned back in the chair and smiled. "She will find you enthralling, just as everyone in the palace does. You have nothing to fear, my love. Though she is probably old enough to be your mother." He laughed, and she joined him. Amestris was much older than she was as well, and the truth was, Xerxes was not much different in age from Mordecai. But wives of kings had no choice when it came to age.

"I am told they have many children." She deftly changed the subject as she fingered the food on her plate. In four years she had yet to produce a child. Was that why he did not call for her as often as he once did? Amestris had since given him a third son and one daughter.

"Yes! The man has ten sons!" Xerxes slapped his knee. "Can you imagine? The woman is barely done bearing one child and she has another."

Esther nodded. "I am happy for them. I wish you had as many." Her words came out in a whisper.

He stilled for a moment, then touched her shoulder. "Esther, look at me."

She did so.

"Vashti had only one son. Amestris has given me three. Some of my concubines and other wives have given me plenty of children. You need not worry about this. You are young. When the time is right, you will give me a handsome son to bear my name. Who knows but that he might even inherit my kingdom?" He took her hand and squeezed her cold fingers.

She intertwined their hands. "Thank you, my husband. I will be content to wait." She forced a smile lest he sense her lingering concern. "This banquet tonight. Will Haman's entire family be there?" From what she had heard, Zeresh would be trouble enough, but ten sons? With a father like Haman, whom she did not trust for reasons she could not explain, what must they be like?

Xerxes turned for a moment to look toward the window. "I had thought only to invite his wife to a small banquet of my closest wives and noblemen. But you have given me a wonderful idea!"

"I have?" Worry snaked up her spine at the unnatural gleam that suddenly appeared in his gaze.

"Of course, I should wait. He isn't expecting it now and I don't have the proper arrangements made, but what better time to announce his promotion over all of the other nobles than when his family is in attendance and the other nobles are there to witness the event? I shall make sure their wives are also included." He kissed her cheek, then stood. "And you, my dear, will be in charge of the women as my first queen once was. Amestris will chide me for it, but you are the one who made me think of it, so you shall have the honor of overseeing the women at the banquet. It is time they learned to listen to my queen." He pulled her to her feet and kissed her again. "This will be a good day!"

She walked with him to the sitting room, where he explained to her all that would be required of her, then he called his servants to send out the invitations to his nobles and their wives. "And include Mordecai for Esther's sake. He is not a noble, but he is her father and as such should be honored."

Esther sat listening, too stunned to know how to respond. Her heart thudded. The man she did not trust was to be promoted tonight because her husband had mentioned that he wanted her to meet the man's wife? Xerxes' thinking was so twisted that she could make no sense of it. If only he would wait, perhaps someone could talk sense into him. But he wasn't likely to listen to anyone other than Haman, from the way things sounded.

She stood again as the servant left, and Xerxes led her to the door. "I will let you get ready for tonight. I don't know exactly what women do to handle these things, but I am certain you will do an excellent job." He took her hand and squeezed. "Thank you, Esther."

She nodded. How to respond to all of this? "I will do my best," she said as she left his chambers and allowed the guards to escort her to her rooms. She had a banquet to plan, and she needed to pray if she hoped to have an attitude that would please the king. Haman was not a man she cared to impress, but the king would notice if she was not as gracious to him as she was to even the lowliest servant.

Why couldn't she trust her husband's choice? Other than her father's concerns, what had the man done to deserve her suspicion? He had never displeased the king and seemed to always be ready to do whatever the king asked. Perhaps it was his overt readiness to please that troubled her most. He was like a man who charmed snakes, though Xerxes was no snake. In any case, she would watch him and his wife, and she would do her best to keep her distance from them both.

"I will not bow to that man," Mordecai told Esther the following week after the king's abrupt announcement. She walked with him in her gardens, and she had sent even the guards away for privacy, though they had orders from the king to hover near. Xerxes had always been obsessed with her protection as well as his own.

"But the king commanded that all of the king's officials must do so. How can you ignore the king's command?" She led him to a gilded bench and sat beside him. "You will get in trouble with the king!" She lowered her voice, leaning toward him.

"The king is my son-in-law. He is not going to harm your father." Mordecai stroked his beard and held her gaze. "But I want you to know my reasons, my daughter, because my decision could affect you."

Her eyes widened. "Tell me."

He glanced about them, then leaned closer to her ear, his voice a mere whisper. "I am no longer willing to hide my Jewish identity. I believe Adonai is displeased with my silence, though I do not regret telling you to keep your heritage a secret. Now that you are queen, I no longer see the need."

She stared at him. "You have kept yourself even from meeting with our people for fear of the king's reprisals." She struggled to comprehend why he should suddenly change his thinking. Her husband and now her father were becoming most confusing.

"I know I have. And I regret that I was not more involved with them, nor had you more involved. Your life might have turned out much differently." He cupped her cheek. "But besides no longer wanting to displease Adonai, I cannot, as a good Jewish man, bow to an Agagite. Haman is descended from our ancient enemies the Amalekites, whom God said to destroy." He glanced around again, for his words came close to treasonous.

"But we didn't." She had heard the stories of her people often from him. Mordecai was a Benjamite, of the same tribe as King Saul, the man God had commanded to destroy Amalek. "You cannot blame yourself for what King Saul failed to do. Even King David failed to completely wipe them out, though he surely tried."

Mordecai rubbed a hand along the back of his neck.

Esther stared at him, the truth hitting her. "An Agagite? You are sure he is descended from Amalek?"

Mordecai nodded. "King Agag was killed by Samuel, not Saul, but if some of his descendants had not escaped, then David would have had no Amalekites left to destroy. And yet he found groups of them during his exile from Saul. What does that tell you, my girl?"

She shifted uncomfortably on the bench, longing to stand but not wanting to draw attention to them from anyone who might be watching from the windows. *This* was why she did not trust Haman. His heritage was that of an enemy of her people. How could she not have figured this out on her own? Xerxes had told her that Haman was an Agagite. But the connection to King Agag of long ago had slipped her mind.

"Somehow Saul allowed more than Agag to be spared," she said. "Or his men were not diligent to carry out the command and some were allowed to escape. Either way, Haman and his family and who knows how many more still exist today." What on earth were they supposed to do about it? "But shouldn't that make you more wary of him, Abba? Shouldn't you bow so you don't invoke his anger?" Powerful men tended to have powerful tempers.

"I've thought of that," he said, meeting her gaze. "But how can I go against the law of my God? He decreed in ages past that He would wipe Amalek from the face of the earth, and yet His people failed to do as He commanded. How can I bow to a man God has cursed? Let God deal with him and do to him all that He has promised. But I will not honor a man God has cursed."

Esther shook her head and fought the temptation to rub her temples. She lifted her chin instead. "I cannot tell you what you should do, Abba. But I fear that man's anger. He has my husband completely seduced into thinking he is good, and I have never trusted him even though I did not know why. And now you would ask me to fear for you? What would I do if Haman has you thrown into prison for disobeying the king's command? Even I cannot be certain you would be spared simply because you are my father."

Mordecai took her hand. She half expected him to push her hair behind her ear as he had done when she was small, but she wore a veil and was too well dressed for him to touch more than her hands or cheeks.

"Do not fear for me, Esther. I did not come to this decision lightly. You need not worry. No one knows of your heritage, and even if I make mine known, Haman will not make the connection. He is too caught up in his own pride for that, plus he would never consider accusing the king's favorite wife of wrongdoing. But you must let me do what I believe God would have me do. And if that means disobeying an order the king ought never to have given, one that goes against the will of our God, then I cannot abide it. I will not do it."

She searched his face for a lengthy moment, memorizing each line, fearing she might never see him again. "I will not fight you on this, Abba. You must do what you believe is right. I only hope you will not hate me if I cannot agree with you. And if I am required to bow to the man, I cannot disobey my husband."

"You must do what you must do," he said, bending close to kiss her cheek. "Now I must go before your guards come back, fearing I have somehow harmed you." He smiled, but she could not return it.

She wished she had never heard of Haman the Agagite. He hadn't done anything to her or her family, but the history was there. The curse of God rested on him. And she could not argue with God.

CHAPTER Twenty-eight

The following day, Mordecai's brave words to Esther were tested as Haman passed through the hall at the king's gate. He walked with head high and did not even glance at the men who groveled at his feet. Mordecai breathed a sigh when Haman's shadow no longer lingered in the hall and his footsteps receded. The other officials stood, but no one seemed to notice that Mordecai had not risen from his seat nor bowed on the tile floor.

He bent his head to his work, ignoring his fellow servants, hoping to avoid any questions. This decision was going to be harder than he'd expected. If asked, would he be able to honestly admit his Jewish heritage as reason for ignoring the king's command?

He pushed the question out of his mind as the day's work consumed him, and finally the time came to leave for home. He slipped down the stairs and headed away from the palace, glancing once behind him to say a silent prayer for Esther.

When he had taken to praying that his actions would not affect her in any way, he could not recall. But her status as queen mollified most of his fears. God would protect her. He had placed her there for a reason, though Mordecai often wondered what that reason could possibly be. Still, the king seemed to favor her, so he let himself trust enough to focus on the things he needed to do. And admitting his heritage and his faith mattered more to him now than it ever had.

He turned down a street toward home, grateful for the brilliant splashes of color in the sunset lighting the way. His gaze shifted at the sight of movement. A man appeared from an adjoining street. Mordecai recognized Roshan, who had served as one of the king's officials for many years. His beard was flecked with gray and his brow bore the lines of age. Had he gotten lost?

"Roshan, this is not your normal route home. Is there something you seek?" Mordecai asked.

"Mordecai, my friend." Roshan came up alongside him and they continued slowly walking in the direction of Mordecai's home.

Mordecai was determined to lead him away from his actual house. The men he worked with need not know where he lived. He had few he would call friend in that place, nor did he trust many of them.

"I have come to ask you a question. I did not want to ask it in front of the other officials lest I embarrass you. We have labored together too long to ruin a good friendship." Roshan's grip on Mordecai's shoulder was strong but brief.

Mordecai stopped to face him, sudden apprehension filling him. "What question is so important that it could not wait until morning?" He laughed lightly. "Surely nothing has happened to be so secretive." No one had seen him. Had they?

"I think it is," Roshan said, his voice quiet and somber. "I noticed that you did not bow when Haman passed by. You did not even move from your seat. And yet the king himself has commanded us to do so. Why is it that one of the king's servants, an official, in fact, feels he has no need to obey the king? Has he given you permission to ignore the command because of your relationship to the queen?"

Mordecai's heart beat faster, and a thin trickle of sweat snaked down his back. So he had not been as unnoticed as he'd thought. "You ask many questions, my friend."

"Do you deny that you did not bow?" Roshan's tone accused him.

"I do not deny it." Mordecai drew a steadying breath.

"Why did you disobey the king's command?" Roshan stepped back, assessing him. "The gods know we would all like to ignore the command. No one likes Haman." He lowered his voice as he spoke the man's name. "No one wants to bow. But we dare not disobey the king, and yet here you are doing just that."

"I am a Jew," Mordecai said. "I bow to my God alone." Never mind that he also bowed to Xerxes as king.

Roshan raised a brow. "And you are allowed to refuse because of this? You are a Jew?"

"Yes." He had already told the man enough. "Now, if you have nothing more to say to me, I will see you in the morning." Mordecai turned and walked toward home, listening for footsteps following him. When he came to a turn, he glanced back, but there was no sign of Roshan. Good.

Mordecai entered his house and collapsed onto a couch,

his strength spent. He had just done exactly what he had told Esther not to do. Would their Jewishness get them in trouble? Persia was an accepting culture. None of Xerxes' ancestors had forced conquered peoples to change their beliefs. Surely he had acted rightly.

But as he searched for food to fill his empty belly, he wondered if God had truly directed him or if he had acted out of his own disdain for Haman. If the truth were known, he did not like the man who had managed to get so close to the king. Agagite or not, Haman was not a man he would ever like or trust.

A week had passed since Esther had spoken with Mordecai, and as she walked the gardens, she could not get his concerns out of her mind. But to defy the king—she feared for him. She realized as she bent to smell a rose that she cared not what happened to her nearly as much as she did what happened to him.

She understood his distrust of Haman, for she shared it. But to defy an order of the king could have dire consequences. What if her cousins were also punished? Hadn't she heard the tales? Wasn't her father aware of what Xerxes had done to others who had gone against him in the past? Was it enough that Mordecai had saved the king from Bigthan and Teresh years ago? The king seemed to have forgotten Mordecai's efforts, for nothing had ever been done to reward him.

Mordecai should be sitting in Haman's seat for what he did. But she could not have suggested such a thing or tell Xerxes her thoughts on the matter. For some reason he had taken a liking to Haman, though most everyone else she met feared or hated the man. Her husband seemed oblivious to his counselor's wily ways.

She left the gardens to begin the day, as dawn would soon awaken the household. Somehow her time alone before day's break brought her a sense of peace she could not get during the day or even at night. There was something refreshing about being the first to greet the dawn.

It was the day itself that troubled her, and her fears mounted with each new dawn. Mordecai needed to rethink his position. Perhaps keep his silence and make an exception for Haman until they could find a way to replace him. Surely in time God Himself would take the man out if his bloodline were truly cursed.

But she could not think of a way to convince her father to do anything different. If life had taught her anything, it was that men would do what men would do, and it was not easy for a woman to influence them otherwise.

Mordecai heard footsteps before he looked up to see Haman and his retinue march past the area where he worked. Again, every official at the king's gate bowed low, lining the hallway. Haman did not look down as he passed, nor did he glance in Mordecai's direction.

Mordecai sighed as the footsteps receded. Did the man just enjoy marching about the palace so men would be forced to bow at his feet? Pompous fool! Amalekite. Agagite. The connection caused the anger to rise within him, heating his face. Why had Haman's ancestors been allowed to live? Why had King David not been able to rid the land of them?

Worse, why was Adonai allowing this man to hold such a

high position near his Esther? Just knowing she had contact with Haman and his wife made Mordecai's skin crawl. Surely something could be done to keep her from interacting with them. But what?

"I see another day, another week of days, has come and gone and still you do not show respect to Haman or bow as he passes by." Roshan stood near the table where Mordecai held a stylus between two fingers, poised to record the goings-on in this room. Yet he had not written a single letter since that arrogant "lord" had disrupted his day yet again.

More men joined Roshan, surrounding the table. "Why are you disobeying the king's command?" one asked. Others repeated the question.

"I am a Jew," Mordecai said, glancing at Roshan. "I do not bow to anyone but my God. Now unless you have something good to tell me, go." He shooed them away with a wave of his hand.

They reluctantly dispersed, but the next day and the next and the day after that, they returned to surround him and ask him the same question over and over again.

"I am not going to bow," he shouted at the end of the week. "Stop asking me!" He wiped his brow, quickly set aside his tools, and left his table, brushing past the stunned men as he left the king's gate. He could not deal with this any more today. They would give him no peace until he bowed, and now that he had taken his stand, how could he go back on his word?

"I won't bow." He spoke to himself to reinforce his decision, which seemed to waver with each passing day. He could not let his guard down, and he could not give in to the affront of his colleagues.

As he slipped into his cool, dark house, he fell to his knees and prayed. Fear crept up his spine, and he questioned his sanity in admitting his heritage and defying the king. Pray God Haman never found out.

Haman entered the king's antechamber, waiting for an audience with Xerxes. Despite his position as most powerful official in the empire below the king, he was still forced to wait to be allowed into the king's presence. Xerxes had become nearly paranoid in recent years, ever since two of his guards attempted to assassinate him. No one could come into his presence without permission, and if they came unannounced, they risked death. Haman only needed to be announced and had not yet been refused, but he took the precaution of not presuming. Zeresh had warned him to take things slowly, to build trust, to win the king's approval whether it took months or years, and he could see now how well her advice had paid off.

At last a servant announced his presence and the king called him into the audience chamber.

"What do you have for me today, Haman?" Xerxes leaned back on his gilded throne, hands clasped beneath his chin. The golden scepter sat leaning against his chair, and guards stood watch in pairs on either side of the throne.

Haman bowed low as he approached the king. He stood, walked a few paces, bowed again, and repeated the process until he came within the boundaries set to keep people at a distance from His Majesty. "I came to see if you would like me to travel to Persepolis to check on your building projects. I could be back within a few days and give you a full report."

He bowed again after he spoke, then stood straight, though he kept his eyes averted from the royal gaze.

Xerxes did not answer immediately, and Haman risked a glance to see that he stroked his chin as though in contemplation. "Yes," he said at last. "I believe I can trust you to check on the projects for me this time. Next time we will go together."

Haman lowered his gaze. "Thank you, my lord king. I will not disappoint you."

Xerxes dismissed him without a word. Haman walked backward from the royal presence until he reached the antechamber, then he gathered his own retinue of guards and began his daily walks through the palace and the king's properties. If he must still grovel before the king, at least he could see others grovel before him. Perhaps if he played his hand well, one day he would wear the crown, but for now he would bide his time and do all he must to keep the king's respect. Slowly, Zeresh had said. Yes, slowly. In time things would go even more in his favor.

As he turned aside toward the king's gate, he stopped. A delegation of officials walked toward him, quickly bowed, then asked to speak with him.

"Tell me quickly. What do you wish?" He did not want his subordinates to think their need for his advice made him glad. Let them think he had better things to do.

"We have a question, my lord," one said, bowing again. He straightened and twisted the belt at his waist.

Nervous type. Haman hated nervous men. "Out with it then."

"Yes, my lord. It seems that there is a man who works at the king's gate, one Mordecai, who refuses to bow when you pass by. He says he does not bow to anyone but his god. He says he is a Jew. Is this something that you, my lord, have allowed because of his beliefs, or is he defying the king's decree without approval?" The man bowed low once again.

Haman stared at the group, heat rising from the bottom of his feet up through his spine, but he clamped back his anger. "Take me to this Mordecai." He had heard the name, probably even met him once or twice, but none of the king's officials had made much of an impression on him. The king had so many men working throughout the palace that even he with his brilliant mind had trouble keeping track of them all.

The group turned and led him down a passage to where Mordecai sat at a table, head bent over papyrus, working like a scribe. He stopped in front of the man and waited. The other officials fell to their knees and touched their foreheads to the stone tiles.

Mordecai did not lift his head or even seem to notice Haman's presence. Could the man not hear the footsteps or feel the crowd near him? But despite several minutes of Haman standing there, Mordecai refused to look up.

At last Haman whirled about and marched out of the king's gate, heart racing, rage pulsing through his veins. The *Jew* had ignored him completely! How dare he! He marched faster, his promise to the king in the back of his mind. He had a trip to plan, and he should not allow himself to overreact because of a mere Jew.

As he entered his house later that night and complained profusely to Zeresh, he realized that one Jew was not enough to pour out his hatred on. Mordecai's actions deserved the full wrath of every Agagite or Amalekite who had ever walked the earth.

"What are you going to do then?" Zeresh asked as she placed a platter of fresh fruit and vegetables and her tasty stew before him. "Seeing Mordecai alone hang for this crime will not satisfy you, my husband. You know this. His people are a threat to our entire family."

Haman chewed a piece of flatbread, meeting Zeresh's wise look. Their sons lived nearby with their families, the start to rebuilding a lost dynasty of Agag. But if he allowed Mordecai to continue to disrespect him, the result would be similar to what Memucan had foretold if Vashti had been allowed to defy her husband. Just as all of the women of Persia would have refused to obey their husbands, so all of the Jews would refuse to bow and perhaps even rise up to harm him.

Mordecai surely knew of the ancient feud between them. It was why he didn't look up, acknowledge Haman's position, or bow before his authority. He knew Haman was an Agagite.

"You are right as always, dear wife. We must find a way to destroy all of the Jews throughout the entire kingdom of Xerxes. There is no other way to ensure our safety." He took a long swig of wine. "It is the only way."

"But you must be sure you pick the right day for such an endeavor, and you must get the king to allow you to do so." Zeresh poured him more wine from a sweating wineskin. "How do you plan to do that?"

Haman dipped more bread into the stew. He had no idea. "I will think about it as I travel to Persepolis. I will have time on the journey, and when I report back to the king, I can give him what I have found and perhaps turn his heart to my request at the same time."

It was possible. Of course it was. Satisfied that the gods were on his side and that he would come up with a solution on this fortuitously timed trip, he continued his meal a happier man.

CHAPTER Twenty-nine

Esther moved about her suite of rooms, trying to destroy the restless feeling that had taken root inside of her the past few weeks. Xerxes had not called for her in nearly a month, and the absence had left her struggling with understanding why. Had her favor with him already diminished in so short a marriage? Had Amestris taken her place? Had he found a new love?

She told herself he was simply busy. Haman had returned from a trip to Persepolis, and the two of them had been in conference about the king's building projects ever since—at least according to her eunuch Hathach.

"What if we work on the mosaics today?" Parisa came up beside her and bowed slightly. "You always enjoy working with the tiles."

Esther stopped her pacing and looked at her maid, then glanced around at all of the women in her service. "Am I that obvious?"

"You seem distracted, my queen. But there is much good you can do even if the king is too busy to call for you," Zareen said. "What did you enjoy doing before you came here?"

"Certainly not mosaics." Esther smiled at Parisa. "Though I have come to enjoy working with them since. In truth, I enjoyed weaving with my ima." Thoughts of Levia caused an ache to settle within her. She missed her family. She missed all that was once so familiar, things that she thought would never change.

"Then we shall order a loom and the finest wool and you can teach us how to weave." Zareen smiled, obviously pleased with her suggestion.

"There will be no problem with such a thing?" She looked from one maid to the next. She had never had to request anything, for every one of her needs was met before she realized she needed or wanted it.

"There will be no problem at all, my queen," Hathach said, coming from a side room where he had likely overheard everything. "I will order a loom and the finest of every kind of thread available. You can weave or create fabric, if that is what you wish for, as long as you like."

She nodded her thanks and sank onto one of the cushioned chairs, extending her legs. Before she could say a word, Shirin stepped forward and bent with bowl and towel and ointments to treat her feet to her ultimate pleasure. Esther leaned back, enjoying the pressure of Shirin's hands working the ache from her feet. If Xerxes had tired of her, at least she had the ability to enjoy the pleasures of royalty.

But even the thought of things to do that she once enjoyed and the sudden overattention of all of her maids did not seem to have the ability to pull her from the melancholy mood that had slipped over her of late. She should not miss the king. It was not like they would ever have an honest love. She was a queen, he a king. They would live separate lives, probably from now on. She would carry on queenly duties, and when he remembered her, she would go to him.

She could not go to him if he did not ask. Even she was not free to simply enter his presence as she once did. Something had changed between them. Did Haman have something to do with it? Or was it Amestris? Where once she had found favor throughout the court, now she wondered just how long that favor would last.

"Bring the lots." Haman stood in the main area of his house with his sons surrounding the outer area. A Zoroastrian priest stood near a table, dressed in his white robe and golden sash, holding the Pur in his right hand. He looked at Haman, his gaze penetrating.

The idea to cast the Pur had come to Haman during his visit to Persepolis, and he had hardly been able to contain his excitement or his anxiety to see what the lots would decide. But Zeresh had warned him that to hurry was to invite error. They needed to be precise, she'd said. They needed the Pur to land on the perfect day and time.

"This must be done with great care and precision so that we know the exact will of the gods," Haman said. "I don't want anything to get in the way of taking action on my enemies." He nodded toward the priest as deep silence settled over the room.

Lamps lit the darkness, as night had fallen during this first month of Nisan. The priest rubbed the Pur between both hands, bowed his head, and tossed them into a golden bowl on the table.

Haman stepped closer, his gaze on the priest, his heart pounding. "What day?"

The priest bent close and took the lamp Haman handed to him. He straightened and shook his head. "They did not land flat. It is impossible to get an accurate reading."

"Then do it again." Haman felt the heat rise from his middle to his face. The rage grew every day, and his patience wore thin.

The priest shook his head again. "I am sorry. The Pur can only be cast once a day. It will have to wait until tomorrow." He picked up the lots, tucked them into a leather pouch, and tied the pouch to the golden sash at his waist.

"The same time tomorrow then," Haman said, waiting for the man's acknowledgment. "We will do it every single day for a year if we must, but I *will* have my day. We will not stop until the Pur is right."

The priest narrowed his gaze. "Such attempts will be costly."

"You need not worry about payment. You will be well compensated, I assure you." Anger bubbled up again at the way the man attempted to control him.

The priest held his gaze. "Nevertheless, a donation to the priesthood will be necessary each week."

Haman forced himself not to flinch. This man was going to rob him of all of his earthly goods if this took too long. But the thought of destroying Mordecai's people overruled his concern for his wealth. Once the Jews were destroyed, he would regain far more than the wealth he now possessed.

"Name your price." He crossed his arms and lifted his chin,

reminding the priest just whom he was dealing with. Agagites did not accept Zoroastrian beliefs, but Haman had convinced Xerxes that his entire family had adopted everything Persia had to offer, including her religion. Yet saying so did not take away his disdain for the practices or the priests.

"One siglos a week ought to cover it." The priest gave him a slight smile.

Outrageous! But Haman merely nodded. The silver he could handle. At least the man hadn't asked for the gold daric. "Consider it done." He would send a servant each week to put the coins in their coffers. For now, he simply wanted this to be over with. He wanted the Pur to give him what he needed. It would do no good to anger the gods or to arbitrarily choose a date without the assurance that he had chosen wisely.

"Very well. I will return tomorrow." The priest turned, bells jingling from his garments, and left the house.

Haman sank onto a couch and put his head in his hands. Zeresh sat beside him and his sons drew close. "Did we do something wrong?" he asked. "How is it possible that we have to do this over again?"

"I am sure it has nothing to do with you, my husband," Zeresh assured him. "That priest is probably purposely misreading them in order to draw more money from you."

"I'm sure that's it, Father," Dalphon said. "The man looked greedy."

His other sons agreed, praising Haman and condemning the priest. Perhaps he should have the priests of Zoroaster killed too. But no. He stopped that thought before it could gain strength.

"We must speak no more ill of the priests," he commanded, standing. "If we dishonor them, the gods will not give me the day that I need. I want their favor, not their wrath. So no more."

His sons each meekly nodded and whispered their agreement. "We will do as you say, Father," Aspatha said.

"Good. See to it that you do. And keep this quiet. I want no one else to know until I can bring the results to the king. If word gets out too soon, all could be lost."

Haman could not even abide that possibility. He would have vengeance on the sons of Abraham for what they had done to his people. He would do whatever it took to destroy them, even if it cost him his life's fortune.

CHAPTER *Thirty*

One Year Later

Esther stood on the roof above her rooms, looking down at the court of women. She had visited Xerxes' harem once but had been met with a sense of mild hostility and never returned. What had happened to the favor she once felt from everyone who saw her?

She glimpsed Amestris and her train of maids emerge from the halls into the courtyard, cross the tiled stones, and enter a door that led to her private rooms. That Esther's rooms were closer to the king's brought some comfort, but what good did it do if she rarely saw him? He had his fill of other women, and perhaps she had grown wearying to him. Less beautiful. She had aged a little, though at twenty-one she was certainly young enough to attract his attention. Had she somehow offended him?

"You are fretting again," Parisa said, coming alongside her

near the parapet. Of her seven maids, Parisa had grown the closest to her, the one she most confided in.

"You read me too well, my friend." She smiled and touched the girl's hand, then sighed and turned away from the court. "I have none my equal here." She glanced at Parisa. "I mean no offense."

"There is no offense to be taken, my queen. I am honored you call me friend, but you are right, you have no equal in this place. You are not equal to the king and Amestris is a queen of sorts, but she is not *the* queen of Persia, as you are. You do realize that gives you advantages to do whatever you want, of course." The girl moved her hand in an arc, as if all of Persia were Esther's for the taking.

Esther laughed. "You exaggerate. I am a bird in a cage here. I cannot travel freely about the city without an army of guards surrounding me. I cannot even walk about but must be carried in a litter. I do have free rein of my rooms, but I cannot visit the king without his request. And the women of the harem favor Amestris. It did not seem as though they did at first, but she has somehow bewitched them to take her side, and I'm not sure what she is up to. Do they plan a coup to unseat me like Vashti?"

Parisa linked her hand through Esther's, something Esther had often allowed her to do, and led her toward the opposite side of the roof, where she could look down on the main palace gardens. "There is always gossip and intrigue among royal circles, my queen." She pointed to the beauty below them. "And it would not surprise me to learn that Amestris intends to somehow, someday take your place. But she has no standing with the king right now. Her sons are her only claim to anything close to the throne. When Darius is of age, and if the king names him co-regent, then Amestris will be someone with whom to contend. But for now, you have nothing to fear."

Esther listened to the whisper of the wind and the call of the birds in the trees below her. Arched doorways lined the enclosed garden, and nobles held conversations in huddled sections of the vast space, their voices blocked by the dense foliage.

"I am not afraid," she said after a lengthy pause. "Amestris is a lonely, bitter woman, and I think if I were in her position, I might feel the same. To marry a man, to bear him children, and then to be set aside by someone so much younger like me . . . well, I just feel sorry for her sometimes."

Parisa chuckled. "Amestris needs no one to feel sorry for her. She is a conniving woman, and trust me when I say that you would do well to keep your distance and never tell her anything. She will use it against you. Even if she tries to befriend you, do not let her. You are the queen. You do not have to be her friend."

Esther met her maid's gaze, lifting a brow, surprised by the outburst. "Has something happened that causes you to speak so sternly? This isn't like you, Parisa." The girl had always been easy to talk to, but she had never spoken against others in the palace.

Parisa looked down as though studying her feet. "It is just . . ." She paused and shifted from foot to foot. Uncomfortable silence followed. She looked up at last and met Esther's gaze. "My queen, forgive me. I know I spoke harshly against one of the king's wives, and it is not my place to give you advice. But there has been talk among the servants, and perhaps it is something you should know."

"Tell me." Esther's skin tingled as a sliver of apprehension slid up her spine.

Parisa leaned closer. "The rumors are old and not possible to prove, but some say that Amestris was behind the plot to remove Vashti."

"That is not new. The gossips have suggested it from the beginning." Esther crossed her arms, slightly relieved but a little put out that her maid would simply relive old stories.

"That is not all. There is also talk that she was behind the plot to kill the king." She lowered her voice. "The one Mordecai discovered."

Esther shook her head. "That was fully investigated, and nothing came to light to suggest such a thing. Could it be possible that the gossips are simply unhappy with Amestris and seek to smear her reputation?" She would need to put an end to this talk. It was not good to speak ill of others no matter how much Esther disliked them. Even Haman was a man she refused to defame out loud, despite how much she disdained him privately.

"There is one more reason, my queen." Parisa bowed her head briefly, and when she looked up, her gaze held fire. The meek maid had been replaced by a woman who could not keep silent.

Esther straightened. "What is it?"

"There is talk that Haman is up to something. He is keeping it very private, but his wife has become quite close with Amestris. One of the guards told Hathach that they are plotting something. He fears it is something against the king." She blew out a breath. "Or you."

"Me?" Esther choked on a laugh. "Why would Haman care about me?" Though she had always wondered if he wanted the king's position. Would he assassinate Xerxes to gain the throne? Would Amestris help him to do such a thing when her son's own life would be at stake? It made no sense.

"Amestris would care to see you deposed. Haman would care to see the king removed." She looked quickly about her and clamped her mouth shut as the other maids climbed the stairs to join them.

Esther bent her head closer to Parisa's ear. "Amestris would not help Haman with such a thing. It would affect Darius. She would not jeopardize her son's future."

The rumors couldn't be true. Though as far as rumors went, Esther tended to trust Parisa more than the others. Why tell her such a thing? What could Amestris possibly see in Haman or his family? Especially his wife? Zeresh made Esther's skin crawl. But then, so did Amestris.

"We will speak no more of this," she whispered as the others approached.

"There you are," Zareen said. "We wondered where you had wandered off to."

Esther turned slowly toward the stairs. "We were just admiring the gardens. But now it is time to get out of this sun and work in the cool of my rooms. I have a new idea for a colorful sash to weave. Are you up to joining me?"

They all spoke at once of their delight, something she wondered at times if they truly meant. But they belonged to her. What else could they do but agree with her? Even Parisa for all of her boldness still called her "mistress." She had no choice but to please her.

Esther sighed. She missed Jola. With her she could be honest. But there was no way she could invite her friend to the palace. Besides, she wasn't sure she could bear to see Gad again. Queen or not, she had still been rejected by a man she once thought had loved her. Much as she now felt with her own husband.

PART FOUR

When Haman saw that Mordecai would not bow down or show him respect, he was filled with rage. He had learned of Mordecai's nationality, so he decided it was not enough to lay hands on Mordecai alone. Instead, he looked for a way to destroy all the Jews throughout the entire empire of Xerxes.

Esther 3:5–6

CHAPTER Thirty-one

Xerxes followed the trumpeters and flag bearers, and his guards flanked him as he entered his audience chamber. A few scribes and servants stood at attention along the walls, but the columned hall stood silent except for the marching feet and the intermittent blaring trumpet. The fanfare was unnecessary when the room stood so empty, but he needed the reminder that he was indeed king. He had too many enemies, too many people he did not trust, and dared not allow even the nobles or courtiers in his presence without individual permission. Was he becoming paranoid since that threat on his life a few years ago? Or was it the continual concerns that his guards had in protecting him that made him overly cautious? Was he simply growing old?

The thought depressed him. Forty-eight years was not so old, was it? He took the steps to his throne and sat, his thoughts taking him to places he did not wish to go. He had plenty of years ahead of him. He simply needed to be cautious lest the assassin's blade find him before his time came to rest with his fathers.

The servant in charge of his appointments approached and bowed. "My lord, Haman waits in the outer court and seeks an audience with you."

"Send him in." Xerxes straightened, his spirits brightening. Haman was a good man. He would bring good news and perhaps distract Xerxes with a new project—something he might build right here in Susa. He'd been considering expanding his palace or adding an additional hall to accommodate greater crowds, but the work in Persepolis was not yet complete, and some of the outlying regions made him wonder if another war might be imminent. They had no reason to balk at his taxation. They were his vassals. They owed him allegiance.

Footsteps pulled his thoughts from their melancholy. War had a way of depressing him, ever since Greece. Without his father to lead, he had never felt quite as adequate. But he could never admit such a thing.

Haman approached, and Xerxes extended the golden scepter. Haman touched its tip and bowed.

"Rise and speak." Xerxes considered briefly having a second throne brought for the man, but thought better of it.

"My lord, I have something of great import to discuss with you." He glanced about and then held Xerxes' gaze. "It is of a sensitive nature."

Xerxes lifted his chin and looked down at him through a slanted gaze. "I think we are safe enough here for you to speak."

Haman nodded. "Yes, of course, my lord." He cleared his throat. Was the man nervous?

"Speak," Xerxes said.

Haman clasped his hands. "There is a certain race of people scattered through all the provinces of your empire who keep themselves separate from everyone else. Their laws are different from those of any other people, and they refuse to obey the laws of the king. So it is not in the king's interest to let them live." He paused and lifted his hands in entreaty. "If it pleases the king, issue a decree that they be destroyed, and I will give ten thousand large sacks of silver to the government administrators to be deposited in the royal treasury."

Xerxes stared at this trusted advisor, trying to imagine what people he could be talking about. Were his fears of assassination coming from this group? How would they search out the true culprits? Destroying the entire people seemed rather harsh. He glanced beyond Haman, his mind whirling. He'd been living in fear since his personal guards had plotted to take his life. Even before that. Since he'd lost Vashti and suffered Memucan's treachery. Was no one to be trusted?

Esther's face came to his mind, and the thought of her smile calmed him. He drew in a deep breath. Esther would agree with Haman. She would want these people who threatened the peace of the kingdom, his peace, his safety, destroyed. She would protect him. Of course she would. He could ask her, but such a thing was not done. He had his nobles and advisors, and Haman was second to him alone. If Haman thought them a threat, then they were surely a threat.

He looked at Haman again and removed his signet ring from his right hand. "The money and the people are both yours to do with as you see fit."

"Thank you, my lord." Haman took the ring and bowed low. "You will not be disappointed once we rid the kingdom of this scourge."

"I am sure I will not." He dismissed Haman and sank deeper into his thoughts, wondering when he had gone from seeking normal advice to becoming so utterly dependent on his advisors. What other king would have given his signet ring to another simply so he didn't have to look into the matter himself? He was a warrior! If these people were a threat, he should assemble an army and go to battle against them even now.

Instead, he had given the job to Haman for the simple reason that he was too weary of fighting. Esther's face came to mind again, and he considered going to her. Yes, that is what he would do. Better yet, he would call her to his rooms for a private banquet and allow her to wipe the fear from his mind and remind him that he was still wanted.

On the thirteenth day of Nisan, a year after Haman had begun to have the priest cast the Pur, he finally stood outside Xerxes' audience chamber, holding the king's signet ring. Better yet, he carried the king's approval to do whatever he wished with the people he wanted to destroy. Xerxes had not even asked what people Haman was talking about.

Haman scratched his head as he pondered the king's disinterest in the details. He'd noticed it often of late, as though the king had little interest in the goings-on in his own kingdom. Had he given up control to Haman more thoroughly than even Haman realized? A sense of giddy delight filled him at that possibility. But one glance at the guards lining the halls and he tamped down his enthusiasm. He had work to do and no time to waste. He hadn't waited an entire year for the perfect day in order to let it slip away unused.

"Summon the king's scribes and tell them to meet me in my offices," he said to the servants standing near. He would work with them day and night if necessary in order to get enough clay pressed with the message in every script and language of every people in all the provinces Xerxes ruled.

He moved through the halls to his offices, which were nearly as big as the king's meeting rooms. Scribes soon sat at tables piled with clay tablets and triangular rods that would be pressed into the clay to form symbols into words. All eyes looked to him.

"Write this decree in every language of every people throughout the entire Persian kingdom. 'Be it known that all Jews—young and old, including women and children—must be killed, slaughtered, and annihilated on a single day. This day is to happen on the thirteenth of Adar next year. The property of the Jews will be given to those who kill them.'" Haman rested his gaze on each man to make sure they fully understood.

"A copy of this decree is to be issued as law in every province and proclaimed to all peoples, so that they will be ready to do their duty on the appointed day." He paced the front of the room, unable to contain his nervous energy, then faced the scribes once more. "This decree is to be sent to the king's highest officers, the governors of the respective provinces, and the nobles of each province. Write this in the name of King Xerxes." He held up the signet ring. "Each document is to be sealed with this ring, so as you finish one, bring it to me. It will be dispatched immediately."

He turned to a guard. "Gather swift messengers to be ready to ride to every province in the kingdom. This decree must go out before the sun sets tonight."

"Yes, my lord," several guards said in unison. They left, and he smiled at the sound of their running feet in the halls outside of his rooms.

Scribes bent over tablets and furiously pressed out every word. Haman sat at a table with the king's ring, and as servants presented the tablets to him, he placed the seal at the top of each decree. He had just created a law of the Medes and Persians that could not be revoked. Not only would the Jews finally be destroyed, but there was nothing anyone, not even the king, could do to stop it now.

After the last clay tablet bore the king's seal, Haman went to his house. Sounds of confusion trickled to him from the king's gate, and he imagined Mordecai reading the decree. A slow smile spread over his face. More voices rose, and sounds of anguish filled the air as the copies placed throughout Susa were read in the fading light of the setting sun.

Zeresh welcomed Haman with a knowing smile and poured him a tall goblet of the choicest wine in the kingdom. The wine he'd been saving for this very moment. He sank onto his couch, put his feet up, drank, and laughed.

CHAPTER Thirty-two

Mordecai stared at the tablet hanging from a nail outside the king's gate.

Be it known that all Jews—young and old, including women and children—must be killed, slaughtered, and annihilated on a single day. This day is to happen on the thirteenth of Adar next year. The property of the Jews will be given to those who kill them.

Xerxes' seal, the imprint of his signet ring, stood out above the words. The law of the Medes and Persians could not be revoked with that seal.

He read the words again and again. *Killed, slaughtered, and annihilated . . . all Jews . . . women and children.*

Why would his son-in-law do such a thing?

A guttural cry rose from deep within him, and he doubled

over and fell to his knees. Right there in front of the king's gate, he rocked and wailed. All the Jews?

More voices joined him as men drew near to read the decree, and soon the entire area near the gate was filled with Jewish men weeping.

"Adonai, where are You? Why have You abandoned us?"

"How will we deal with this? Where can we go?"

The questions rose and fell around him as men cried out, then seemed to realize there was no answer, no getting away from this terrible decree of death.

Mordecai tore his clothes and sat in despair as the sun descended, until at last he gathered his strength to stand. He pulled the tablet from the wall and headed home. He stumbled, drunk with grief and pain, as the realization hit him that this was his fault.

He straightened, his mind clearing, but the pain in his heart deepened as he stopped and looked back toward the palace. Haman was behind this. The man hated him and his unwillingness to bow to an Agagite. But to hate so much that he would destroy an entire people because of one man's actions?

He forced his feet forward again, hurrying now. Had his sons seen this? Should they do something to escape Persia before the day in question? But where could they go that wasn't under Persian control? Even Jerusalem was not held by Israel alone. Persia controlled the area, and it was only by the good grace of the kings that the exiles had been allowed to return and rebuild. Would his people in Jerusalem suffer the same fate as those throughout the kingdom?

He entered his dark house, missing Levia all over again. Yet at the same time, he was glad she had not lived to see this day. She would have encouraged him to bow rather than to act so foolishly as to anger a mortal enemy. Why had he been so proud? He should have thought of Esther. What had possessed him to think he could reveal his heritage and not expose hers? Just because she was queen did not mean she was immune to this decree.

And yet, hadn't the Jews always faced enemies? If the Lord had not helped them throughout the generations, they would be no more.

Would God help them again, here? In a land where they had been sent for disobeying His laws? In a land where they had stayed instead of returning to the place He had prepared for them?

He fell again to his knees, weeping, nearly dropping the clay. He sat up. He must save the decree to show his sons. To show Esther.

Esther. She must be told. Shut up in the palace, she very likely did not know what her husband had done. But she was the only one with access to him. The only one who might be able to talk sense into him.

He leaned back on his heels and swiped at his wet cheeks. He must go to her. But he could not simply walk into the palace and ask to see her. Things had changed in recent years, probably because of Xerxes' paranoia. Even an audience with the queen had to be set up days or weeks ahead, though he was her father.

But word would surely reach her soon with all of Susa in an uproar. He would don sackcloth and pour ashes over his head and sit outside of the palace gate. Someone would surely tell her. And she would listen. She must. If she didn't, he did not know what else he could do.

The following morning, Mordecai put on burlap and ashes and walked into the city with a loud and bitter wail. He passed through the Jewish section, only to be met by men and women sitting or even lying in their courtyards weeping, wearing sackcloth, and grieving as he was.

"So you have heard?" Jola's father asked as Mordecai passed his house.

Mordecai stopped and showed the man the clay tablet. "It is all I think about." He swallowed hard. He could not tell even this trusted friend the truth of what he suspected. Or the blame he cast on himself.

"I heard talk that Haman has promised the king ten thousand pieces of silver once we are killed. No doubt he plans to take whatever he can from those who do his deed for him." Jola's father cast a glance toward his house. Weeping could be heard from inside.

Mordecai shook his head. He should have known. Jola's father worked inside the palace and probably had heard this sooner than he had.

"What can be done? Surely as the queen's father you can do something." The man held his gaze, imploring.

Mordecai feared he would crumble and weep in front of him. "I don't know. I doubt Esther knows of this yet. I am on my way to see if I can get the message to her now."

Jola's father simply nodded and turned back to his house.

Mordecai passed by merchants and walked down one of the king's major thoroughfares toward the palace. His cries grew louder with every step. Ten thousand pieces of silver!

No wonder Xerxes had agreed to such a plan. Did the king even know what was behind this plot?

He stopped at the gate of the palace, where guards stood watch. No one in mourning could enter the palace, so he sank to the earth near the gate and continued to weep.

A contingent of guards marched toward the palace, their swords visible at their sides, the sun glancing off their helmets. Behind them, Haman strutted, a satisfied expression on his face. More guards followed behind and some walked beside him. That was new. Perhaps that smug smile wasn't quite so confident. Did he think his life was in danger because of the decree?

But who could touch the king's favorite? Certainly not the condemned Jews, or they would pay for it with their lives before the time set by the decree.

Mordecai watched as Haman glanced in his direction. For the briefest moment their gazes met. Mordecai stopped weeping long enough to show his utter contempt for the man. Let him gloat. Whether Mordecai and his people lived or died, Haman would not go unpunished. God would personally deal with him. Surely He would.

Haman marched on, his smile never dimming, and soon passed out of sight into the palace.

All of the Jews. The thought brought bile to the back of Mordecai's throat. *Please, Adonai.* He began his bitter cry once more, silently praying that someone would notice him and tell Esther.

"My queen," Zareen said, entering Esther's rooms out of breath. "There is news." She fell at Esther's feet.

"Tell me quickly." Had something happened to Xerxes? If he were sick—or worse, had died—what would become of her?

"Mordecai sits at the gate to the palace in sackcloth and ashes and is weeping bitterly." Zareen knelt, hands clasped in her lap.

Esther drew in a sharp breath and stared at her, now grateful that they were at eye level, for she needed a moment to accept the girl's statement. "What could possibly be wrong?" She jumped up as nervous energy overtook her, hurried to the window, then turned quickly away. It afforded no view of the palace gate where Mordecai presumably sat.

"Send him clothes at once. He can change, and then they will allow him into the palace. I will meet him in the king's antechamber." She hurried to her dressing room and Parisa followed. "Help me to dress. Nothing overdone. My father will not care what I look like."

"Others in the palace might, mistress." Parisa gave her a look that reminded her of the many people she might happen upon during the long walk to the antechamber.

"Perhaps we will have my father come to my gardens instead. Yes, that will be better. Tell one of the eunuchs to catch up to Zareen and give her the new instructions."

"What do you mean he refused the clothes?" Esther looked from Zareen to the eunuch who had accompanied her.

"He refused them," she said again. "He would not explain why. Not to us, in any case." She lowered her gaze as though she felt she had failed Esther.

"It's not your fault, Zareen. My father can be stubborn." An understatement to be sure. She moved again to the window, wishing she had a better view, anger at the situation bubbling within her. What could have possibly happened to cause Mordecai to act this way?

Fear rushed through her, making her knees weak. Something was seriously wrong. And not knowing was worse than knowing. She whirled about. "Send Hathach to me."

Zareen hurried from her presence, the eunuch a short distance behind her. Xerxes had given Hathach to her, and she trusted him. Few men had proved as loyal. At least she hoped he could be trusted, for she had no one else.

Moments later Hathach appeared in her chambers and bowed. "You asked for me, my queen."

"Yes, I did. I need you to go to my father, Mordecai. He sits at the palace gate in sackcloth and ashes. He refused clothing from me in order that we might meet, so I need you to go to him and find out what is going on and why he is in such despair."

"I will go now." He bowed again and disappeared, but her fear did not abate.

CHAPTER Thirty-three

Mordecai looked toward the palace, his view blocked by the impenetrable gate fortress. Dressed stone encased in a thin layer of hammered gold enfolded the columns, which stood like watching sentinels. Guards decked in battle array stood dwarfed beneath them.

Mordecai's tears still wet his beard, and he looked at the burlap covering his frame. Groans rose as he looked at the tablet he held in shaking hands. He was weak from fasting, though he knew he would grow far weaker in days to come, for he would not eat until Esther at least tried to save her people. Surely she would once she heard the truth. Wouldn't she?

Her maid had indicated Esther's distress over his appearance. But he could not don wealthy clothing at a time like this, even to see his daughter. She must see the seriousness of the situation. But how to make her see?

A loud wail burst from him again as he studied the words

before him, all thoughts of Esther gone for a brief moment. *Oh Adonai, how can You save Your people from this? If Esther is not willing to help . . . please, Adonai, do not let the influence of her position keep her from remembering her heritage, her people.*

His prayers came silently as he rocked back and forth. He stopped abruptly at the sound of hurried footsteps and looked up to see Esther's eunuch Hathach approach. He attempted to stand, but Hathach sat near him on the tiled square in front of the gate.

"My lord Mordecai," he said in that cultured voice he had. "My mistress, Queen Esther, has sent me to find out exactly what has happened to cause you, her father, such grief. Please tell me so I can relay your message to her."

Mordecai assessed the eunuch a moment. He had met Hathach several times. If Esther trusted him, he would have to do the same.

He handed the copy of the decree to Hathach. "This was posted to the walls of the city gate and in other places throughout Susa. I have been told that it has gone out to every province of the kingdom, written to every official and governor and noble in every language and script of the people. This is surely Haman's doing, though it bears the king's seal, so it cannot be revoked even by the king himself. I'm also told that Haman has promised ten thousand pieces of silver to enhance the king's treasury once the Jews—all Jews, even women and children—are annihilated. This is set to happen a year from now on the thirteenth of Adar."

Mordecai drew a breath, his voice hoarse from weeping. He swallowed. "You must go to Esther and explain everything to her. Then you must tell her to go to the king to beg for mercy, to plead for the lives of her people."

Hathach held the tablet and silently read the words. He looked at Mordecai, a brow lifted in question. "Her people, my lord? Are you telling me that the queen is a Jew?"

Mordecai lifted his head, determined to show strength. Perhaps he had been wrong to tell Esther to keep her heritage a secret. Her own maids and eunuchs could turn against her. But he was done hiding. And besides, right or wrong, his decision had been made months ago. He may have erred by refusing to bow to Haman, but he had not erred in determining to side with his people. With his God.

"You understand my meaning correctly," he said, holding Hathach's gaze. "Will you do as I have asked?"

Hathach could lie to Esther. Both Esther and Mordecai were putting much faith in a man Mordecai did not know well. How did he know that Hathach wouldn't go to Xerxes and tell him the tale instead of Esther? What if Xerxes truly had sided with Haman in all of this? A knot filled his empty stomach at the thought, but he did not flinch as he waited for Hathach's answer.

"I will do as you say, my lord. And may your God be with you." Hathach stood, tucked the tablet into his robe, and walked through the gates where Mordecai could not follow. Now he would wait to learn Esther's answer.

"What did he say?" Esther rose to meet Hathach and motioned him to follow her into her gardens, away from the ears of her maids and other eunuchs. At the look on Hathach's face, a cold dread filled her.

Hathach stood while Esther sat on a bench in a secluded part of the garden. He handed the tablet to her. "Mordecai gave me this and asked me to give it to you."

She read the words. Stopped. Read them again. She looked up at Hathach, shock rushing through her. "Tell me what he said."

"He said that the decree went out to every province in the kingdom, sent to every official, governor, and noble, and spread to all of the people in order to prepare them to kill every Jew on the thirteenth of Adar next year. Even the women and children. That explains the uproar we have heard in Susa."

"I heard no uproar." Suddenly she hated the seclusion of these walls that kept her prisoner from the goings-on of everything around her.

"The servants can hear things from their quarters better than you can, my queen. Susa is in confusion, and Mordecai has asked me to tell you that you must go to the king, plead for mercy, and beg for the lives of your people."

She glanced beyond him. "He told you I am a Jew."

"Yes, my queen." His voice held kindness. "Your secret remains with me. If you do not wish the others to know, you are safe here, no matter what happens in the rest of the land."

His loyalty warmed her, but how could she hide in her palace prison while her people, her own father and cousins, were slaughtered outside? Surely God would judge her for such a thing. But she couldn't just approach Xerxes.

She rose and strode the decorative walkway, leaving Hathach to wait for her. How could this have happened? How could Xerxes have trusted Haman with his signet ring? Although the king's ring was clearly stamped above the decree, the evil behind the plot was surely not her husband's. Did he even know what Haman had done? He trusted that man far too easily. And Mordecai had indicated that Haman was behind this. Of course he was. She would still investigate, but she knew it in the depths of her being. Haman hated the Jews. And he hated her father. Mordecai's refusal to bow to Haman . . . was that what had sparked this impossibly horrible crime against her entire race?

She turned slowly about and walked back toward Hathach, her mind whirling, her fear rising. She wished she had the power to help, but how could she? She couldn't just go to the king without a summons.

"Have you made a decision, my queen?" Hathach bowed slightly, concern etched along his dark brow.

"You must return to Mordecai and give him this message. Tell him that all of the king's officials and even the people in the provinces know that anyone who appears before the king in his inner court without being invited is doomed to die unless the king holds out his gold scepter. And the king has not called for me to come to him for thirty days." To admit that she had not been in her husband's presence for a month—and this was not the first time—caused the ache to return to her heart. She missed the early years of their marriage when he had spent every possible moment with her. When she felt that he might even love her. Now they were living separate lives, like distant ships on the sea. Rarely did those ships draw close enough to touch, let alone speak. Had he truly grown tired of her?

"I will give him your message, my queen." Hathach bowed and left.

She stood in the gardens alone except for guards at the very edges of the doors. They could not hear her words, but they watched her. And she was not in the mood to be watched.

She walked back into her rooms, sank onto her favorite couch, and waited.

Mordecai observed people coming and going from the palace, some giving him curious looks or shaking their heads in disgust. Let them look. He didn't care what they thought of him. They could not act against him for a year, and perhaps there would be deliverance before that time.

He slowly rose to his feet and walked to the center of the square, where a large fountain stood. He cupped his hands and drank, slaking his thirst. As he turned to reclaim his spot, he saw Hathach walking toward him. He followed the man away from the crowd that milled about.

"I gave your message to the queen." Hathach cleared his throat and relayed Esther's words to Mordecai.

Mordecai examined the man a moment, then lifted his gaze toward the clouds scudding across the heavens. Was she refusing to help then? Or was she afraid she would be killed trying? The irony settled over him. She would be killed in a year if not now, but if she did not try, who was left to save their people?

Adonai?

But the heavens were silent. Still, he could not believe that the enemy of God's people would get away with destroying them. God had always promised a deliverer. He had promised it since the garden when Adam sinned. He had always saved a remnant of His people, even when they sinned against Him so grievously. Surely He would do so again. With or without Esther.

He looked into Hathach's eyes. What if Esther was the

person God had placed where she was for this moment? "Tell my daughter this: 'Don't think for a moment that because you're in the palace you will escape when all other Jews are killed. If you keep quiet at a time like this, deliverance and relief for the Jews will arise from some other place, but you and your relatives will die. Who knows if perhaps you were made queen for just such a time as this?'"

Hathach rubbed his chin, as though to speak to his queen in such a way might cost him his head, but he slowly nodded and his expression changed to one of admiration. "You are a wise man, Mordecai. Your words hold great wisdom. I will relay your message to my queen."

CHAPTER Thirty-four

Esther sprang to her feet the moment the door opened and Hathach stepped across the threshold. She returned to the garden and he followed her.

"Tell me what he said." She did not sit this time but stood with him in a different secluded area far from the guards.

He paused. "You may not like what he said."

"I often don't like what he tells me. Speak." Her heart pounded, and she fought the impatience of not knowing.

Hathach told Esther what Mordecai had said, and she felt the blood drain from her face. She looked about for a place to sit, but they were far from benches. Hathach took her arm and led her to one, where she sat hard, feeling as though Mordecai's words had knocked the breath from her. He was right, of course. How could she have ever thought it possible that she had become queen on her own? Surely God had put her here for a reason. Hadn't she always known it? And now the reason could not be more obvious or the need more great.

The thought of approaching Xerxes unannounced and uninvited sent a ripple of fear rushing through her.

"I do not want to die," she whispered, not looking at Hathach. She was young. Had never even borne a child.

"Of course not, my queen. And you do not have to do as Mordecai requests. Your secret is yours, and I have promised to protect you."

"But what of the women and children who have been dealt the certainty of death by Haman's decree? They deserve life as much as I do." She looked at him, but he merely nodded. What could he say? He was loyal to her alone, not to the thousands of Jewish people who had one year left to live.

"My life is not my own," she said after a lengthy pause. "I *am* a Jew, and the God of my people has given me this opportunity." She could risk her life and save her people or die trying. But her life would not last long on this earth if she did nothing.

She straightened and smoothed imaginary wrinkles from her royal robe. "Return to Mordecai and tell him this: 'Go and gather together all the Jews of Susa and fast for me. Do not eat or drink for three days, night or day. My maids and I will do the same. And then, though it is against the law, I will go in to see the king. If I must die, I must die.'" She ignored the dismay on Hathach's face, released a long-held breath, and stood.

Hathach walked beside her into her chambers, then left to do her bidding.

Mordecai stood when he glimpsed Hathach emerge through the arch of the palace gate. He met him and walked with him to a secluded area outside of the square.

"What did she say?" He had no patience to wait for the eunuch to speak. His heart had pounded since the moment he had declared what Esther must do. And he had questioned whether she would listen in the many moments since.

"She said to tell you to gather all of the Jews in Susa to fast from food and drink for three days, night and day. She and her maids will do the same. Then she will go to the king." He paused, his brow furrowed. "She added, 'If I must die, I must die.'"

Mordecai felt the tension seep from his shoulders, but as he studied Hathach's expression, he frowned. "You do not approve of her decision."

"It is not my place to approve or disapprove of what the queen decides to do." He rubbed the back of his neck. "I did promise to keep her secret and to protect her should she decide to remain silent. I cannot tell you that I find this choice to be a wise one."

Mordecai scratched at the burlap above his shoulder. "You have every right to feel as you do, and I thank you for your willingness to protect my daughter. But she is doing her part to protect far more people than simply herself. Tell her I will do as she has asked."

Hathach simply nodded, and Mordecai turned to walk back toward the area where most of the Jews lived. He understood Hathach's devotion and felt gratitude toward the man. But this was far bigger than Esther's safety. If they did nothing to save their people, God would surely judge them. God had given Esther a great gift and position that no one else could claim.

So he would do as she asked. He would fast, and he would pray. Oh how very much he would pray.

Esther ordered her guards to find her a copy of the scroll of Isaiah, something Mordecai had memorized and taught to her but that had not been in the forefront of her mind in years. She needed its comfort now, if such a copy could be found without giving away more than she intended. She also ordered the guards to keep everyone from entering her rooms for three days. Only her maids remained with her. Not even Hathach joined them.

"I am going to ask you to do something for me," she said as the girls gathered around her, sitting on the floor at her feet. "What I am about to tell you will not leave this room until I am able to tell the king. So for the next three days, you will remain with me. The guards have orders to keep anyone from coming in or going out."

Parisa tilted her head, her expression curious. Zareen's brow furrowed in obvious concern. The others had expressions ranging from wide-eyed fear to anxiety. But none spoke as they waited for her to explain.

"How many of you are aware of the decree that Haman sent out in the king's name to destroy the Jews throughout the kingdom?" She searched each face.

"The servants can talk of nothing else, my queen," Parisa said. "The news has thrown Susa into utter despair."

"And what is the general feeling among the servants? Do they side with the decree?" Fear of the response niggled at the back of her mind, but she shoved the feeling away. She must be strong, whether her maids agreed with her or not.

"Most everyone in the palace does not like the man, my queen," Mahin said. "The truth is, most people think he is arrogant and no one trusts him. But they fear him. He has great power." Her words ended in a mere whisper.

Esther nodded. "Then you will understand when I tell you that I, too, fear him. And I fear what will happen when I attempt to approach the king in three days without an invitation."

Gasps came from each young woman.

"No, my lady, you can't!"

"You risk your life!"

"Why would you do such a thing?"

She raised a hand to silence them. "Because I must do something to save my people." She let her comment hang in the silence.

"You are a Jew," Parisa said at last. "You are also in danger."

"Whether I am in danger or not, I do not know. No one knows of my heritage. Only Hathach and you. But soon I will tell the king, because if I do not speak for those who cannot speak for themselves, who will? I cannot remain silent when the lives of women and children and all of our men could be lost in less than a year."

"But if the king does not receive you . . ." Mahin did not finish the sentence.

"Then he will never know," Zareen said. "And your people will be lost."

"It is a risk I must take." Esther looked beyond them. "This is why I am asking all of you to fast with me for three days. Do not eat or drink, night or day. Then I will go to the king."

"Anything, my queen," Parisa said, leaning closer to Esther's feet. "We will do whatever you ask."

Murmurs of agreement followed Parisa's remark, and Esther breathed a prayer of thanks for their loyalty. She did not ask her maids to pray to the God they did not know. Although she had not asked her father to pray either, she knew he and the other Jews would do nothing less.

She would also pray as she fasted. She would pray the prayers of King David when he begged for release from his enemies. Though she had no copies of the Torah or the Hebrew poetry, she would pray what she remembered from her childhood.

And perhaps she would pray words of her own making, as David had done. Didn't God respond to a seeking heart? Didn't He hear the cries of His people?

Surely the God who saw Hagar in the desert could see her in the palace. Both of them in circumstances they had not chosen. Yet God had met Hagar there. Esther would fast and hope that He would meet her too.

On the third day of the fast, Esther awakened with the dawn and picked up the scroll they had found for her. She read again the words that had burned within her for three days.

> No, this is the kind of fasting I want:
> Free those who are wrongly imprisoned;
>   lighten the burden of those who work for you.
> Let the oppressed go free,
>   and remove the chains that bind people.
> Share your food with the hungry,
>   and give shelter to the homeless.
> Give clothes to those who need them,
>   and do not hide from relatives who need your
>   help.

> Then your salvation will come like the dawn,
> and your wounds will quickly heal.
> Your godliness will lead you forward,
> and the glory of the LORD will protect you from behind.
> Then when you call, the LORD will answer.
> "Yes, I am here," he will quickly reply.

She drank in the words. Though her whole body begged for water, she refused to quench her thirst with anything other than Isaiah's words. She had no appetite despite her days without food. Only resignation and a sense of commitment resided inside of her, in a place of strength she did not know she possessed.

The hour of decision had come, and she would know before the sun rose to its midday height whether she would live or die. Strange how one felt about life when its end could be so close.

She rose and bathed, and Parisa helped her to dress in her royal robes. Shirin pulled her hair into a style reminiscent of her first night with the king. Mahin covered her glowing black tresses with a colorful veil. Hettie placed the royal crown on her head and a ring on her finger. Rosana tucked jeweled sandals on her feet. And Jazmin spritzed the faint scent of lavender over her clothes.

Peace settled over Esther as Zareen held the golden mirror before her. She was ready. As ready as she was going to be. Olive oil moistened her lips, lest she appear as though she had been mourning. The king must not know that yet.

"Shall we go with you?" Parisa asked, concern etched in her gaze. None of them looked at peace—not like the peace that Esther felt—but none of them had prayed as Esther had prayed, at least not with the knowledge she had. How could they? They had no idea what trials her people had been through. They did not know the history the Jews had with Haman's people or how the Amalekites had attacked them when they were vulnerable on their journey out of Egypt. Hostility had existed between the Amalekites and the Israelites ever since.

She looked at each one, cupped each dear cheek. "You have been a blessing to me these past three days. But now it is up to me to attempt what I did not think I could ever do." She drew in a breath. "If I do not return, please know that I could have chosen no better maids. But do not mourn for me. Mourn for my people, and do what you can to tell your family and friends that we are not your enemies. Perhaps you will make a difference in my place."

She turned and headed toward the door to the sound of their quiet weeping. She straightened as she opened the door and met the guards standing there. "Take me to the inner court of the palace."

Two guards glanced at her, their expressions grim. But they did not try to dissuade her. She knew better than most what the law said. They could be escorting her to her final moments on earth. But neither guard spoke as they walked with her down the long hall and around several bends until at last they came to the inner court. She moved past them and stood alone, looking toward the throne, where her husband sat facing the entrance to his hall.

She watched him, trying to read his expression, her confidence threatening to waver. Time stilled as she waited. He looked her up and down, and then slowly a smile lit his face. He extended the royal scepter to her.

Relief flooded her, and sudden weakness in her knees added to her already weak state. But she stood taller, straightening her spine, and pushed one foot in front of the other down the long corridor toward the throne. At last she reached the end of the tile, where no one other than the king was allowed to pass, then bowed low, extended her right hand, and touched the end of the golden scepter.

"Queen Esther, my love. What can I do for you? What is your request? I will give it to you, even if it is half the kingdom!" It was a common saying of favor, even if he did not literally mean it.

Yet his words were far more than she had dreamed in her most desperate prayer. Her breath longed to escape in a rush, but she held herself in check. "If it pleases the king," she said, offering him a gentle smile, one he would surely remember, "let the king and Haman come today to a banquet I have prepared for the king."

Xerxes kept his expression neutral, but she saw the appreciation in his eyes. How she missed time with him.

He held her gaze for a lengthy moment, then turned to his attendants. "Tell Haman to come quickly to a banquet, as Esther has requested." He looked again into her eyes, his own shining with the joy she so dearly missed. "Is there anything else, my love?" he said softly.

"The king is already most gracious to grant my request." She sensed a desire in him to say more, but she knew he wouldn't. She bowed low and backed from his presence, her heart singing.

Now there was much to do to have a banquet ready for the

king by eventide. She left the inner court and hurried down the halls, her guards barely able to keep up. First she must have water. Then a date and some cheese. "Send for all of my attendants and servants," she told the guards as she flew down the hall. "We have a banquet to prepare."

CHAPTER Thirty-five

Haman looked up from the clay tablets he'd been working through all morning, but the answers he sought still eluded him. The measurements for the tower he intended to propose to Xerxes simply would not fall into the right calculations. What was he missing? The tower would be a testament to Xerxes' greatness, and Haman would have the distinct privilege of knowing he had designed it. If things went well for him, he might even convince Xerxes to have his own name inscribed beneath the king's in the cornerstone.

But he would never get anywhere if he could not get the measurements to fit for the way he wanted it designed. He cursed under his breath at the same time a servant knocked on the door.

"What is it?" he barked without looking up.

Footsteps drew slowly nearer. Haman lifted his head to see his trusted attendant standing with head bowed, hands clasped in front of his thin frame. "What is it?" he said again, gentling his voice.

"My lord, the king has sent word to tell you to come quickly and prepare to join him for a banquet that Queen Esther has planned for both of you this very night." The man leaned back as though he needed to keep his distance.

But this was excellent news! "This night?" He laughed. The king would surely approve the tower now, especially since the queen wanted to include him in her company. "Of course I will go. Come to my house and help me to dress in my best robes." They weren't exactly royal garb, but close. His lacked the golden threads woven through the purple or the wide golden cuffs and hem. But they were still highly valuable, above all others in the kingdom.

He stood abruptly, pushed the tablets aside, gave orders for a servant to carefully put them on the shelf, then followed his attendant toward home. What an absolutely fortuitous day! Surely the gods were shining down on him. He had taken great care to appease them, and this decree he had set out to keep was a holy war against the enemies of his people.

Despite what others may say of him—and he knew they talked, for gossip was impossible to keep from him—he knew he was a favored one. He would go far in the kingdom. And this banquet tonight was just the beginning!

Esther moved gracefully about the small banquet room connected to her personal chambers. She had chosen this place above the larger banquet hall at her disposal for the intimacy it would afford. Three people did not need an entire hall. No, this room would suit her purposes well. After a meal of yogurt soup, duck with pomegranate and walnut sauce over barley, stewed spinach, and baked apples, they could move to her receiving room and enjoy wine in the comfort of a more private setting.

That Haman would be joining Xerxes caused her stomach to knot, and she prayed she would be able to eat lest she appear sorrowful to the king. Haman must not know the purpose of this gathering. Not yet. Not tonight.

But the thought of his presence in her rooms made her skin crawl. She had managed to avoid much contact with the man. But now she must be strong, play the perfect hostess, even smile at this enemy of her people.

If she didn't, if she gave any hint of displeasure, he would go away suspicious instead of happy. And she did not want him to question the king or put false thoughts in his mind. Sadly, she did not know whether she could trust her own husband to listen to her over Haman.

She moved a goblet that sat too close to the edge of the table and walked to the window that overlooked her gardens. Her gaze slanted heavenward. The sun had begun its descent toward its place of rest. They would be here soon. She looked back and surveyed the room once more. Sconces stood along the walls, casting the perfect ambient light.

She stepped into her chambers, where Parisa met her. "You look lovely, my queen," her maid said, bowing low. "Remember that we will be near—all of us. And we will pray to your god that he will grant you favor."

"Thank you, Parisa. Tonight is simply a test. Tomorrow we will know." Why she needed two days to tell Xerxes, she was not sure she could explain. But she knew he enjoyed a surprise, and at times when she had teased him in the privacy of his rooms, he had laughed with delight. Tonight she wanted his heart to be merry. To remind him what she meant to him. If God was willing, tomorrow he would grant her request.

Footsteps coming from the hall outside her rooms startled her out of her contemplation. She looked at Parisa, who simply nodded her assurance. She could do this.

Guards opened the door to the small banquet room, and Esther met both men as they entered behind the guards, who remained standing along the sides of the room. She bowed to the king, then dipped her head toward Haman. "Thank you both for coming." Her hand moved in a sweeping motion toward the food-laden table. "Please take a seat."

The king sat first on a plush couch, where he could recline as he ate. Haman sat on a similar, small couch beside him, and Esther sat opposite them—an upset in protocol, but one he allowed since in essence he was her guest. Servants began first with the soup, then continued with every Persian dish Esther had specifically chosen. She knew the king especially enjoyed the duck, and she was delighted when he praised her choices.

"The food is excellent, my love," Xerxes said, licking the sticky sweetness of the pomegranate sauce from his fingers.

"Thank you, my lord. Would you both like to join me in my receiving room for the wine?" She stood and motioned to an adjoining room.

Xerxes stood first and smiled. "Of course." He followed her, placing one hand at the small of her back. He leaned close. "Thank you for doing this. I have neglected you of late, and soon we will remedy that." He straightened as they entered the chamber. Haman lagged slightly behind.

Soon the three of them were laughing and talking over

one of the king's best wines. After the sun had fully set and the stars poked through the latticed windows, Xerxes turned to her. "Now tell me, my love, what you really want. What is your request? I will give it to you, even if it is half the kingdom!" His voice held enthusiasm, and she sensed he was merry from a little too much wine. Definitely not the right time to speak her heart.

She smiled demurely. "This is my request and deepest wish, my lord. If I have found favor with the king, and if it pleases the king to grant my request and do what I ask, please come with Haman tomorrow to the banquet I will prepare for you. Then I will explain what this is all about."

Xerxes gave her a curious look, assessing her. Esther held her breath as the silence lingered, but a moment later he smiled. "We will do as you request."

She smiled in return, slowly releasing her breath. "Thank you, my lord. I promise, I will tell you everything then."

"I count on it," he said.

As they left, Esther's heart pounded with relief and fear. One more day. Tomorrow she would know whether the king would smile on her or allow her and her people to die. At least then she would die knowing she had done all she could.

CHAPTER Thirty-six

Haman strutted through the palace halls, head held high, barely able to hide his delight at his good fortune. The gods were definitely smiling on him! His careful planning and work to rid the earth of evil had surely found favor in the heavens.

Or perhaps the good that had come to him was a result of his own hard work. If he considered it long enough, he knew deep down that he deserved the power now afforded to him. It had taken him years to rise to this position, and it was no small feat for him to grant the king's every ridiculous wish just to fall into his good graces. Finding new rooms for him to inhabit after the war with Greece, simply because the king could not bear Vashti's memory, had seemed an impossible task. And a foolish need. But he had done it! He alone had pulled it off. And his rise to power had improved ever since.

And now to think Queen Esther wanted his company! The thought made him nearly skip down the hall, but he forced himself to remain dignified. He moved through the main corridors toward the palace gate and smiled with satisfaction as each man fell to his knees, head to the tiled floor.

Until his gaze came to rest on Mordecai still sitting at his table, not bothering to look up. He would *still* ignore him? The man should be groveling at his feet, asking him to destroy the decree! How dare he act as if this was nothing?

Haman stared for the longest moment, rage bubbling from deep within him. But he tamped it down. It would do no good to make a scene in front of the rest of the men, who were showing their respect. He would rise above and find a better way to deal with Mordecai.

He left the palace, flanked by his guards, and walked to his home, which was in the wealthiest section closest to the palace. His guards remained stationed around his home. He could take no chances with his safety or that of his family. Not as long as the Jews lived. Any one of them might attempt to assassinate him before the year passed and the decree could be fulfilled.

"Zeresh, dear wife, I have wonderful news!" Haman entered the house and kissed her cheek.

Zeresh smiled, but her eyes held skepticism. "Tell me," she said, cupping his cheek. She would believe him, but he needed a greater audience than his wife with whom to share what had happened today. And he needed advice regarding Mordecai.

"I will. But first, gather my friends. Especially Artabanus. This news requires advice that goes beyond the two of us."

Artabanus was one of his closest allies—one of the few he trusted. Was he becoming like Xerxes, who trusted so few? He shook the thought aside. He would wait for his friends until they could also hear this news and give their advice. He turned Zeresh about and pushed her to hurry, while he sat and allowed servants to wash his feet and bring him wine.

The sun had long since set and Haman had finished his first goblet of wine before all of the men entered his house. Zeresh stood in a corner, watching. She was useful to him, and she had given him ten sons, but sometimes her tongue tempted him to beat her. She should respect him more than she did. But he held those thoughts in check. Mordecai was a far greater evil than a little disrespect from his wife. Still, she ought to have learned from Vashti's downfall to be a little wiser with her tongue.

"You called for us, my lord?" Artabanus spoke while the others bowed. Even his friends respected his high position.

"Yes. I have need of your advice." He motioned for them to sit on cushions about the room, then took the seat of highest prominence. "As you know, the gods have blessed me with great wealth and many children. I have been given many honors by the king, even promoted over all of the other nobles and officials in the land." He paused to look each man in the eye.

They all nodded, each gaze holding the proper awe.

"And that's not all!" He paused again, drawing out the effect. "Tonight Queen Esther invited only me and the king himself to the banquet she prepared for us. And she has invited me to dine with her and the king again tomorrow!"

Artabanus clapped in a gesture of triumph, while murmurs of congratulations and smiles filled the faces of his other friends. Even Zeresh's gaze held an expression of awe. He smiled. Good. Perhaps he could overlook her caustic tongue a while longer.

He waited until the men quieted again, then frowned, his posture downcast. "But I called you here because this is all worth nothing as long as I see Mordecai the Jew just sitting there at the palace gate."

"He should not be allowed to get away with how he treats you," Artabanus said.

"Why the king puts up with him all these years is hard to understand," said another.

"Some say he is closely related to the queen. Though he is only her adoptive father." This from Zeresh.

"That makes no difference. He does not rank as high as Haman, and relative or not, he must bow," Artabanus insisted.

Haman listened with deep satisfaction as the discussion moved about the room, each man growing bolder and more in Haman's favor as the wine flowed and the night waned.

At last Zeresh spoke again. "Set up a sharpened pole that stands seventy-five feet tall, and in the morning ask the king to impale Mordecai on it. When this is done, you can go on your merry way to the banquet with the king."

All of his friends turned to Zeresh, then faced Haman. Artabanus voiced their agreement. "Zeresh speaks wisely, my lord. An ingenious plan!"

Haman smiled. What a perfect solution! He would not need to wait a year to be rid of his nemesis. The queen would not even know until it was too late, and by then he could surely appease her somehow. Or convince the king to do so.

"Do it," he said, leaning back in his chair. He faced his attendant. "Have workmen called this very night and build the pole. I want it done before dawn."

Xerxes flipped over in his bed, pounded the pillow beneath his head, and switched sides again. This constant tossing was not helping, and the more he moved, the more the covers tangled around him and his body grew heated.

What could Esther possibly want that she would hold two banquets to tell him? Why not just come out and say it? And why Haman? Granted, he had promoted Haman to a high position, but he had to admit he would have enjoyed a banquet alone with his queen. It had been too long, and he needed her company once more. But he couldn't come out and say so in front of Haman.

Blast! He flipped over again, certain that sleep would never come by trying. He swung his legs over the side of the bed and sat up.

An attendant appeared at his side. "How can I help you, my lord?"

The man had remained awake as well, as Xerxes required several attendants to stay awake as he slept. Guards did the same outside of his doors.

"It is obvious that I will not sleep this night unless I get drunk or call a woman to my bed, neither of which appeals to me tonight."

"Perhaps some reading, my lord?" the attendant suggested.

Xerxes nodded. "Yes. Perfect. Bring me the book of the history of my reign and have someone read it to me." Not all of his attendants could read, so one must be found who did.

"Yes, my lord. Right away, my lord." The man hurried off to do his bidding while Xerxes rose and paced the room. Energy could be released by movement. Perhaps he could wear himself out with walking.

But the image of Esther, so unwilling to make her request,

baffled him. Something troubled her. She would not have risked her life to approach him for a trifle. Whatever the issue, it surely held great significance. He would almost think she toyed with him, but she would not toy with her life just to tease him back to her bed.

What do you want, my love? He would give it to her. He cared not what it cost him, he would give it to her. She had already won his heart and his decision by stepping into his inner court. Nothing she asked of him would be too great.

But his decision to grant her desire did not ease his sleeplessness, because the not knowing was keeping his mind churning.

A scribe appeared with his attendants sooner than he expected, and he breathed a sigh of relief. Good. He sank onto a couch as the man carried several clay tablets into the room and spread them onto a wide table.

"'In the year that Esther became queen, Mordecai son of Jair, who works at the king's gate, uncovered a plot to assassinate King Xerxes,'" the man read. "'Bigthan and Teresh, two of the eunuchs who guarded the door to the king's private chambers, devised the plot. Mordecai brought the news to Queen Esther, who is his daughter, and she carried the news to the king. Bigthan and Teresh were executed once the plot was confirmed.'"

Xerxes sat straighter. This reading was doing nothing to aid his ability to sleep. He remembered this incident. Years had passed, but he had become more aware of his own safety since. And he had always considered Mordecai of value because of his help, of more value than a mere father-in-law.

He stroked his chin, forcing his mind to recall the details. Esther had worried about him, fearful that Bigthan and

Teresh would act before she could bring Mordecai to him to explain what he had heard. He could hardly believe such faithful eunuchs would want to kill him, so he'd instructed Haman to search for the truth. Haman had confirmed Mordecai's words.

"Continue," he said, wanting the scribe to finish the story. But the words turned to something unrelated to the plot against his life. "Wait." He held up a hand. "What reward or recognition did we ever give Mordecai for this?"

His two attendants spoke before the scribe could open his mouth. "Nothing has been done for him," they said.

He looked at them, noting an intensity in their eyes he had not seen before. "You recall this incident well."

They nodded. "Yes, my lord," one said. "Mordecai was not rewarded for his part in uncovering this plot. Somehow the incident was recorded and forgotten."

Xerxes abruptly stood. He moved to his dressing rooms, his attendants following. "I will dress for court now." Never mind that the sun had yet to rise or that sleep had utterly eluded him. He must do something about this lack. How could he go another day without honoring the man who had saved his life? How foolish he had been to forget all about it until now.

Was this what Esther wanted to ask of him? If it was, he would do something before she could even speak. He would show her how much he valued her by honoring her father. But how?

His attendants fitted his royal robe over his arms and tied the belt as his mind whirled. Jeweled sandals were tied to his feet, more jewels were attached to his arms and neck, and the golden crown was placed atop his head.

Guards surrounded him as he moved through the halls to

his inner court and ascended his throne. He couldn't promote Mordecai to the highest position without dishonoring Haman. He could make Mordecai one of his officials, but then he would be under Haman, and that didn't seem to be an improvement to his current state.

He looked at one of his attendants, frustrated with his train of thought, and saw a shadow pass the latticed window of the adjoining court. "Who is that in the outer court?" Perhaps one of his advisors was up early and could advise him.

"Haman," the man said.

"Bring him in," Xerxes ordered.

Haman. Good. Just the man who could tell him what to do.

CHAPTER Thirty-seven

Haman stood in the king's outer court, his heart pounding, excitement pouring through him. He hadn't even bothered to pass by the king's gate where Mordecai sat, for the sun had barely risen and the officials would not yet have arrived. He was early. He knew that. The king was probably still asleep in his bed, but he would wait. He had looked up at the grand stake in his courtyard and felt such calm this morning that he could hardly think that tonight its use would be far less calm for Mordecai.

Laughter bubbled from within him, but he held it back. He would relish the moment after he had secured the king's permission. For now, he would simply relax in knowing that his nightmare was almost over. With Mordecai gone, he could easily wait a year for the rest of the Jews to be annihilated. Of course he could. He had patience. Hadn't he proved that with all of the waiting he was forced to endure with Xerxes?

The man was the slowest decision maker he had ever seen. A child would make a better king.

But he never said such things aloud. Those words would mean the end of his own life, and he would be the one impaled on a stake, not his enemy.

The door to the king's inner court opened, and a guard summoned him into the room. So soon? He followed in silence, surprised to see the king sitting in royal splendor upon his throne, the scepter like a sword in his hand.

He assessed Xerxes' expression. Was this a good time to ask for his request? Obviously the king had something on his mind. He would wait to hear him out. He approached and knelt.

The king extended the scepter. "What should I do to honor a man who truly pleases me?"

Haman reeled a moment with the abruptness of the question. Xerxes could be known to quickly speak his mind, but so early in the day . . . Whom else would the king want to honor more than him? Perhaps he intended to promote Haman to an even higher position, though the only thing left would be to make him co-regent.

He must want something less glamorous. I must speak carefully. Just because he was smarter than the king didn't mean he could let on to things that the king would assume he did not know.

Haman hid a smile. "If the king wishes to honor someone, he should bring out one of the king's own royal robes, as well as a horse that the king himself has ridden—one with a royal emblem on its head." He watched the king and saw the light brighten in his eyes. "Let the robes and the horse be handed over to one of the king's most noble officials. And let him see that the man whom the king wishes to honor is dressed in the king's robes and led through the city square on the king's horse. Have the official shout as they go, 'This is what the king does for someone he wishes to honor!'"

Xerxes clapped his hands, startling Haman. "Excellent!"

Haman held his breath, waiting for the king to give the order to honor him just as he'd suggested.

But the king's gaze never left his. "Quick!" he ordered. "Take the robes and my horse, and do just as you have said for Mordecai the Jew, who sits at the gate of the palace. Leave out nothing you have suggested!"

Haman felt the blood drain from his face, and his knees weakened. For a moment the room began to spin, but he caught himself. He must remain strong.

"Yes, my lord. I will do as you say." He hurried from the king's presence, his heart pounding so hard he felt as if it were running ahead of his thoughts. This could not be happening! This was not at all what was supposed to come of this meeting. He should be walking away with the assurance that Mordecai would be raised on the stake in his courtyard this very hour.

He slowed his steps as he neared the king's rooms where an attendant would choose a robe for him to place on Mordecai. Had he truly heard the king correctly? Surely this walking nightmare was simply that. He would awaken and it would end.

"May I help you, my lord?" the attendant said.

He drew in a breath and gave the man his request.

"Here you are," the attendant said, draping the robe over Haman's arm. The weight of it nearly caused him to lose his balance. His mind whirled, and envy hit him like a fist to his gut. The glorious garment belonged on him. Not Mordecai. *Never Mordecai!*

He stumbled through the halls, dazed, his guards conspicuously missing. Was he not worth guarding any longer? Where had his servants disappeared to? Worthless eunuchs!

He continued through the palace to the stables. "I need one of the horses the king has ridden," he told one of the groomsmen.

The man looked him up and down, apparently satisfied with Haman's royal insignia etched into his robe, and went to find a black steed, sleek and strong. Perfect. *For me. Not Mordecai.*

He clenched his fists around the robe and felt his jaw throb from forcing back the curses he longed to spew. He attempted to draw a shallow breath, unable to breathe deeply. This was not real. The king had made some horrible mistake. That had to be it. Xerxes had lost his senses, and Haman happened to be near enough to take the brunt of his foolishness.

He shook himself and walked the horse the groomsman had brought toward the palace gate. Fine. He would appease the king again. Hadn't he done so over and over? But his face heated as he reached the steps to the area where Mordecai worked. How could the king humiliate him like this? He handed the reins to a guard and sluggishly climbed each step, certain he would die of mortification when he reached the top and faced his enemy.

He stopped at Mordecai's table. "Mordecai, son of Jair."

Mordecai looked up, eyes narrowed, assessing him. "Yes?"

"The king wishes to honor you." He held out the robe and beckoned Mordecai to stand.

Mordecai slowly stood, his brows drawn down, his lips in a grim line. "What is this about?"

Haman drew in a breath, forcing his exasperation at bay. "I told you. The king wishes to honor you. Let me put this robe on you. The king himself has worn it. Then you are to come with me to ride the king's own horse. I will guide you through the city streets."

Mordecai still hesitated, but at last he allowed Haman to dress him. Haman then led the man down the steps to the waiting horse, watched him climb atop the magnificent steed, and took the reins from the guard. His gut knotted worse than before, and for a moment he thought he would be sick. But he squared his shoulders, lifted his head, and walked the horse through the city square, shouting, "This is what the king does for someone he wishes to honor!"

Mordecai sat atop the king's mount, holding tight to the saddle for fear his limbs would betray him and he would fall off the giant animal. Its sleek coat shone in the morning sun, and the proud tilt of the animal's head told the world that he belonged in the king's stables. Mordecai had no doubt that the beast would defeat any foe in battle, or at least be an asset to the king.

But it was Haman's voice shouting as he led them like a small parade through the streets that held Mordecai in shock.

"This is what the king does for someone he wishes to honor!" Haman's voice rang loudly at first, when they were nearest the palace. As they moved through the city, his tone softened, until he glanced at the guards surrounding them.

Then he cleared his throat and shouted the words until his voice grew hoarse.

Mordecai saw people exit their houses and merchants step from their booths to watch. Haman's face had darkened into a deep shade, nearly purple, when he first approached Mordecai that morning. How awful the man must feel to be put in this position.

Mordecai lifted his gaze heavenward. *Adonai?* What was happening that God would allow such a thing? And why was he being honored in the first place? Even if there was a good reason, why would the king appoint Haman to act like a servant leading him? Haman was the king's highest official. He had the king's ear.

It made no sense. But Mordecai enjoyed the attention and Haman's humiliation just the same. When they came to the Jewish quarter of Susa, Haman nearly stumbled over the paved stones. His voice, nearly gone now, continued to call out the king's words. Mordecai could see the shocked looks, the angry expressions, even hatred aimed at Haman, as they passed each home. Surely Haman felt it too.

God had humiliated his enemy before his very eyes. But this was simply one day. Tomorrow the edict would still stand and Haman would still pass by, demanding everyone bow to him. Nothing had changed, despite the magnificent horse beneath him and the fleeting sense of power he felt because of this moment.

It was only a moment, after all. Much more must happen before the Jews were free of this nemesis that was Haman . . . and all the evil he had created.

Haman stopped at the king's gate, allowed Mordecai to dismount, took the robe from him, and returned the items to their proper places. His mind whirled with the events of this awful day. How could things have possibly gone so wrong? Had the gods decided to no longer find favor with him?

He attempted to stand up straight as guards walked him home, but the moment he entered his house, he hung his head, dejected.

Zeresh met him in the sitting room. "What happened?" Her tone said more than her question. Had she already heard but was simply waiting for him to tell her?

"Call for my friends and advisors."

She handed him a goblet of wine and went to do as he asked.

He drank in silence, fuming, fearing. What could all of this possibly mean?

The sun had dipped lower in the sky by the time his friends and advisors had gathered. Zeresh took her place along the wall once more.

"I went to the king this morning," Haman said, searching each man's face. "I had planned to ask him to allow Mordecai to be impaled on the stake in the courtyard, as all of you suggested I do." His brow furrowed as he briefly wondered if following their advice was the cause of all of this trouble. Had one of them warned the king of his request? But no. None of them had access to Xerxes as he did.

"When I entered the king's chambers, he asked me what should be done for the man the king wants to honor. Of course, I could think of no one he would want to honor more than me, so I suggested he dress the man in a robe the king himself had worn, have him ride one of the king's horses, and order one of the officials of the kingdom to go with the man throughout the kingdom and shout, 'This is what the king does for someone he wishes to honor!' I expected him to call an attendant to do just that for me, but in the next breath, the king ordered *me* to do as I had suggested for Mordecai! *Mordecai!* I had no choice but to obey, but the entire day was completely humiliating." He drank from his cup and watched them.

"Since Mordecai—this man who has humiliated you—is of Jewish birth, you will never succeed in your plans against him," Zeresh said. The others agreed.

"It will be fatal to continue opposing him," one of the men said.

The news felt like a giant blow to his gut, and though he had already expected this answer, he had hoped for better. For a suggestion on how to reverse his fortunes.

As the men were still agreeing among themselves, the king's eunuchs knocked on his door.

Haman's attendant answered and approached him. "It is time to attend the queen's banquet, my lord."

Haman slowly rose, light-headed and caught by an intense inner fear. But there was nothing to be done. He could not refuse such a summons. He took one look back at his wife and friends, shook his head, and followed the eunuchs to the palace in silence.

CHAPTER Thirty-eight

Amestris heard the knock and sat up, listening to what her attendant was saying to the person on the other side of the door. A servant spoke in urgent tones, but she couldn't make out the words.

At last her attendant approached her and bowed. "Mistress Zeresh, wife of Haman, is asking to meet with you, my queen. What would you have me say to her servant?"

Zeresh was seeking her out? So urgently? "I will see her. But not here. We will meet near the king's stables." It was a place she could go to speak with people outside of the palace and not arouse suspicion. And she could always explain away her sudden interest in horses.

"Very well, my queen." The man rose and gave her message to the servant, then helped her to prepare for her secret meeting.

Amestris determined on the walk over to keep her relationship with Zeresh cooler than it had been in times past.

Haman had done many things of late that could go for or against him, and she didn't want to be caught having any relationship with him or his family should things not go well.

She and her attendant arrived with Zeresh already there, pacing the small area outside of the stable gates.

"Zeresh. What a surprise to see you like this." Amestris extended a ringed hand and allowed the woman to kiss her fingers. "What is so urgent?"

"Did you hear about the way the king treated my Haman today?" Zeresh wrung her hands and gave Amestris an imploring look.

"I have heard nothing. I have been in my apartments all day. Has the king done something displeasing to Haman?" She raised a brow. She really should pay better attention to court gossip. But since Esther's crowning, she rarely saw her husband, and until her sons were grown, she had little reason to pursue her place as queen. Once Darius was of age, she would do what she must to claim her rightful place.

But the look in Zeresh's eyes told her that she should have paid more attention to the political goings-on. The palace was usually abuzz with news that had anything negative to do with Haman. No one liked the man, including her. But then, she suspected not many liked her either. It was the way of things in royal circles.

"The king forced my Haman to parade about the city, leading Mordecai the Jew on the king's horse, wearing the king's robe." Zeresh lowered her voice. "To ask such a thing of a servant might make sense, but to force his highest official to do such a thing . . ."

Amestris felt the niggling sense of doom begin across the back of her neck, causing a slight headache. This was not like Xerxes at all. Did he not read his own edicts that the Jews were to be eliminated? Why on earth would he honor one?

"This is not good, is it? I knew it the moment he spoke, and then the eunuchs came to take him to Esther's banquet— "

"Wait. Esther's banquet? What banquet?" Why hadn't she heard of it? Surely her choice to remain away from the court of women was no reason her servants should not keep her abreast of things like this! Anger simmered, but she pushed it down. She would deal with her eunuchs later.

"The queen invited the king and my Haman to a banquet yesterday and today. And tonight as we were speaking, the eunuchs came to take Haman to the banquet. I don't trust her, Amestris. Whatever can we do?"

Amestris ignored the slight of Zeresh using her given name instead of addressing her as "my queen" as she usually did. She drew herself up and looked down at the sad woman. Zeresh had the makings of becoming a strong ally. But it was obvious that Haman's fortunes were turning against him, and Amestris was not about to be part of helping him, for good or bad.

"I'm afraid if Haman is with the king and queen, there is nothing to be done, Zeresh. You know as well as I do that no one approaches the king upon pain of death. If the queen is holding a private banquet, I'm sure she will give her reasons if she has not already done so, and we will hear of it. Perhaps Haman will be honored and your worry will be for nothing."

Zeresh slowly nodded. "Perhaps." Though by her look she did not think so.

"I must go. I wish I could help you, but I fear there is nothing I can do." She turned and marched toward her waiting attendant, the one she trusted to keep her secrets. Once inside the palace, guards would join her and she would pretend she had been to the gardens. It was a good arrangement when she needed it. She should have used it when she had met with Memucan long ago. But she need not think about what was past any more than she need think of Zeresh or Haman. She would wait to hear what fate awaited them, but Haman was no longer someone with whom she wished to have any contact.

She entered her rooms and sank onto the cushions, weary of life's dramatic turns. "Tell me if you hear any news of Haman," she told her attendant. "And I want to know about this banquet Esther planned for the king and Haman. Do not leave out any detail."

"Yes, my queen." The man left to find her answers.

Mordecai stopped at the threshold to his house, his mind still whirling with the day's events. Dusk had fallen, and the neighborhood buzzed with the sounds of families talking and the scents of food cooking. But this was the second day of Esther's banquet, and he had no appetite for food until he found out how things went.

He opened the door to the quiet house, but moments later he turned and walked out again. He moved in the shadows past his pagan neighbors to the Jewish quarter, where men and women spoke in lower tones and the atmosphere was weighted with the heaviness of fear.

He knocked on the door of his son Taneli's house and was greeted with warmth. Niria set a place for him to eat with them, but he refused the food.

"I thought we should pray," he said, looking at Taneli. "Gather your brothers and let us pray for Esther tonight."

"We have prayed and fasted as she asked, Abba. Do you fear those prayers were not enough?" Taneli glanced at his wife and young children.

"The children can eat—you may all eat if you wish. But after today, I am confused by the display of honor from the king when he seeks the very lives of our people." He ran a hand through his hair. "And I thought it might not hurt to seek the Lord on Esther's behalf one more time. Surely her family can pray for her."

Taneli nodded. "I will go to get my brothers, Abba. We will pray for our Hadassah."

Mordecai released a sigh and leaned into the couch in the sitting room. Surely Adonai was up to something to cause his honor on the same day as Esther's banquet. Surely He had heard their many prayers for their people. But praying one more time couldn't hurt.

CHAPTER *Thirty-nine*

Xerxes walked ahead of Haman through the palace halls to the queen's apartments. One glance at Haman when the man had finally appeared had startled him, but he did not show his surprise. What had caused Haman's cheeks to pale and his eyes to lose the merry shine he'd grown used to would have to remain a mystery. He would ask him later what troubled him. For now, all he could think of was what Esther wanted from him. She would not have gone to all of this trouble for no reason. And he sensed in his spirit that it was something that caused her great distress.

Had she also had trouble sleeping last night? He should have called for her, but the timing had not been right. Besides, he was glad to have finally honored her father for saving his life. How he could have overlooked that at the time still appalled him. Had Haman's suggestion been enough? Perhaps he should promote Mordecai to a higher position.

He could make one up if he could not find someone who needed replacing.

They stopped at the door to Esther's banquet room, and he smiled in delight when she herself welcomed them.

"Thank you for coming again, my lord." She bowed low, then rose with such grace it took his breath. How beautiful she was!

"I would never have refused you." He took her hand and kissed it, something kings did not do, but he did not care. She was his bride, and right now he wished Haman was at the bottom of the sea so he could be alone with her. But he acknowledged Haman's presence as Esther's attendants seated them, and he spoke with him of superficial things as the food Esther had prepared was set before them.

Esther sat opposite them. He watched her, amused with the careful way she ate and concerned with the tense way she held herself. She was normally so relaxed in his presence.

At last they moved to her sitting area, where her attendants poured the wine in goblets of shining gold. He savored the rich tartness on his tongue. Haman held his cup without drinking. Esther's cup sat on a low table beside her.

Xerxes set his cup down as well and leaned forward, his gaze piercing hers. "Tell me what you want, Queen Esther. What is your request? I will give it to you, even if it is half the kingdom!"

Esther stood, walked away from Haman, and knelt at Xerxes' feet. She lifted her hands in supplication, her dark eyes earnest as she held his gaze. "If I have found favor with the king," she said, her words respectful, humble, "and if it pleases the king to grant my request, I ask that my life and the lives of my people will be spared. For my people and

I have been sold to those who would kill, slaughter, and annihilate us. If we had merely been sold as slaves, I could remain quiet, for that would be too trivial a matter to warrant disturbing the king."

Utter silence filled the room. Not even an insect or night fowl twittered or squawked or chirped in the gardens just beyond the open window.

Xerxes stared at her in numb disbelief. "Who would do such a thing?" he demanded. "Who would be so presumptuous as to touch you?" Surely he had not heard her correctly. No one would *dare*!

But she was speaking again, and her words snapped him out of his wild thinking. "This wicked Haman is our adversary and our enemy," she said.

Xerxes looked at Haman as if seeing him for the first time. If the man had been pale when he first arrived at the palace, he had gone nearly white with Esther's statement. Which meant there was guilt there. Somehow he was responsible for this travesty.

No longer able to stand the man's presence, and needing to think, to understand, he jumped to his feet, rage pulsing through him. He stalked through the doors to the palace garden. How had Haman become Esther's enemy?

My people and I have been sold to those who would kill, slaughter, and annihilate us. Was this the group of people Haman had come to him about a year ago, complaining that they were a threat to his nation? His wife's own people?

How had he trusted this man so fully? He should have questioned him, asked for more details. He would never have allowed such a thing if he hadn't trusted Haman so completely. What a fool he was!

And yet, how dare this man go behind his back and use his own animosity to convince his king to annihilate innocent people? He must get to the bottom of this. He believed Esther with all of his heart, but he must know more, must ask the questions he did not ask at first. Must put a stop to this.

He paced the garden, the rage building. No more thinking. Haman deserved to die for this. And if he could muster a drop of patience, he might ask the man's excuse before he commanded his execution.

Esther returned to her couch and reclined, her position allowing her not only to watch Haman but to nod to her guards at any hint of fear the man might evoke. She did not relish this moment alone with her enemy, and an exposed enemy was often a more deadly one. But her guards stood near with swords in hand. Haman could see them as easily as she could.

Xerxes needed this time, for his hot anger would surely explode if he did not think this through. And how could she expect him to just trust her word? He might love her, but he had trusted Haman for years. Why should he trust her now?

She longed to look toward the gardens in hopes of glimpsing him, of assessing his reaction, of guessing what he might do. Would he order Haman's execution? But she dared not look lest she lose sight of her enemy.

"My queen," Haman spoke, startling her. He leaned forward on his couch, no longer reclining but sitting as if ready to jump up toward her. She tensed. "Please, my queen. I did not know any of this. I did not realize . . . I was simply trying to handle an unfortunate situation . . ."

"You mean you wanted to get back at my father by destroying our people." She glared at him, and he seemed to fight to keep his balance.

He fell to his knees and drew closer. "No, my queen. I did not think of you . . . that he was . . . I did not realize he was your father, and I admit I was wrong to let my anger grow so strong. But please, have mercy on me." He glanced toward the gardens, then moved closer and fell at the foot of her couch, his arm brushing her gown. "Please, my queen. The king is going to demand my life if you do not speak up and spare me. I will do anything you ask. I can give you riches. I will undo what the edict has done. I will give your father greater honor than I have today."

Esther shifted, uncomfortable with his nearness, but just as she was about to nod to one of her guards, the king burst through the doors, his face red, his hands clenched, and a scowl drawing deep lines upon his brow. "Will he even assault the queen right here in the palace, before my very eyes?"

Esther leaned further into the couch as Haman fell backward. The king's attendants who had accompanied him stepped forward, lifted Haman to his feet, and covered his face with a black cloth.

One of the king's eunuchs faced the king. "Haman has set up a sharpened pole that stands seventy-five feet tall in his own courtyard. He intended to use it to impale Mordecai, the man who saved the king from assassination."

Xerxes stared at Haman's covered face for a short breath. He stepped closer, took Haman's ring finger, and removed his signet ring. "Impale him on it!"

The guards carried Haman out, limp and weeping, and did as the king commanded.

Xerxes looked to where Esther had been sitting and noticed her place empty. He glanced about and found her pacing the very stones in the palace gardens where he had been.

He approached slowly. She stopped. "I didn't know," he said, his voice hoarse. "I should have been more observant of his actions."

"You had no reason not to trust him. He had done his best to prove himself to you." She knelt at his feet, causing him to feel uncomfortable.

He took her hand and pulled her up.

"I should have told you my heritage from the start. I am sorry."

He kissed her and held her close. "You have done nothing wrong. It is I who trusted an evil man. He will not hurt you ever again." He patted her back, the fear of almost losing her rising within him, making him nauseous. He held himself still until the feeling passed. "I am giving Haman's property to you," he said, deciding at once that he had to do something to make it up to her. "All that he had is now yours." He turned the signet ring over and over on his finger, then released Esther and took her hand in his.

"There is something I should tell you. That is, I should remind you, for you already know it." She sat on the bench he indicated and he sat beside her.

"Tell me." He cupped her face in his hand. "I will still give you anything you ask."

"It is not a request." She searched his face. "You know that Mordecai is my adopted father, but he is really my cousin. He is Jewish, as am I."

"Mordecai saved my life." Xerxes traced a line along her face. "Just today I had Haman honor him through the city streets. I read again about the way he discovered the plot to kill me."

"Yes. I remember."

"I should have honored him sooner, but with my mother's death . . . " He let the words linger, wishing again he had been better to her. How is it he seemed to fail every woman he loved? He shifted in his seat. "Let us go inside and call for your father. It is time he is properly rewarded." They stood and walked slowly into her rooms again. "We will meet with him in my chambers, and then you will stay. I want your chambers moved to better quarters. I cannot abide the thought of Haman having set foot in these rooms. I will place you nearest to me. You need never fear approaching me again."

She turned and faced him, touching his face, smiling into his eyes. "You honor me more than I deserve."

"I honor you far less than I should. Now come. There is still much to be done."

CHAPTER *Forty*

The king's actions against Haman sent a ripple of shock through the entire palace of Susa. Amestris took Darius and Artaxerxes to Atossa's former chambers. She knew Zeresh had been worried, which had caused Amestris to sense trouble brewing, but this! Haman's screams still rang in her ears, and she sought her mother-in-law's apartments, farther from the outer walls, for quiet. *Please let there be quiet.*

"What's going on, Maman?" Darius asked. "Why is everyone running and crying and whispering?"

She looked at her twelve-year-old son and wrapped one arm about his shoulders. She pulled his brother close with her other hand. "When we get to your grandmother's rooms, I will tell you."

Her guards hurried her along, and Amestris's pulse raced. She had considered Haman a possible ally to help her make Darius co-regent. True, he was young, but kings could never be sure of the future, and though Amestris did not doubt that

Darius would rule one day, she wanted control now. She wanted a say in the things Xerxes did. Esther held far too much sway over him, especially if she had the power to have the most influential man in the kingdom executed.

A shiver worked through her. She reached her mother-in-law's empty chambers and entered. The rooms were still strange without the imposing presence of Atossa, but Amestris felt a connection to the woman here even now.

She closed the door behind them, walked the boys to the center of the room, and sat them beside her on the couch Atossa had once favored. She looked at Darius, then at Artaxerxes. "To answer your questions," she said, looking again at her firstborn, "your father's advisor Haman has been executed." She had imagined a better way to say it, but they would be men soon enough, and they needed to know the truth.

Darius scrunched his brow, a habit Xerxes did when things troubled him. "But why? I thought Pedar liked Haman."

"He did. But Haman did something that put Queen Esther in danger, and your pedar could not abide such behavior." Would he have protected Amestris and her sons the same way?

"I like Queen Esther," Artaxerxes said quietly. "I'm glad Pedar protected her." The boy, about a year his brother's junior, was still so innocent. And much too loyal to Esther. Esther had made it a point to get to know all of Xerxes' children, and Artaxerxes had taken to her quickly and easily.

"Yes, well, Esther is a fine person, and as your father's wife, she should be protected. Just as you and I should be protected. This is why we have guards who follow us everywhere." She patted each boy's hand. "And there are things we must do to ensure that in the future things like this don't happen again, to any of us."

"Like what, Maman?" Darius lifted a brow.

"Like finding a wife for you. We must make an alliance with your uncle and wed you to his daughter." The thought had come to Amestris some time ago, but she loathed Xerxes' brother Masistes and had held off, considering Darius's young age. But now she must do something to make Darius's coming rule secure in case Esther conceived. Esther was clearly Xerxes' favorite, but Amestris was the mother of his heirs. She must make Xerxes see the importance of this.

"I thought marriage came when I'm older. Like twenty." Darius twisted to face her. "I don't want to marry, Maman."

Amestris smoothed his brow with one hand. "I know, my son. It will only be for legal reasons. You will not be expected to be man and wife until you are of age. But we must have an agreement. And by marrying your cousin, you keep the line of kings in the family as it should be."

Darius looked unconvinced, but at last he nodded. "My cousin Artaynte, right?"

"That's right." The girl was about Darius's age, the oldest of Masistes' daughters. "We will send word to Bactria and confer with your uncle. Then I will approach your pedar. For now, let's allow this mess with Haman to quiet down. Your father will be in no mood to discuss these things until there is peace again. This will be our secret—the three of us." She pulled each boy close and breathed in their scent, relishing this moment. It was a difficult business raising sons and ensuring their future. But it was one she cherished, and she was not about to let Esther or anyone else stop her from seeing her son sitting one day on his father's throne.

Mordecai dressed in his best robe and sandals and even added a golden armband. The king's guards waited in his courtyard, and he wished not for the first time that Levia were there to help him make the best choice of clothing. He had no time to summon one of his daughters-in-law to advise him.

He looked in the bronze mirror, turned side to side, and decided nothing could be done with his hair despite his attempt to trim it. The king could not be kept waiting.

The guards moved at a brisk pace through the streets of Susa, entered the palace gate, and led him to the king's private chambers. He had been in this room only once, when he had told the king of the plot to kill him. He bowed low before the king, then Esther, hiding his surprise at seeing her seated beside Xerxes on a cushioned couch.

"Mordecai, please sit." The king pointed to a chair opposite them.

Mordecai did as he was told and folded his hands in his lap.

"Esther has told me of your relationship to her in detail, and as you know, just this morning I was made aware again of how you had saved my life so many years ago. But a ride through Susa's streets led by your enemy is hardly a just way to honor you." The king pulled his signet ring from his finger and looked at it. "I can think of no better honor than to put you in charge of all that Haman did for me. You will be the highest official in the kingdom, second to me."

Xerxes handed his signet ring to Mordecai. Mordecai looked at it, dumbstruck, but held out his hand to accept it lest he seem ungrateful for the offer. He felt the weight of it in his palm, then quickly placed it on his index finger.

"I am honored, my king. I will do whatever you ask." He bowed his head, feeling as though he should kneel, but Esther spoke before he could do so.

"I am giving you charge of Haman's property, which the king has kindly given into my possession. You can manage it for me, can you not?" Esther's smile dissolved any sense of discomfort he felt.

"Of course." He returned her smile and shifted slightly in his seat. He thought to ask what was to become of Haman's wife and sons, but the bigger issue remained. The decree that Haman had written in the king's name still existed. If they could not undo that, the Jews were still in danger of annihilation. But he sensed the king's mood had shifted, as though he believed the problem had been solved with Haman's demise.

He looked at the ring again and decided his concerns could wait a few days. He now had the authority to speak directly to the king, and right now, though they had summoned him, he recognized the king's desire to be alone with Esther.

"I will give you instructions tomorrow," Esther said, looking from Mordecai to the king.

"Or the next day," the king said, his gaze fixed on Esther's.

"If there is nothing else then . . ." Mordecai hesitated, for he did not want to leave them without a dismissal.

"There is nothing else. Welcome to the palace, Mordecai."

He rose, and an attendant walked him to the door of the king's chambers.

Outside in the hall, the attendant spoke. "The king will have rooms made for you in the palace. You will use Haman's official quarters for your business, but sleeping and living quarters will be set up per the queen's instructions."

Mordecai nodded. "I will wait to hear from the queen on

this matter." Tonight he would sleep in his own home, which he much preferred.

The ring weighed heavily on his hand as guards escorted him to his residence. They would stand watch until he occupied his new rooms in the palace, where they would guard him. Common sense told him that he had to make the move for the king's and queen's convenience. He needed to be accessible to them, and he had no desire to live in Haman's house. Esther would know that.

He glanced at the stars before passing over the threshold. *Thank You for intervening and using my Esther to help her people. I will trust You to complete the work soon.*

Whether or not they talked about Him in Susa, God had become very real to Mordecai, and he knew that without Adonai's intervention, there would have been no night like this one. And without Adonai's future help, there would be no rescue in days to come.

Esther walked beneath the marble columns of the palace, the light of a new dawn filtering through the latticed windows that marked the eastern wall. Her seven maids walked behind her, quietly talking among themselves. Esther ignored the chatter. Weeks had passed since Haman's death and Mordecai's new promotion to ruling high official. Weeks that had seen a change in her status with Xerxes, the nobles, and the women of the harem, but had seen no change in the edict against her people. And Mordecai reminded her often that something more must be done.

The prospect of going again before the king to beg for one more favor did not sit well within her. And then her monthly time had prevented her from coming into his presence, so she had lain awake many a night praying, but no answer came. She needed a distraction.

"Are you sure you want to visit the children?" Parisa said, drawing up beside her. Extra guards walked with them, as Xerxes had doubled the number since Haman's plot was uncovered. If she could, she would call for her family and visit her nieces and nephews again. But for now, the children of Xerxes would have to fill the emptiness she often felt with no child of her own. At least she could enjoy watching the children and feel somewhat normal again.

She glanced at her maid, her closest friend in this place. "Yes, I'm sure. They bring joy, and right now I need to stop thinking about what to do next." All she did these days was think, give orders, confer with Mordecai, and pray about how to approach her husband one more time. Things were going so well between them. How could she risk ruining that?

"I am sure they will be happy to see you." Parisa showed Esther a bag filled with playthings for the youngest of Xerxes' children. "Shirin has the gifts for the older ones, if they are there."

Esther nodded and smiled, her step lighter as they drew closer to the king's harem and the area where the children lived with their mothers or were tutored by the king's eunuchs. She followed her guards into the common area and listened as Hathach announced her presence. Doors opened and Xerxes' children hurried to greet her. Another more ornate door, set apart from the others and not as readily connected to the harem, opened moments later. Amestris entered the courtyard, dressed in regal attire.

"She still resents you," Parisa whispered in her ear.

Esther glanced at the woman who should have been queen, if she'd had her way. "I know. She is, after all, the mother of Xerxes' heir." Xerxes had told her that Vashti's son had visited him on a rare trip to Persepolis, but the boy would never be king, even if Xerxes wanted him to be. Atossa had made sure of that by bringing Amestris into Xerxes' life.

As Esther met Amestris's gaze, she sensed not only animosity but also fear in the woman's expression. Did she think Esther would bear a son to take Darius's place?

She turned again to the children and distributed the gifts she had brought. Some of the mothers thanked her while most remained silent. Of course, they did not speak because she was their queen and must speak to them first.

She looked at Parisa. "I don't know what to say to them." For the first time since Xerxes had chosen her as queen, she felt as though she had fallen from a sense of favor to one of fear. She held power she had never known before. The king had listened to her over Haman, and no woman had ever held such sway over the king in all of the years these women had known him. Even Vashti could not have persuaded him against Xerxes' nobles. But Esther, by God's grace, had prevailed against Haman.

"Perhaps just smile and greet them," Parisa whispered.

Esther nodded, then turned to each woman, smiled, and asked how they fared and if they needed anything. She spent the morning getting to know these women who had shared her husband's bed—some more than once—and had borne him children but did not hold his heart. Not even his rightful wife, Amestris.

When she turned to Amestris, she was surprised the woman had waited. Her sons were nowhere to be seen. Esther masked her disappointment, for she had come to favor Artaxerxes.

"Amestris," Esther said, offering her a genuine smile. "Thank you for waiting."

"You are the queen. I would not want my husband to discover that I dishonored his wife." Her tone matched the narrowed look in her dark eyes.

"He would not have discovered such a thing from me." Esther clasped her ringed hands together. "I am surprised Darius and Artaxerxes are not with you."

Amestris's eyes narrowed further. "They left early with their tutors." She clamped her lips shut, obviously unwilling to say more.

"Well, thank you for the visit. I wish your boys well as they prepare to help their father." Esther took a step back.

"And one day rule in his place," Amestris said, as though the news was something Esther needed to be reminded of.

"Of course. Xerxes fully expects Darius to follow in his steps." He did, didn't he? She had spoken for the king without truly knowing what he thought. If she were to bear a son, might his thinking change? Would the people accept a half-Persian, half-Jewish king?

"A fact I have ensured he will not forget." Amestris's eyes held a calculating look.

Esther debated whether to say more, whether to show her ignorance of what had gone on in the king's chambers during her seclusion two weeks before. "I wish you well then." She turned before she could appear curious and left the court, her robes and her maids trailing behind her.

When they were far down the hall, nearing her chambers, she turned to Parisa. "What do you think she meant? What did I miss these past few weeks?"

Parisa glanced about, then spoke quietly. "Amestris spent

time with the king while you were secluded. Rumor has it that they have sent to Bactria to secure a bride for Darius—a cousin, daughter of the king's brother. The marriage will make the kingdom stronger and Darius's right to rule greater. No doubt Amestris has planned it all along."

"But Darius is still a child of twelve." Such things were done, of course, but Esther still found what went on in royal circles unsettling. Would Amestris wish Xerxes dead just so her son could reign and Amestris could help him rule? If something happened to Xerxes, what would happen to Esther, to Mordecai? To her people if this edict was not revoked?

"It is an alliance in name only for now. But it is not unusual," Parisa said, interrupting her thoughts.

"No doubt Amestris is quite pleased with herself." Esther reached her rooms and entered after the guards opened and inspected the area. She sank onto her couch as servants brought her food and cool water.

"She has been scheming to be queen since she married the king. For whatever reason, the king will not give her what she desires, so no doubt she pines for the day when her son will rule." Parisa offered her a tray of cheese and figs.

"Well, there is nothing to be done about it, and what happens in the future with the next king is not my immediate concern. It is time I meet with my father again to go over some plans that cannot wait." She glanced at Hathach.

"I shall summon him right away." He turned to leave, but Esther stayed him with a hand.

"Wait a bit." She fingered a slice of goat cheese, staring at it as though it held the answers to her silent prayers. "I need some time alone first."

Hathach nodded and returned to his place along the wall near her gardens. He would watch her as she strode about the grounds. And prayed. Time alone meant she needed Adonai, and she needed guidance as only He could give. If only He would give it.

CHAPTER Forty-one

Mordecai left his new living quarters at the palace and walked to the offices that had once belonged to Haman. He paused at the entrance, still struck by the strangeness of it all. To sit where his enemy had plotted his demise, to wear the ring he once wore, to hold the power he once wielded . . . He glanced toward the tall ceiling. To thank Adonai here felt wrong. He would do so later, when he could walk outdoors and look at the heavens. But his heart held gratitude just the same.

He nodded to the guard who kept the room secure and entered the chambers. Clay tablets and records Haman had kept were things that would take months, perhaps years, to document. For now, he set his attendants to helping him uncover every piece of writing related to Haman's decree. If there was anything missing that needed amending or changing, he wanted it in hand before he met again with Esther.

They could not afford to wait much longer, but he also

could not approach the king without every detail. That Xerxes seemed to feel no need to do anything since Haman's death left a hollow feeling in Mordecai's middle. He would still act, wouldn't he? He could not possibly think that killing Haman was enough to protect the Jewish people.

But Xerxes had a habit of acting quickly and then forgetting a problem still existed, until either he missed what he'd driven away or something jarred him into realizing it was still a problem. Exactly what Mordecai needed to do.

What he needed Esther to do.

He rubbed the back of his neck, his thoughts troubled. He did not want to concern Esther in this matter again any more than was needed. He had hoped that Xerxes might have broached the subject or Esther might have had reason to bring it up to him in their time alone. But when he had spoken with her last, nothing had been said or changed.

He bent over a letter his attendant handed to him from one of Haman's friends.

Most Excellent Haman,

Greetings in the name of your friend and servant Artabanus. I trust you are well and that your plan against the Jews is nearing a date to complete the task. Troublesome business, these priests and the casting of the Pur. I do agree that you need the blessings of the gods before you begin this enormous endeavor. May the gods grant you favor soon.

As you know, I am in contact with the king's wife from time to time, and she is deeply concerned about the line of succession for her son to wear the crown once the king departs this earth. It would be in your best interest to help her in any way you can to ensure an easy transfer of power long before such a time comes. It will not be an easy task for you, of course, but one you will find more agreeable than this business with the Jews. Her son deserves to rule, and any of his other children, even if one is born to the current queen, cannot usurp his reign. She is depending on your help.

Consider my words, for they are wise, and you know of whom I speak. She will not take kindly to you discarding her wishes.

The gods be with you.

Mordecai read the script three times, trying to take it all in. Who was "she"? Amestris? One of Xerxes' many wives? He shoved back his chair, clutching the tablet, and walked to the window, then moved toward the gardens. He must mean Amestris, for who other had a son old enough to consider wearing the crown?

Who else would Artabanus be in contact with? He had heard of the man but did not know him. Memories of years past surfaced, and he considered the times Haman had traveled to Persepolis to bring reports on the building projects to the king. Vashti had been exiled there, but that rumor was of long ago. Surely she had been moved outside of the king's immediate realm since then. But what if she hadn't? Could Artabanus be in league with her to see *her* son rule in his father's place? Vashti's son had been born before Xerxes was crowned king, so no one had ever considered such a thing, but he was the oldest. Might Vashti have designs on the crown to make up for her years of exile?

He rubbed his forehead to forestall a headache. In any case, the future king did not matter nearly as much as seeing the Jews' fate changed. He must get Esther to speak once more to the king. And if Artabanus had conspired with Haman or even approved of Haman's desire to see the Jews destroyed, he must be found and destroyed as well.

How many other friends of Haman were enemies of the Jews?

He reached the garden, then did an about-face, returned to his office, and summoned an attendant, who bent on one knee at his approach. "Yes, my lord."

"Find out what has become of Artabanus. I want his every move traced, and when he is found, bring him into custody by order of the king." He sat at his table, quickly pressed instructions in clay, and sealed it with the king's ring.

His attendant took the tablet, bowed again, and hurried to do his bidding. The list of Jewish enemies could be far greater than Mordecai once thought. He stood, left his office again, and took the long walk to Esther's chambers.

"I have never heard of Artabanus," Esther said as she walked with Mordecai in the palace gardens that afternoon. "That is, I do not know many of the nobles' names, especially those who were close to Haman. I fear a queen is only told what her servants tell her or the king decides to divulge. Xerxes and I never talk about the kingdom or the problems he is facing with anyone in it. We do not talk about war either. Only building projects and intimate things." She felt her cheeks heat and looked away. "Even then, it is only when he calls for me that we speak. I still do not have the freedoms I had the first few days after

Haman's death. It is as though he has returned to the way things have always been."

They stopped near an almond tree, and Mordecai glanced around. Esther drew in a breath, the fragrance giving her a sense of peace. But peace could be misleading, and she knew they could not let the atmosphere lull them into thinking all was now well.

"What else do you know, Abba?" She briefly touched his arm.

"Artabanus could be as big a threat to us as Haman was, with the exception that he does not hold the power," he said. "But he has been conspiring with someone, probably Amestris. Though I've wondered if even Vashti could be meeting with him. One of them wants to see their son named Xerxes' crown prince and heir. In either woman's case, once Xerxes is gone from the earth, it would allow one of them to take your place." He looked at her, his brows knit in a frown. To lose her place before she could save her people would have dire consequences for all of them.

"But Xerxes is well. And is guarded to the point of obsession." She smoothed her robe and briefly wondered what to do with her hands.

"Assassination plots can come from anywhere, my daughter. You know even the king's own eunuchs conspired against him not so long ago." Mordecai rested one hand on her shoulder. "I have sent men to find this foe Artabanus, but this also means we cannot wait to approach the king again. You must go to him, Esther." He took her hand and held it. "I know it is not easy for you, and I do not wish to risk your life, but surely Xerxes will look on you with favor if you but ask."

Esther placed her hand over her father's. "You want me to appeal to him again to beg for the people."

"Yes."

She lowered her hand and turned away, walking along the garden paths. She glanced to the side, but Mordecai did not follow. *Oh Adonai, why must I do this again? Why could not the first time have been the end of it? Must relief from evil come in stages?*

She lifted her gaze to the cloudless sky and felt the slight warmth of the breeze, a sign that summer would soon be upon them. In less than a year, her people would be condemned to slaughter if she did not act. Her people. Her family. How could she bear it?

A deep sigh escaped as she turned back and walked toward her father. "I will go," she said, feeling the weight of anxiety in her middle. "I will do my best to plead with him, even if it costs me his favor."

When had his favor mattered so much to her? Were her feelings for him so strong? But the very idea of love caused her to fear that he did not return the feeling. While he was attracted to her, he was also attracted to many women. She had always wanted her husband to be hers alone. But queens should not hope for such a thing.

"We shall pray as we did before," Mordecai said, interrupting her thoughts. "We shall pray and fast for three days. Then you can approach the king once more."

Esther nodded, though she wondered if her maids would be as willing to fast as they had the first time. "Very well. We shall ask our God to intervene. Then we will see what He will do."

On the third day, Esther again entered the inner court near the king's throne. He saw her and summoned her at once. She fell at his feet, weeping.

"What can I give you, dear Esther? Ask me anything, up to half of my kingdom."

"Please, my lord, do something to stop the evil plot devised by Haman against the Jews. Otherwise, I and my people will soon perish from the earth."

The king held out the scepter to her, and she stood. "Speak," he said, clearly expecting her to say more.

Esther recalled the words she had crafted with Mordecai. "If it pleases the king, and if I have found favor with him, and if he thinks it is right, and if I am pleasing to him, let there be a decree that reverses the orders of Haman son of Hammedatha the Agagite, who ordered that Jews throughout all the king's provinces should be destroyed. For how can I endure to see my people and my family slaughtered and destroyed?" She watched him as she spoke, forcing her emotions in check. The very thought of her nieces and nephews, her cousins, their wives, her friends. . . she could not bear it.

"Call Mordecai the Jew," the king said to a waiting attendant, startling her. Esther moved to the side as the king indicated. Moments later, Mordecai appeared before them both.

Xerxes looked from one to the other. "I have given Esther the property of Haman, and he has been impaled on a pole because he tried to destroy the Jews. Now go ahead and send a message to the Jews in the king's name, telling them whatever you want, and seal it with the king's signet ring. But remember that whatever has already been written in the king's name and sealed with his signet ring can never be revoked."

"Thank you, my lord," Esther said, bowing once again at his feet.

Mordecai knelt as well. "May my lord King Xerxes live forever."

The king extended the scepter to both of them, and they rose. "You have my blessing."

Esther and Mordecai walked away from the king's audience hall and stopped in a private alcove. "See what our God has done?" Mordecai asked, searching her gaze. He cupped her face and smiled on her with fatherly affection.

She nodded, feeling like a child again under his tutelage. "Our God is mighty. And His ways are beyond understanding."

"Now we will trust Him to help us write the decree to undo the damage our enemy has done." Mordecai kissed her cheek and left her with her guards to return to her chambers, while he sent word to the king's secretaries to meet with him the next day. They had much work to do.

CHAPTER Forty-two

Two months had passed since Haman's decree had sent the Jewish people into a tormented frenzy. Mordecai pondered all that had happened as he moved from Haman's smaller offices to the king's royal receiving chamber. Esther's servant Hathach approached as Mordecai looked about the room, silently thanking Adonai for bringing them to this place.

"The queen has asked if you need anything, my lord." Hathach bowed low, then rose. "I am here to serve you for as long as you need me."

Never mind that he had his own attendants. It was like Esther to want to help him. And he suspected that she wanted to be kept informed by one she trusted. Hadn't Hathach been her go-between with Mordecai since the start of this mess?

"I am grateful for your help," Mordecai said. "I have summoned the king's secretaries to appear here on the twenty-third day of Sivan to begin the work on a new decree. Please make sure the lighting is arranged well, and plenty of clay tablets, triangular rods, tables, and anything else the secretaries need for writing are ready and waiting for them. They will bring their own tools as well, but I want more than enough."

"It will be as you say, my lord."

"And send someone to the stables. The groomsmen need to ready every fast horse bred for the king's service and summon every courier to be ready to ride. As the decrees are written and sealed, they will go out." Mordecai longed to run a hand through his hair, but the headdress stopped him. He twisted the ring on his index finger instead, his mind whirling. Had he covered everything? He wouldn't know until the scribes began.

"I will go there myself, my lord," Hathach said. "I will make sure all of your attendants have followed your orders, and you will have everything as you have requested."

"Thank you, Hathach." Mordecai dismissed the eunuch, then walked with his guards to his own offices to begin a list of things the decree must include. He would write it himself, then go over it with his advisors, then dictate it to the secretaries, all in two days. The king's edict would give the Jews in every city the right to assemble and protect themselves, the right to destroy, kill, and annihilate the armed men of any nationality or province who might attack them and their women and children, and the right to plunder the property of their enemies.

It was good. This would give his people the edge they needed to defeat those who hated them. He released a sigh. Once this was done, he would search for Artabanus. Both issues weighed on his heart and mind, but the decree pulled the hardest.

The Jews must be allowed to do to their enemies everything their enemies were allowed to do to them. On the same day. If he let the Jews kill their enemies a day early, they would be guilty of a greater evil. If he forced them to wait a day, they could all be dead. He must give them the chance to defend themselves, to fight back against evil, not create it or be destroyed by it.

Two days later, the king's receiving area was filled with secretaries writing the king's words, which were actually Mordecai's words. As soon as they were written, a servant handed them to Mordecai, who sealed them and gave them to another servant, who rushed them to a waiting courier.

The thundering sound of racing horses came from the open windows as they hit the stone pavement and ran through Susa's city gates. Cries of joy rose in the city as copies of the decree were fastened to the walls of the king's gate and at prominent places throughout the capital.

Esther stood near, watching the frantic work. Awe that God had used her for this moment caused joy to rise up within her. When she heard the singing and laughter of the people outside, she wanted to weep and dance at the same time.

Was this why You placed me here, Adonai? She had always wondered what possible reason there could have been for her to be so chosen. Surely other women were more beautiful than she. Surely other women had captured Xerxes' heart. With a Persian wife in Amestris who had given him sons, there had been no need for him to seek another wife. Even if he missed Vashti, it wasn't like he needed more.

And yet here she stood, watching her father, second in

command to the throne, write letters to every satrap, governor, high officer, and noble in all 127 provinces of her husband's kingdom. All because God saw fit to use her.

Her. Hadassah.

Her face heated with the humbling thought. How unworthy she felt, yet how blessed.

She glanced to the side at the sound of marching feet. Guards appeared, leading the king. He approached Mordecai, said something she could not hear, then turned and walked toward her.

She bowed low when he stopped near her. "My lord king."

He took her hand and raised her to her feet. "Queen Esther, my star." He smiled into her eyes. The guards stood at a distance, and she felt her heart pick up its pace at the way he regarded her. "You have done what no other woman has done in saving your people. You are brave and strong, my love."

She searched his face, reading sincerity in his eyes. "Thank you, my lord. I am honored to think that I have found favor with you."

He shifted to stand beside her, and they both watched Mordecai and his team work in a system that moved without a hitch. "Your father is well organized."

"He has always been that way, though his wife helped to keep him in balance, peace be upon her." She laughed lightly.

He leaned close to her ear. "A woman has a way of giving that balance to a man."

A warm feeling filled her. In all of her years at the palace, she had never had a moment like this. Alone with Xerxes in a crowded room was unheard of. Alone with the king in his chambers was entirely different. But this . . . this felt like camaraderie, like what Mordecai had had with Levia. Like what she had dreamed of in a marriage.

And yet she knew it would not last. This was a moment for now, not forever. Soon he would return to his duties and she to hers. But this day, when the Jews would at last have a chance at liberation from their enemies, was one she was grateful to see with her husband.

Mordecai did not even glance their way as they looked on the work progressing in relative silence.

"We must celebrate when this day is over," Xerxes said, taking her hand. "This time I will hold a small banquet to include your father and your family, but you need not fear. It will not end as your banquet with Haman did."

"That is very kind of you, my lord." Her entire family to meet the king? "Thank you."

He nodded, squeezed her hand, and left her side, leaving her feeling somewhat bereft. But she clung to the memory of his presence, even as she watched the precision of the scribes working with the servants and her father pressing the king's ring into the pliable clay, affixing his seal.

Whatever happened after this day and on the thirteenth of Adar, she had no choice but to trust that God saw. He would either spare her people or not. But she could not believe that He would abandon them now. He had brought them this far. Surely He could be trusted to carry them through to victory.

Epilogue

Esther noted the lines on her husband's face, deeper than in times past, as she watched him from the couch in his private chambers. He sat near, his brow drawn.

"What troubles you, my love?" In the ensuing years since the Jews' victory and the establishment of the festival of Purim to celebrate and remember, she had grown accustomed to using more intimate terms with him. Theirs was a marriage of companionship and intimacy, though to her sorrow she had never been able to bear him a son. Amestris's son Darius would wear the crown after his father, as she had always suspected.

"Do I look troubled?" He smiled. "I am sorry. It is the rumors, I suppose. There are always those who are whispering around me, and when I demand to know of what they speak, I suspect they lie to me. There are few I trust."

"I hope you know that I am still trustworthy." She would have added that Mordecai was as well, if not for the fact that he had passed into Sheol the year before. "I do wish my father were still here to help you, though."

"He was a man I trusted more than any other." Xerxes ran his ringed hand through his graying hair. "I cannot say that I even trust my own sons."

He did not say that his sons had good reason not to trust him, for rumors abounded that Xerxes had committed adultery with Darius's wife, his own niece. Esther had never been able to prove the accusation that had come from Amestris's tongue. Darius, however, appeared less kind to his father, his attitude cooled, their relationship strained. Could the rumors be true?

"Perhaps you would like me to rub your temples or your feet?" She offered him an alluring smile.

He returned her look with an ardent one of his own. "Perhaps you can do me a greater favor than that." He leaned forward and took her hand. "But first there is something I want to tell you."

She nodded. "I'm listening."

"I am troubled because I fear for you."

"Me?" She could not tell him that she, too, had feared for herself in this place with her father gone. Though her cousins now worked in the king's employ, she did not see them as often as she had her father. And rumors had arisen that Artabanus had returned to somewhere in Persia. That, coupled with Amestris's lies or half-truths or whatever they were, did not give her confidence in her own safety.

"Yes. If something happens to me and my son sits on the throne, Amestris will not take kindly to you. In that day, if you hear of my death, I want you to flee. I have guards already aware of my decision to whisk you away from Susa. I will not risk your life if mine is taken."

She could not pull away from the earnest look in his eyes. "There would be no need to take me from Susa, my lord. I could slip away and return to my cousins. They would hide me in their homes and perhaps take me to Jerusalem, far from anyone in the palace. Even your guards would not need to know."

"Your cousins work in my service." He scratched his head as though pondering her words. "They could get you away."

She nodded. "I would trust them with my life." She paused. "And only them."

He looked at her, understanding in his gaze. "It is settled then. Warn them. Tell them to make a plan to get you to safety should the need arise. And tell them to go as well. It will not be safe for anyone related to you once I am gone." He intertwined their fingers. "I wish this were not needed."

"Kings have many enemies. I understand."

"You have been my favorite wife, even above Vashti." He leaned close and kissed her.

"And you have been my favorite husband." They both laughed. "But I believe my favorite and only husband has better things to do with his favorite wife than worry about her safety." She tugged him to his feet and kissed him. "The king and queen need some time to be completely alone," she whispered.

He smiled and led her to his sleeping quarters. As he held her in his arms and kissed her the way he had the night of their wedding, she wondered how long she would have him. He was not old, but he was right about the dangers he faced. He had many enemies from many corners of the kingdom. One day they would act, and she would not be able to protect him. She had no idea whether God would deliver him from such threats or not. But she set them aside to enjoy this moment.

As dawn broke the next morning, she looked on Xerxes with a love she had never felt before, love and gratitude to Adonai. She had not wanted this life. Would not have picked it, given the choice. But she could not deny that God had been with her all along and chosen her to live with this man for this season in history.

As she gazed on her sleeping husband, then toward the sun peeking through the curtains surrounding them, she smiled. Her life was not her own. She belonged to her Creator. The plans He had for her were for good and not for evil. To give her and her people a future and a hope.

Note to the Reader

Esther's story in Scripture is a familiar tale. Jewish readers will know every part, as it is reread or retold each year at the celebration of Purim. Christian readers know Esther as one of only two women in Scripture with book titles bearing their name. Esther is famous for being the woman who did the right thing at "such a time as this."

In my version of Esther's story, you may wonder where I came up with some of the characters and plot points, or why I left out the end of the biblical account. I tried something different with this novel in that I wove secular history into the biblical story. The reason I have not done this in previous novels is because there is little outside history on the more ancient stories in Scripture. But Xerxes is a historical figure, as was his father, Darius I, and his grandfather Cyrus, all of whom are named in the Old Testament.

Herodotus, the Greek historian, wrote of Xerxes and his wife Amestris and the five children she gave him. Other sources also mention Amestris along with Xerxes' mother,

Atossa. But these outside sources disagree on the timing of dates, so I chose the ones that fit best with my version of the story.

Secular history does not mention Vashti or Esther, however. Scholars have tried to guess whether either Vashti or Esther was, in fact, Amestris. But the picture the historians paint of Amestris is not the kind of woman I could envision either Vashti or Esther to be. Amestris was said to be cruel. (I left those cruelties out of the story.)

Since Amestris was the mother of Darius II and Artaxerxes in the historical record, and because Artaxerxes is the one who actually became king in his father's place, I did include these two children and briefly mentioned another son and one daughter in Esther's tale. I did not wish to bog down the narrative by adding her last son or the details of their lives.

Artabanus is also written of in history. It is said that he conspired against Xerxes, assassinated him, and told Artaxerxes that Darius had killed him so that he could reign as king. Artaxerxes had both Darius and Artabanus killed and took the crown for himself. Palace intrigue is often bloody and messy.

The tale of Xerxes' adultery with Darius's wife is also from the annals of history. Whether it is true or not is debatable.

The Bible does mention Artaxerxes, and he was apparently kind to the Jews. So even if he did as the historians say, he ended up ruling nearly twice as long as his father and was apparently a good king.

Amestris probably helped her son at least in the beginning and perhaps ruled as queen for a time. We do not know for sure. The sources outside of Scripture are subject to interpretation, especially Herodotus because he was Greek and likely held a grudge against the Persians, who had tried and failed to conquer Greece under Xerxes' rule.

So we return to the biblical tale, and as I studied it alongside other recorded history, I decided that Amestris had to be separate from Vashti and Esther. So I wove her story into Esther's story. I hope you enjoyed the mix of history and Scripture.

Originally, I had written the entire account from Scripture into Esther's story, but for the sake of poetic license and because the book of Esther is somewhat anticlimactic, I chose to leave out the actual war where the Jews defeat their enemies. I also left out all but a brief mention of the installment of the celebration of Purim, which is still celebrated in Jewish households today. I did not do this to leave out Scripture but to make the fictional account end on a positive and less bloody note.

One last comment: In the story I refer to "like the dawn." This is in reference to the midrash comparison of Esther to a hind and the dawn, based on Psalm 22:1:

> "For the leader; on *ayelet ha-shahar* [literally, the hind of the dawn]," which the Rabbis apply to Esther. . . . She was compared to the dawn, for just as the dawn breaks at the end of each night, so, too, Esther [i.e., the miraculous delivery of the Jews] came after there had been no miracles [during the period of exile and darkness].*

I realize that this is more explanation than I normally give, but I hope it helps you to understand the difficulty Esther's

*Tamar Meir, *Esther: Midrash and Aggadah*, Jewish Women's Archive, accessed July 22, 2019, https://jwa.org/encyclopedia/article/esther-midrash-and-aggadah.

story presented and a few of the more interesting commentaries behind it. Mostly, I hope you read the biblical account of Esther and see that though God's name is not mentioned—as so many people point out—His handiwork is visible on every page. Sometimes our God works in the silence. Let us never think that His silence means He isn't watching or doesn't care. He is there. He knows where we are. And He is always willing to guide us as He did Esther when we are faced with the darkness before the light of the dawn. He can make each one of us like the dawn, showing His light each and every new day.

In His Grace,
Jill Eileen Smith

Acknowledgments

I have been asked many times during my years of writing biblical fiction to write a story about Esther. I always declined for two reasons:

1. Her story has been done *many* times.
2. I did not think I could bring anything new to the retelling of what had already been written.

But time has a way of changing our perspective. With ten novels on the lives of other biblical women under my belt, I thought, *Can I do this?* A lot of women in Scripture fascinate me, and Esther is one of them. Still, even after I signed the contract, I wondered, *What was I thinking?*

I must admit, I think this way with every novel. But this story was one of the most challenging of them all. So I want to thank Revell for believing in me again. Thank you, as always, to my editors, Lonnie Hull DuPont and Jessica English. My deepest gratitude to each one of the teams that support my work—in particular, Michele Misiak, Karen Steele, Gayle Raymer, and Erin Bartels—and so many more.

Thank you to Wendy Lawton for believing in me from the start. If not for your faith in *Michal*, we would not be here today.

Much gratitude to my critique partner, Jill Stengl, who answered my desperate plea to brainstorm when I was pretty sure the story was awful and I would never find enough words. If you read Esther's biblical account, it *looks* long, but it's really not. Everything takes place in a few years, some of it even days. I wanted to give this story depth, not filler. As always, Jill helped me to see a way to do that.

A special thanks to my prayer team—Emily, Ann Marie, Keeley, Ruth, Miriam, and Pam. You were there when I needed prayer most.

To my sons, daughters-in-law, granddaughter, and coming grandchild—you will always be closest in my heart. I am grateful to God for each one of you every day that I live.

To Randy—thanks for reading every book and for listening to me moan over every first draft. I love doing life with you.

Above all, Adonai—You seemed silent in Esther's story, and You also seem silent in ours now and then. Yet You are there. You proved it then, and You prove it over and over again to us when we open our eyes to see. Thank You for choosing to use Esther at the right time in her day, so that we might believe You can use us as well when we come to our "such a time as this."

Jill Eileen Smith is the bestselling, award-winning author of the Wives of King David, Wives of the Patriarchs, and Daughters of the Promised Land series, as well as *The Heart of a King* and the nonfiction book *When Life Doesn't Match Your Dreams*. Her research has taken her from the Bible to Israel, and she particularly enjoys learning how women lived in Old Testament times. Jill lives with her family in southeast Michigan.

Contact Jill through email (jill@jilleileensmith.com), her website (www.jilleileensmith.com), Facebook (www.facebook.com/jilleileensmith), or Twitter (www.twitter.com/JillEileenSmith).